FIRST STRIKE

The four men were clinging to a single life jacket bag. McKellip. Eggert. Moore. Adams. They told each other there was nothing to worry about. The sea was calm. The water was warm. The rescue planes would arrive soon.

Suddenly McKellip shrieked. Horror swept over his face. "Something bit my leg!" he babbled.

He felt down with his right hand, his left hand clinging to the life jacket bag.

He pulled up the hand. Absolute terror was on his face. "My God, something bit my leg clear off! Right below the knee!"

McKellip was the first one. Soon there would be hundreds more . . . as the days and nights of frenzied killing went on and on, and only the savagely determined few could hope to survive this devastating attack of the one creature more deadly than man. . . .

TERROR AT SEA

Terror at Sea

DEAN W. BALLENGER

A SIGNET BOOK
NEW AMERICAN LIBRARY
TIMES MIRROR

NAL BOOKS ARE AVAILABLE AT QUANTITY DISCOUNTS WHEN USED TO PROMOTE PRODUCTS OR SERVICES. FOR INFORMATION PLEASE WRITE TO PREMIUM MARKETING DIVISION, THE NEW AMERICAN LIBRARY, INC., 1633 BROADWAY, NEW YORK, NEW YORK 10019.

SIGNET, SIGNET CLASSICS, MENTOR, PLUME, MERIDIAN AND NAL BOOKS are published by The New American Library, Inc., 1633 Broadway, New York, New York 10019

First Printing, April, 1981

1 2 3 4 5 6 7 8 9

PRINTED IN THE UNITED STATES OF AMERICA

THIS IS A NOVEL BASED on a true incident. On July 29, 1945, while traveling between Guam and Leyte, Philippine Islands, the heavy cruiser U.S.S. *Indianapolis*, commanded by Captain Charles B. McVay III, was torpedoed and sunk by the submarine *Nakapo*, commanded by Lieutenant Commander Mochitsura Hashimoto of the Imperial Japanese Navy. More than eight hundred members of the *Indianapolis*' 1,195-man crew survived the sinking, to be thrown into the warm waters of the Pacific. There they drifted helplessly, awaiting rescue for five days as they were attacked and eaten by sharks at the rate of a hundred men per day. The following is a fictionalized recreation of that ordeal: the greatest tragedy in U.S. naval history and the most awesome confrontation between sharks and men ever recorded. With the exception of the two captains, Commodore Vernon F. Grant, Dr. Lewis L. Haynes (the *Indianapolis*' senior medical officer), Father Tom Conway (the *Indianapolis*' chaplain, who did not survive), Japanese Rear Admiral Hiroshi Matsubara, and the rescue ships' captains W. G. Claytor and A. H. Nienau, the names and characters described are the products of the author's imagination. Similarly, the specific incidents and dialogue have been totally created by the author, within the factual accuracy of the story's date, places, and principal events.

The author has personal familiarity with the historical events used, having been assigned as a Navy correspondent to Air-Sea Rescue, Marianas, and having participated in the rescue of the *Indianapolis* survivors recreated in this novel. The author subsequently interviewed survivors about their experiences for the Naval Board of Inquiry, which was immediately ordered to convene in Guam by Admiral Chester Nimitz, Commander in Chief, Pacific.

1

THE *Indianapolis,* A HEAVY CRUISER of the United States Navy, was zigzagging toward the Philippines. It was a calm tropic night. The seas were rolling gently. Fleecy altocumulus clouds drifted over the big warship.

She was a silent, gliding shadow. She had no running lights, no porthole or deck lights. "I hope the moon doesn't come out," Quartermaster First Class George Adams, who was at the wheel in the navigation bridge, said to Chief Quartermaster Larry Keefer, who was making entries in the navigation log.

"You still spooked, for chrissake?" Keefer asked, looking over at the man at the helm.

"Fuckin' right I'm still spooked," Adams said, spinning the helm to port. He would keep it at port a little longer this time. Never zigzag in a pattern, he always said.

"Why don't you relax?" Keefer said. "There are no Japs around here."

"Is that a fact?" Adams said. "You got a directive from the Imperial Gook Navy that says the Pacific Ocean is now our private swimming pool?"

Adams swung the wheel to starboard. He had changed his mind about keeping the big ship at port.

"I don't need a directive," Keefer said. "Everybody knows there isn't a Jap this side of the north chop line."

"Everybody might be wrong," Adams said, his lips tight.

He looked up at the moon peeking through a cloud. He looked at the chronometer on the bulkhead above the helm. Three hours until dawn. This was the worst time. The most dangerous time.

The cruiser's four screws, propelled by geared turbines, churned the sea at sixteen knots. The *Indianapolis* (CA35) was an old girl by Navy standards. It was nearly thirteen years since she was commissioned on November 15, 1932, as the first major Navy warship authorized and completed after the London Treaty of 1929, which limited naval armaments.

"You're worrying for nothing," Keefer said. "In the first place, the way you zigzag—I've got to admit you're good at it—we'd be a real tough target. In the second place, suppose we get hit. You want to remember the *Indy* is not exactly a floating pumpkin. In fact, I'd bet a month's pay, unless they're awful damn close, a torpedo couldn't bust through our belt armor."

The *Indianapolis* was, indeed, a tough ship. She had four-inch belt armor, four-inch decks, and three-inch splinter protection on her antiaircraft batteries. She also had a four-plane aviation unit capable of depth-bombing any Japanese submarine with the audacity to attack the big cruiser.

"Those new Jap oxygen-propelled torpedoes could go through our belt plate like it was cardboard," Adams said. "I've been reading about them."

"For chrissake . . ." Keefer mumbled, turning back to the log. Adams bugged him. Always worrying. Always thinking the worst of every situation.

There was, generally, a relaxed feeling among the officers and enlisted men of the *Indianapolis*, and Keefer shared it. The war in Europe had ended. The war in the Pacific was in a doldrum while preparations were being made for the final assault, the invasion of the Japanese home islands, which would not be until, at least, November. More than three months away.

Adams changed zigzag. Maybe there weren't enemy submarines south of the chop line. But maybe there were.

The *Indianapolis,* midway between Guam and Leyte, on the east coast of the Philippines, glided through the rolling seas. Most of her crew of 1,195 officers and men were sleeping.

Adams continued to worry. The *Indianapolis* did not have submarine-detection gear. Cruisers didn't need this equipment, the Navy Department had decided. Cruisers relied on speed. What submarine could menace the *Indianapolis* or any other cruiser at twenty-eight knots? The best Japanese submarine had a cruising speed of fourteen knots, seventeen for short runs.

But the *Indianapolis* had orders to proceed at no more than sixteen knots. This was a fuel-conservation measure. Every drop of oil to feed the *Indianapolis'* four turbines had to be brought from mainland USA.

Adams, expert at zigzag, kept the *Indianapolis* veering port, then starboard. Left, then right, then again and again, meanwhile maintaining a westerly course.

Adams was a worrier. He admitted it himself. But he was competent. He was the ship's best helmsman and the way he zigzagged, the *Indianapolis* would not be an easy target for a Japanese submarine.

A small man, not much more than four inches over five feet, Adams had an intelligent, almost handsome face. But the thing you noticed most about George Adams—before the war a parts-department employee for an Omaha Ford dealership—were his ears. They stuck straight out, at right angles to his head, like sonars perpetually listening for enemy beeps.

"Ears," the other Navy men called him. It had infuriated him at first, in boot camp at the Great Lakes Naval Training Station where it had started. But he had become used to it. He didn't care anymore. What he cared about was surviving the war. He had a son in Omaha he had never seen. He wanted to see that little guy. He wanted to play ball with him, fish with him. But right now he just wanted to hold him in his arms and love him.

Tears came to Adams' eyes. Would this war ever end? Four years Adams had been a part of it. It had been almost two years since he had seen Karen. It was rough for her, raising little Gary by herself and without much money.

He had been in ship's company on the *Indianapolis* for more than three years. He and the *Indianapolis* were veterans of just about every enemy area in the Pacific. The *Indianapolis* had destroyed, in a horrendous explosion, a Japanese ammunition ship in the Aleutians. She had bombarded enemy islands in the Pacific, including three of the Japanese main islands. Her gunners had shot down Japanese bombers at Tarawa, Woleai, Iwo Jima, and Okinawa.

The *Indianapolis* had been badly mauled at Okinawa, and Adams kept thinking about this. It could happen again, not necessarily the same way but perhaps, next time, fatally. The war, Adams always said, would not be over until it was over.

The *Indianapolis* had laid a week-long bombardment on the heavily fortified Japanese bastion Okinawa from her eight-inch main batteries. Meanwhile her gunners, during this week, shot down six Japanese bombers and fighter planes.

On March 31 the Japanese, trying desperately to sink the *Indianapolis,* very nearly succeeded. A kamikaze pilot survived the big cruiser's gunfire and crash-landed on the main deck. The kamikaze bounced off the steel-plated deck and plunged, ignominously, into the sea.

But the kamikaze's pilot had released his plane's one great bomb just before he landed on the deck. It penetrated the deck plate, crashed through a sleeping compartment, a mess hall, fuel tanks, and exploded in a tremendous burst under the hull, blowing two gaping holes in the hull and killing nine men.

Damage-control parties quickly contained the flooding, but the *Indianapolis* was finished as an assault ship. She limped back to the great navy yard at Mare Island on the West Coast, eight thousand miles, where crews worked around the clock to repair the damage.

When they finished, Navy inspectors said, the *Indianapolis* was "better than new." Mare Island artisans had added the most modern radar and radio equipment and fire-control devices.

Adams, changing the big cruiser's zigzag from port to starboard, quit thinking about the son he had never seen. The ship's captain, Charles Butler McVay III, was coming into miral Chester Nimitz, commander-in-chief, Pacific (CincPac), ordered a Board of Inquiry to convene at Guam. He also ordered the author, the Navy Correspondent who had participated in the rescues, to interview survivors and prepare their reports for the inquiry.

The Navy had to find out quickly what had happened and be able to present its case to the public, which would soon be asking why no attempt was made to rescue the survivors during those horrible five days although rescue planes and crews were less than five hundred miles away.

Captain McVay was charged by Secretary of the Navy James Forrestal with "Culpable inefficiency in the performance of duty." Specifically, he had failed to cause a zigzag course to be steered and after the torpedoing he did not order "such timely orders as were necessary to cause said vessel to be abandoned . . . by reason of such inefficiency many persons on board perished with the sinking of said vessel."

The hearing was held in Washington, D.C., and the captain of the Japanese submarine that had sunk the *Indianapolis*, Lieutenant Commander Mochitsura Hashimoto, was flown from Japan to testify.

Captain McVay was found guilty of negligence. The court sentenced him to lose a hundred numbers in his temporary grade of captain and to lose a hundred numbers in his permanent grade of commander.

The court's verdict was not well received by the U.S. public. Columnist Earl Lindley wrote: "The fact is that the greater part of the loss of life in the disaster was due to a failure on the part of others to notice that the *Indianapolis* was overdue at Leyte and to begin a search. The Navy has not brought before a court-martial anybody responsible for this costly piece of negligence."

Captain McVay was assigned to New Orleans two months after his trial to become chief of staff and an aide to the commandant of the Eighth Naval District.

He retired from the Navy on June 30, 1949, at the age of fifty-one and was given a "retirement promotion" to rear admiral.

On April 1, 1946, the U.S. Navy towed the *Nakapo*, the

Japanese submarine that had sunk the *Indianapolis*, sixty-two miles out to sea and blew her up with explosives.

The men who survived the terrible ordeal of the sharks meet intermittently as the USS *Indianapolis* Survivors Association.

The last meeting was held in Indianapolis, Indiana, in August 1980.

"Two-sixty-two degrees true, sir," Adams said.

The captain went out the navigation bridge's hatch and toward his sea cabin, which adjoined the bridge. Before he went into his cabin his eyes swept the warship's weather deck. Enlisted men were sleeping everywhere. It was too hot below for sleep. The *Indianapolis* was twelve degrees above the equator.

Keefer and Adams watched the captain go into his cabin. Then Adams said, "He's nuts, if the war isn't over."

"It wasn't his idea," Keefer said. "It was somebody there at Guam. At CinCPac. Besides, what's worrying you? They wouldn't have said secure from zigzag if they didn't know what they were doing. Which means there isn't a Jap this side of the north chop line. And that's a long way from here."

"How do they know there isn't?"

"For chrissake, Ears. For one thing, nobody has seen them. Somebody would, if they were horsing around here. One of our ships or planes would at least see some indication."

Keefer took a cigarette from a pack of Camels on the log desk and tossed the pack to Adams. "The way I put it together, the Jap Navy's subs, the few they got left, are guarding the home islands. They figure we're going to invade anytime now."

Adams looked out at the moonlit sea. His lips became tight. "I hope you're right. It would be a terrible damn thing to be torpedoed now when we've got the war practically won."

Keefer put a match to his cigarette and took a drag. "That would be a bitch of a deal, all right. After all we've been through, and then to get it on the homestretch. But we're working up a sweat for nothing. I'll bet—a month's pay—the Man got the word the war's over and he's keeping it until he makes a formal announcement to ship's company tomorrow."

Adams lit his cigarette. "I hope you're right. It would be damn hard to take being zapped because some desk jockey decided we didn't need to zigzag anymore."

"You got zigzag on the brain."

"Listen, Keefer, I've got a kid I've never seen. I want to at least see the little guy. I don't want some dude at CinCPac screwing my chances."

Keefer, who had been assistant manager of a J. C. Penney store in metropolitan St. Louis, sucked on his cigarette. He was a tall, lanky man, six-feet-two. His features were craggy and generally jovial, but now his face was grim. "You're lucky you got somebody to go home to. That bitch I was married to . . ." Keefer took another drag on the Camel and exhaled it through his nostrils. "She wiped me out. That shyster she hired cleaned me like a chicken. He glommed my house and my car and the money we had in the bank which included the hundred bucks I was sending home every month."

Adams looked anxiously out over the moonlit sea. "If there's a Jap out there he'll have it easier than easy. The most half-ass torpedoman they've got couldn't miss."

He was aware that the *Indianapolis* had, as naval engineers say, a small metacentric height. In layman's language, very little water in her hull would capsize her. Just one torpedo could sink the big warship. This was a major worry for a man who wanted, more than anything else, to see his infant son.

"Barbara better not be there when I get home," Keefer said. "Her and that four-F phony she tossed me for. You know what eats at me, Ears? I hired that wife-stealing son of a bitch. I put him in shoes. Made him the shoe department manager just before I got drafted. I'll bet he was shacking with her before I even got to boot camp."

Adams held the big warship's helm at 262 true. Almost straight west. "If I thought McVay was sleeping," he said, "I'd zigzag until dawn."

"I wouldn't if I were you," Keefer said. "They'd bury you for disobeying a direct order. You'd be a grandpa before you got out of the brig."

"We're in the worst possible place to get it," Adams said. "Six hundred miles from Guam. Five hundred to Leyte."

"Get off of it, will you?" Keefer said. "For chrissake, you worry too much."

2

ABOUT TWO THOUSAND METERS NORTHEAST of the *Indianapolis* a powerful submarine of the Imperial Japanese Navy was cruising just below the surface, her night periscope sweeping the rolling seas.

She was the *Nakapo*, a modern submarine of the Imperial Navy's newly designed I-class. She was a big ship, twice the size of a German U-boat, bigger than U.S. Navy submarines of similar class. Longer than a city block and thirty feet wide, she could cruise fifteen thousand miles without refueling. She had six torpedo tubes in her bow and carried eighteen torpedoes of the deadly 95 type. These torpedoes were oxygen-fueled and capable of silent, wakeless kills at a range of almost five miles. Propelled at the terrifying speed of forty-four knots, each torpedo had a twelve-hundred-pound explosive charge in its nose.

Lieutenant Commander Mochitsura Hashimoto, thirty-six, the *Nakapo*'s captain, was a frustrated and embittered man. The war, which had seemed so glorious for him and for Japan in its beginning, had turned to tragedy. The Americans, the tricky bastard sons of dogs, were winning. No doubt of it. Worse, they were destroying Japan in the process.

If only he could make a kill. Sink an important American

ship. At least he would feel he had done something for Japan. Until now, late in July 1945, he had been a failure. He hadn't sunk even an American raft.

Hashimoto of the Imperial Japanese Navy had been born in scenic, historic Kyoto, the eighth child of a Shinto priest who had a hard time supporting his large family, even with the government's subsidy for clergymen of the state religion.

Hashimoto was graduated from high school at the age of eighteen and decided to join the Navy. A brilliant student, he had little difficulty entering the Japanese Naval Academy on Etajima island in Hiroshima Bay. Four years later in 1931, he was graduated. Japan was embarking on its Greater Asia Co-Prosperity Sphere, and it seemed Japan would soon rule Asia and, perhaps one day, the world.

Hashimoto served in several naval units and in 1940 he was assigned a submarine command. Before he went to sea with this proud command he married the daughter of a wealthy Osaka businessman who gave birth within a year to the first of four sons.

The next year, 1941, Japanese forces attacked Pearl Harbor and Japan found itself at war with the United States. "We will quickly and easily defeat the Americans," Hashimoto said to fellow naval officers, echoing the general opinion held among the Japanese armed forces.

But the Americans weren't decadent, cowardly, or without will, surprising the Japanese who had been told these things, and the war soon changed from high adventure to bitter combat, then fear of Japanese defeat.

In May 1944 Hashimoto was given his finest assignment, command of a just-built submarine of the most modern engineering—the *Nakapo,* an underwater killer superior to the best submarine in the United States Navy.

The night of July 29, the *Nakapo* was midway between Guam and Leyte, far south of the north chop line, an area in which no Japanese submarines were supposed to be.

Petty Officer Second Class Toshi Nokamura, on duty at the night periscope, swept it around listlessly. This was boring duty. He would be glad when it was finished.

Lieutenant Soyei Miyamoto, the navigation officer, sat at the navigation-chart table in the little steel-wall compartment. On the bulkhead back of him a Rising Sun flag had been painted. Below it were the words, WE WILL WIN THIS WAR AGAINST THE AMERICAN BARBARIANS.

Nokamura began another sweep with the night periscope. He saw something unusual. He swung the periscope back to it. He stood straighter and looked intently. Then he turned toward Miyamoto. "Sir," he said excitedly, "I think I saw an American warship!"

Miyamoto leaped up from the chart table and darted to the periscope. The petty officer stepped aside and Miyamoto looked into the periscope. He adjusted it slightly. A look of surprise came over his face. "It *is* an American warship. No doubt of it."

He turned to Nokamura. "Don't take your eyes off of it. Not even for a moment."

"Yes, sir! I mean, no, sir," Nokamura said.

He went to the periscope and Miyamoto darted back to the navigation desk and swooped up a mouthpiece of the *Nakapo*'s voice pipe system.

"Captain Hashimoto . . . Captain Hashimoto . . ." the navigation officer shouted into the voice pipe. "Enemy warship sighted!"

Moments later Captain Hashimoto burst into the navigation compartment. He was an intelligent-looking man, short in stature and somewhat stocky in the Japanese tradition. He was wearing a duty uniform with his rank insignia.

"It's either a battleship or a heavy cruiser, sir," Navigation Officer Miyamoto said. "Twenty degrees in the east."

Captain Hashimoto went quickly to the night periscope. He pushed Nokamura away and looked into it. He adjusted it slightly and looked again. Then a smile relieved his grim face.

"Incredible," he said, his eyes still in the periscope. "Absolutely incredible! No zigzag. No change in true line. Maintaining the same speed."

He looked back at his navigation officer. He was smiling. "I wouldn't believe it if I hadn't seen it myself. There is no way we can miss."

Very suddenly Captain Hashimoto's smile faded. "It's bait for a trap. It has to be. The Americans are not so stupid that they would make an easy target of so major a warship."

He looked into the periscope again. He swept it 360

degrees, then reversed the sweep, both very slowly, very thoroughly. "I don't see anything," he mumbled. "Not a damn thing."

He turned toward Miyamoto. "I want a report from the hydrophone watch. Immediately!"

"Yes, sir," Miyamoto said.

The lieutenant, not quite five feet in height and terribly bowlegged, ran out of the navigation compartment. He came back a minute later with Lieutenant Seiho Yamashita, who was in uniform, and two shorts-wearing enlisted men.

"Don't just stand there like a donkey," Hashimoto bellowed to the hydrophone officer. "Give me your report!"

"I have nothing to report, sir," Yamashita said.

"Nothing?" Hashimoto bellowed. "Listen to me, you incompetent idiot! Out there, only two thousand meters distant, an American warship is underway at fifteen or sixteen knots. And you didn't hear it!"

"Sir," Yamashita said, "the Americans are clever devils. They have recently devised a means of making the sounds of their surface ships' propellers blend with the normal sounds of the sea."

This was the case with the *Indianapolis*. Its fire-room crews were running the big cruiser's propelling screws unevenly. The forward engine-room crew was turning the two outboard screws 168 turns per minute. The after engine-room crew was turning the two inboard screws at 163 turns per minute.

This produced a choppy pattern. To enemy hydrophones it sounded no different from myriads of other underwater noises.

"However," Yamashita said, "the Americans cannot deceive us concerning their submarines. At least with any device we have heard of. We can detect them every time. And we have had no indication of their presence in this area."

"You are sure?"

"Yes, sir," Yamashita said. "Absolutely sure. No trace whatever of American submarines."

"When was your last determination?"

"Just before you summoned us here, sir."

"Are you positive?" Hashimoto demanded. "This is of utmost importance, Yamashita. The glory of Japan, the lives of all of us, and the life of the *Nakapo* depend upon your competency!"

Yamashita was offended. He considered himself an efficient and dedicated hydrophone officer. Perhaps the best in the Imperial Navy. His men monitored every moment of every hour. Except for the Americans' trickery with their surface warships, not even a small school of fish escaped the hydrophone crew's vigilance. But Yamashita did not show displeasure at Hashimoto's questioning. He had learned long ago to maintain a bland expression in the presence of superior officers. "I am absolutely positive, sir," he said.

Captain Hashimoto was clearly excited. He kept biting his lips. But he was indecisive and it was apparent to everyone in the little compartment. They stood, waiting, for his command.

"Return to your duty station," Hashimoto said to his hydrophone officer. "Report anything. I repeat, anything! Immediately. Bring it to me directly."

"Yes, sir," Yamashita said.

He bowed. The two enlisted hydrophone-watch crewmen bowed and followed Yamashita back to their station.

"I can't believe it," Captain Hashimoto said to his navigation officer. "It's almost as though the Americans are deliberately making a target of themselves."

He went to the periscope, roughly shoved Petty Officer Nokamura aside, and looked into the periscope. He swept it around, 360 degrees. Then again. Then he looked steadily at the *Indianapolis.*

Without taking his eyes from it, he said, "Miyamoto, I want my executive officer. And the torpedo officer."

"Yes, sir," the navigation duty officer said quickly. He ran out of the compartment and returned with the executive officer, Lieutenant Commander Haruko Yomura, and the torpedo officer, Lieutenant Nagu Tashida. Both were about thirty. Both were wearing shorts and split-toe sandals.

"Here they are, sir," Miyamoto said to Captain Hashimoto, who hadn't taken his eyes from the night periscope.

Hashimoto turned from the periscope. His lips became tight. This could be the most important moment in his career and these officers looked like they had just got out of a brothel. Damn them! He'd reproach them later, tell them to look like officers at all times. Regardless of the tropic heat an officer of the Imperial Japanese Navy . . .

The hell with all this, Hashimoto reflected. For now, anyway. "Look! Both of you," he said.

Commander Yomura came first to the periscope, as befitted his rank. He looked into the periscope. A smile creased his broad Oriental face. "Incredible," he said.

He stepped aside and Lieutenant Tashida looked into the periscope. He looked for a long while, professionally. Then he turned to Captain Hashimoto. "It is providence, sir. The kind of target I've always wanted."

"Do you think you can hit it?" Hashimoto demanded.

"Unquestionably, yes," the torpedo officer said, grinning with anticipation of the kill. "There is no way I could miss that big American!"

It was a cruiser, he said. A very large one. Its sinking would be a major loss to the United States Navy.

"You sure it's a cruiser?" Hashimoto demanded.

"No doubt of it whatever."

"She is still on true. At about two hundred sixty degrees," Lieutenant Miyamoto, who had gone to the periscope, said.

"Wonderful! Keep watching here," Captain Hashimoto said. He turned to the other officers. Before he could give them his orders, Petty Officer Nokamura said, "I informed Lieutenant Miyamoto the moment I discovered that American cruiser, sir."

He was piqued because the officers were treating him as though he didn't even exist, and here he was, the man whose vigilance had discovered the big U.S. warship. He wanted everybody, especially Captain Hashimoto, to know this.

"Shut up," Hashimoto bellowed, glaring at the petty officer.

"Yes, sir," Nokamura said. He was burning. He wished he had joined the Army. Maybe in the Army his vigilance would be appreciated.

The captain turned to the officers. "I've gone this whole war without a kill. But this big American cruiser will more than make up for it."

His eyes glinted. He smiled, exposing his gold-capped teeth, four in front, where people could see them. Two above, two below. "We're going to close in to fifteen hundred meters, then salvo all of our six tubes."

"That will be an overkill, sir," Torpedo Officer Tashida said.

"That's the way I want it," Hashimoto said excitedly. "I want to be sure. I've got to be sure!"

"Yes, sir," Tashida said. He bowed and quickly left the compartment. Six torpedoes into that sitting duck was stupid, he reflected while he hurried to the torpedo tubes. What the hell did Hashimoto know about torpedoes? It would be better to fire four. At fifteen hundred meters, with those new type-95s, even four would be an overkill. Then get the hell out of here. Very likely there were other American ships in the vicinity. As big and sturdy as the I-class submarines were, they were still vulnerable to depth charges. And unlike many Japanese officers, Lieutenant Tashida had no desire to die for the emperor. Ten thousand years of eternal bliss, the emperor had said, for men who die in combat. Bullshit, Tashida reflected; he would rather enjoy the rest of his natural life here on earth.

The Submarine Attack Force of the Imperial Japanese Navy was an efficient, well-trained organization, so it was but a very little while before the *Nakapo* was fifteen hundred meters—about five thousand feet, less than a mile—from the *Indianapolis,* and every man on the big I-class submarine was at his battle station.

Captain Hashimoto was looking through the night periscope. Executive Officer Yomura and five other officers were in the little navigation department. Their faces were taut. Any moment now, Hashimoto would give the command to fire the torpedoes.

Damn, this was exciting! The first kill for the *Nakapo!* The first, in fact, for all the officers on the big submarine except Torpedo Officer Tashida and Communications Officer Kagemura.

For interminable moments Hashimoto looked into the periscope, his tongue kept gliding over his lips. His hands kept clenching and unclenching. He wanted to be sure. One hundred percent sure.

"Stand by to fire," he said finally.

More tense moments elapsed. Then Hashimoto said, "Fire!"

Lieutenant Tashida salvoed six torpedoes. The *Nakapo*

shuddered and rolled several degrees to port, then to starboard, from the recoil of so many of the big torpedoes leaving their tubes at the same time.

Hashimoto, his feet spread because of the roll, kept looking through the periscope. The other officers stood tensely, their faces grim.

Petty Officer Nokamura was in the little compartment, too. He was, technically, still on duty. Still the night periscope watch. His eyes were on Captain Hashimoto. Why doesn't the son of a bitch say something? he reflected. Why doesn't he tell us what's going on?

"Those new oxygen-fueled torpedoes don't make any wake at all," Hashimoto said, breaking a nerve-racking silence. "I wish they did. I'd like to see where they are."

We'd like to know, too, Executive Officer Yomura reflected. If we miss with all of them—and it's possible . . . everything is possible in war—then we have got our balls in a trap. That big American will come like a bat out of hell and we'll be lucky if we survive her depth bombs.

Hashimoto's eyes were still in the periscope. He smiled. His smile broadened. Without taking his eyes from the periscope he said excitedly, "We got her! Below her forward turret!"

The officers hoorayed. So did Petty Officer Nokamura, but before anybody could remind him that this was improper Captain Hashimoto said, almost shouting, "We got her again! Just below her aft turret!"

Captain Hashimoto was practically dancing, his feet tapping the deck below the periscope. But he kept looking. "Three hits," he yelled. Then he said, "A hell of an explosion. Must have been their ammunition!"

Hashimoto turned away from the periscope. He began to dance around the little navigation compartment. His smile widened. His gold teeth showed. "We got her," he shouted. "We got her!"

He danced back to the periscope and pushed away Petty Officer Nokamura, who had returned to it, reasoning that he was still on duty and his duty consisted of periscope watch.

The captain looked into the periscope. "We got her good," he announced. "She's listing and she's on fire in three places."

He turned to his officers. "Let's go back to Japan," he said happily.

3

WHILE THE SIX DEADLY TORPEDOES from the *Nakapo* sped silently, without wake, toward the *Indianapolis*—which was less than a mile from the big Japanese submarine—Quartermaster First Class George Adams verified the cruiser's course and speed on the instruments forward of the helm.

Two-sixty-two degrees true, Captain McVay had said. Sixteen knots.

The *Indianapolis* was on course and at the proper speed. But Adams had an uneasy feeling. He wished the captain hadn't ordered him to secure from zigzag. The way they were going, they would be an easy target.

Chief Quartermaster Larry Keefer was lolling on the chair in front of the log desk smoking a cigarette. He was thinking about his wife, who had deserted him for a 4-F.

"I think I'll stay in the Navy," he said. "I don't have anything to go home for anymore."

"What about your career with J. C. Penney?" Adams asked. "Don't let Barbara sweep you under the rug, man. There's other women."

"You've got something there, I suppose," Keefer said morosely. "I suppose what I ought to do—"

He didn't say the rest of it. A horrendous explosion occurred forward of the navigation bridge.

Fragments of steel and the body of a deck watch hurtled through the glass of the navigation bridge's forward window. The concussion flung Adams against a bulkhead. It knocked Keefer onto the deck.

Blood dripped onto Adams' face from a gash in his brow inflicted by a fragment of the shattered forward window. He stood dazedly, staring at the mangled body of the boatswain's mate who had been blown into the navigation bridge.

Keefer, sprawled on his belly on the deck, his left flank bleeding, began to get to his feet. He stopped, on his hands and knees, and stared at the dead boatswain's mate. "My God . . ." he said.

Then another torpedo hit the *Indianapolis*. The big ship shuddered. A great ball of orange flame billowed up over the starboard side. Adams was thrown by the explosion's concussion onto the glass-littered deck of the navigation bridge.

He got to his feet and looked out at the upsweeping orange flames. "Jesus Christ . . ." he croaked.

He lurched over to Keefer, who was sitting against the bulkhead where he had been hurled by the second explosion. He pulled Keefer to his feet. They staggered toward the forward window. "For chrissake," Keefer said, "where's the bow?"

Fifty feet of the big ship's bow had vanished. On its edge were curled, ragged steel deck plates. Between this explosion-torn steel and the navigation bridge were bodies of wounded and dead men who had been sleeping on the deck.

"It's my fault," Adams said. "If I'd stayed on zigzag, they wouldn't have got us."

Keefer didn't reply. He was staring, mouth open, at the carnage forward of the bridge. Bodies and pieces of bodies were everywhere. Men were lurching toward battle stations, most of them barefooted and in shorts. The bong-bong-bong of the general-quarters alarm rose above the screams of the wounded and the shouts of officers.

"Fuck what the captain wanted," Adams said, "I should have stayed on zigzag."

A third explosion occurred. It was aft of the bridge. A column of water rose above the deck on its starboard flank.

Whole sections of four-inch steel deck plate were ripped like cardboard. Bodies and fragments of bodies hurtled against bulkheads and over the rails.

A splinter of deck plate came through the navigation bridge's aft window. It impaled Keefer in his chest. Part of it went out between his shoulders, the other part protruded from his chest.

Adams looked dazedly at the dead chief's body. He looks like a bug with a pin through him, like bugs I used to prepare for high-school entomology class, Adams thought. He laughed. Goddamn, that's funny. Old Keefer there, looking like a bug with a pin through him.

Then Adams came out of it. "Oh, God, Larry," he babbled. He and the chief had been beach buddies. Whenever the *Indianapolis* docked, they hit the taverns together. Sometimes they just went sight-seeing. Mutt and Jeff, people called them because of the disparity in their size.

Adams took his eyes from his dead friend. He staggered toward the helm. I'm still on duty, he reflected. I've got to get back to the wheel. The old girl's hurt bad, the way she's listing. The deck in here's got a hell of a list. But maybe we can keep her afloat . . . get her somewhere safe.

Screams and shrieks, the crackle of flames and small explosions came up from the ship's interior. "I should have stayed on zigzag," Adams said aloud.

He came to the helm just as Captain McVay, wearing shorts and shoes, their laces untied, staggered into the navigation bridge. He looked at the bodies on the deck. "We should have stayed on zigzag," Adams said. "You shouldn't have told me to secure."

McVay's lips became tight. He stepped over Keefer's body, looked back at it, then went to the navigation bench. "Where the hell's the charts?" he shouted, looking over at Adams.

Adams turned toward the navigation bench. Nothing was on it. "I don't know," he said. "I hadn't noticed they weren't there. They must have gotten blown out."

McVay's tongue flicked over his lips. This is a bad thing. Real bad. His brow furrowed. He tried to think of the best course for his terribly damaged ship. "Ulithi is closest, I think. It's about three hundred miles. Maybe we can make it. Adams, set a course—"

He didn't finish. Adams had made a terrifying discovery. "Sir," he cut in, anguish on his face, "the wheel just spins."

He spun it to show McVay that it was no longer functional.

"Christ . . ." McVay said.

The captain went to the phone on the port bulkhead. He picked it up. There was no response. He looked back at Adams. "Go down to Radio One and tell them to send a distress to CinCPac. Tell CinCPac we've been torpedoed and give them our location." Dismay swept over McVay's features. "What the hell *is* our location? Jesus, Adams, I hope you know!"

"Latitude twelve north, longitude one-thirty-five east," Adams said. "At least that's what it was the last time I looked. Which was just before we took that first torpedo."

"Great," McVay said, relief coming out on his harried face. "I was sleeping when they hit us. I didn't know how long I'd been sleeping, so I didn't know where we are. Get below, Adams, and tell them to send immediate surface and air rescue. And every submarine in the vicinity!"

Adams didn't wait for the captain to go out of the navigation bridge first. This was no time for rules and regulations. He went onto the weather deck. "My God . . ." he mumbled, looking at the carnage.

He hurried toward the light-lock hatch that opened onto a ladder going down to the ship's radio-operations rooms.

The deck of the big cruiser was a shambles. Everywhere were flames, choking smoke, dead and wounded men, shrieks of agony, pleas for corpsmen, the crackle of flames, shouts of petty and commissioned officers, scurrying men, the continuing general-quarters alarm.

Adams came to a corpsman who had spread a medic kit on the deck. He was injecting morphine into the wounded men around him. Before Adams could step through these men on his way to the light-lock hatch, Alan Brecht, pharmacists mate first class, looked up at Adams, and at the gash in his brow. "For chrissake," Brecht said angrily, "you only got a scratch. Get the fuck outta here!"

"I didn't come for treatment," Adams said. "I've got a Mayday for CinCPac." He stepped over the last of the patients.

"Hey, Adams," Brecht said. Adams looked back at him. "Put this on your forehead," Brecht said, tossing a bandage to Adams.

Adams didn't reply. Brecht wouldn't have heard, anyway. He was jabbing a morphine needle into a shrieking yeoman whose legs had been mangled and who had just come out of the numbing shock of his hideous injuries.

Adams kept going, meanwhile putting the bandage on his brow.

The ship was canting more than five degrees starboard. Adams slipped, almost fell, while he walked through blood that flowed from a mutilated corpse.

Intense flames were roaring from the cruiser's four-plane aviation unit. Always at ready, with full tanks of gasoline, the burning planes were shooting flames far up into the tropic night.

The planes were in a cut-down section of the hull, amidships. It had been cut out especially for the big old cruiser's planes and catapults. More modern cruisers had flush decks; their planes and recovery hooks were on their fantails.

"Christ," Adams muttered, looking at the burning planes. They were supposed to kill any Japanese submarine that attacked the *Indianapolis.* They hadn't even been untied. A frightening thought occurred to Adams. Depth bombs were attached to each of the planes. The flames would detonate them. This would be a disaster for anyone in the vicinity.

Adams hurried toward the hatch that led to Radio One, detouring around rents in the canting deck, debris, wounded and dead bodies, and a fire-control party.

Adams came to Chief Boatswain's Mate Lewis Bradley and two seamen who were removing a life raft from its bulkhead toggles. Flickering flames from the burning planes made these men seem to dance in the dark, predawn July night while they struggled with the big raft. "Give us a hand, Adams," Bradley said. "I want to get this rig away from those fuckin' depth bombs."

"I can't help you, chief," Adams said. "I'm on a hurry-go to the radio shack. The Man's orders."

Bradley, trying to bend a damaged toggle, said without looking at Adams, "Anybody notified CinCPac?"

"I don't know," Adams said, going past Bradley and his men. "That's what I'm supposed to find out."

"For chrissake, get the lead outta your ass," Bradley said, lifting his corner of the raft off its bent toggle. "If we don't get help we're up the fuckin' creek!"

He looked over his shoulder. He saw an enlisted man who appeared to be uninjured. "Hey, you," the chief bellowed. "Come here!"

The enlisted man went to Bradley. He grabbed a corner of the big raft, and he and the others carried it toward the aft starboard rail.

A deck plate under them ripped open. Flames burst up out of this split in the heavy steel plate. The chief and his men were engulfed by them. They dropped the raft and staggered away screaming and clawing at the flames on their bodies.

"I should have stayed on zigzag," Adams groaned, looking at the burning men. "No matter what, I should have stayed on zigzag."

The chief, blinded by the flames that had seared his face, groped toward midships. Brecht ran toward him. Before he got to him, the doomed chief collapsed onto the canting deck, on his back. His arms and legs pumped up and down. He screamed for someone to help him. Then, suddenly, he was still.

Brecht bent over him, then went back to the men he had been treating.

Adams looked at the chief's body. It was sliding down the deck. It would slide under the starboard rail and into the sea. At least he didn't suffer very long, Adams reflected, continuing toward the light-lock hatch.

Adams came to the hatch. A very young ensign, one of several who had joined the ship's company at Mare Island, shoved an arm across the hatch. "What are you trying to do?" the ensign said, his voice shrill and near hysteria. "Run away? Get over there and help get number-two lifeboat—"

"Sir," Adams cut in, "I've got to get down to Radio One, Captain McVay's orders."

"Show me his orders. You better have them, too, sailor!"

"Jesus Christ," Adams said, "do you think he's got time to write anything? It's a distress message. And I've got to—"

A ghastly shriek terminated Adams' explanation. Adams

and the ensign turned toward the source of the shriek. A damage-control man, running across the deck, had fallen onto a jagged, upthrust section of deck plate. It impaled him. He shrieked his agony while he tried to pull himself off the jagged steel shaft that had skewered him.

Adams glanced at the ensign. He was staring, eyes distended, mouth gaping, at the unfortunate man. "Get over there and help the poor bastard, you rank-happy boob," Adams said.

The ensign didn't respond. He kept staring at the awful sight of the skewered man.

Adams opened the light hatch and went down its ladder. The ensign put his hands over his eyes, turned from the dying sailor, and leaned on the bulkhead, his forehead pressing its gray steel.

His shoulders heaved. It was all too much for this boy-officer.

4

ADAMS CAME OFF THE LIGHT-LOCK hatch's ladder onto the narrow passageway of a sloping deck just below the torpedoed ship's weather deck. Hatches on both sides of the passageway opened into compartments housing control and administrative functions. One of them was Radio One.

It was aft about a hundred feet. Adams ran toward it on the down-slope side of the passageway, frequently steadying himself with a hand against the bulkhead.

The deck was hot. Wisps of smoke came up from seams cracked by the concussion of the torpedoes' explosions. "There must be a hell of a fire below," Adams muttered. He could hear crackling noises, the screams of injured or burned men—perhaps trapped men—and the shouts of a fire-control party.

"Goddamn!" he said. His feet were so hot he could hardly keep going. He lifted his right foot and felt the sole of his shoe. He jerked his hand away. It was too hot to touch. He went faster. The quicker he got there, the quicker he could relieve the anguish of his feet.

The ship's list increased. Twice Adams stumbled. Each time he was careful not to break his fall with a hand thrust onto the deck. Instead, he lurched against the bulkhead with a shoulder, regained his balance, and ran on down the passageway.

He came to Radio One. He darted inside. He was dancing from the heat of the passageway's deck. He plopped onto a chair and peeled off his shoes. Then he looked around. Radio One was a shambles. Typewriters, receivers, and other equipment had been toppled onto the deck.

Chief Radioman Paul McGinnes was at a desk, earphones on his head, a microphone in his hand. He was talking into the microphone. His face was grim and tense.

Back of him, Radioman First Class Jody Phillips was tapping the key on a manual transmitter that resembled an oldtime telegraph outfit. Radioman Second Class Jay Philburn was wearing earphones and turning dials on a panel of dials, buttons, and switches.

McGinnes took off his headset. "Yeah?" he said, looking over at Adams.

"Contact CinCPac," Adams said. "Captain McVay's orders. Tell CinCPac to send relief on the double. Tell them we're twelve north lat, one-thirty-five east long. And hurry, chief, we're in a hell of a shape."

McGinnes, a craggy-faced redhead with a crew cut, glared at Adams, who was sitting on the chair massaging his feet, which he had drawn up onto the chair. "What the hell do you think we've been doing! Just sitting on our ass enjoying the heat? Man, we can't receive or send."

Adams slipped his shoes back on. "I'd better phone the bridge and give McVay the word."

"You won't phone anybody," McGinnes said. "Nothing works anymore. Even the sound-power phones don't work. You're going to have to hotfoot it topside and deliver the good news in person."

"You get any kind of word out? McVay's going to ask."

"Not one fuckin' word. And we tried everything. Right now, Phillips, there, is transmitting on our emergency battery outfit. On five hundred kilocycles. The international distress frequency. But we've got no way to know if he's getting through to anybody."

"How about Radio Two?"

"There isn't a Radio Two anymore, Adams. Something exploded inside their compartment. Those guys are just pieces, not to mention what it did to their equipment."

"I'll hightail topside and give McVay the scoop," Adams said.

"How's it up there?" the chief asked.

"Rough," Adams said. "They laid it on us deluxe. You guys better not screw around too long down here, as long as you're not doing any good anyway."

"We gonna abandon?"

"It looks to me like it's just a matter of time," Adams said. "The whole damn bow's gone. You heard anything from damage control?"

"We don't know nothing, except we've been trying to get out some kind of word."

"Well, don't wait too long," Adams said.

He went out Radio One's hatch onto the passageway. The *Indianapolis* had listed twenty degrees. The deck of the passageway was so hot it was buckling. "Jesus . . ." Adams croaked, going as fast as he could, each step burning his feet.

The ship lurched. Adams almost fell onto the sizzling deck. The list had increased. It was twenty-five degrees now.

Agony swept over Adams' face. The soles of his shoes were smoking. His feet were killing him. He kept going. He had to get topside to tell Captain McVay that no radio message had been transmitted and none could be sent.

Water, coming from somewhere forward, began to trickle along the passageway's hot metal deck. It created steam. Visibility became almost zero. Its flow increased. The water went above the tops of Adams' shoes. It felt good. It cooled his feet.

But that rapidly rising water wasn't good, Adams realized. It meant that the *Indianapolis* was taking water. If flood-control parties couldn't stop it, the big cruiser would soon be sinking.

Adams, his feet feeling better, kept going down the listing flooding passageway. He went as fast as he could. He was worried about the water's rise. He looked at the coaming of the hatch of an abandoned office, the big cruiser's code room. Water was lapping over the coaming.

Adams' unease became fear. It would be a horrible way to

die, trapped down here. He tried to go faster. The water was above his knees. This slowed him terribly.

He came to the ladder that led down here from the light-lock hatch on the weather deck. The hatch was open. Tongues of flames from a fire on the deck licked down the ladder several feet from the hatch.

Maybe, Adams reflected, if I soak myself in the water down here, I can make it through those flames. He scooped up water in his hands and threw it up onto the ladder, as far as he could, to see how hot it was. The water sizzled and quickly became steam.

"You can't make it that way, mate," someone said.

Adams looked over his shoulder. Joe Hanley, gunner's mate first class, his face and shirt smeared with grease, was standing in the passageway's water. "I know a way out," Hanley said. "Up the tube in Powder Room Four. That's it just over there."

He pointed to a hatch to show Adams the location of Powder Room Four.

Adams looked back along the passageway. "Can we take the guys in Radio One?"

"No," Hanley said. "They couldn't get here before this water would be over their ears. We've got to go right now. You coming with me or not?"

Hanley had a grim, impatient expression on his grease-smeared face. But, God, Adams reflected, what about McGinnes and the other men in Radio One? Somebody ought to warn them they'd be trapped if they didn't get the hell out. But what good would it do for Adams to warn them if neither he nor the radiomen could escape? The way the water was rising he might not even get to the radio room, much less get back here and up the powder-room tube.

"Last call," Hanley said. "This baby's going topside."

"Lead off," Adams said, looking down the passageway toward Radio One.

He sloshed through the water, now well above his knees, behind Hanley, and soon they were in a powder-storage room. Bags of powder were stacked against a bulkhead. Water was sloshing on them as high as Adams' waist.

Hanley pointed to a powder-bag-size hole in a metal turret. "We go in there and up the ladder. You can't see the ladder, but it's inside. It'll take us up to the pointer's cage on the forward eight-inch turret."

Adams looked at the hole.

"Get going, mate," Hanley said. "We ain't got the whole fuckin' day!"

Adams, Hanley behind him, squirmed into the powder-bag hole and moments later they climbed out into the forward eight-inch gun turret.

They got to their feet and looked over the splinter shield. "We got us another little problem," Hanley said, his eyes sweeping the carnage, "which is getting our ass off this boat before she sinks."

Adams' eyes darted over everyone he could see from the gun turret. "I've got to find the captain. I've got to tell him Radio One—Two's shot to hell—couldn't get word to CinCPac."

"Did they get anything off to anybody?"

"They don't think so," Adams said.

"In that case," Hanley said, biting his lips, "we better find us a couple life jackets."

The *Indianapolis* was listing forty degrees to starboard. She was going to drown, no doubt of it now.

"I've got to find the captain," Adams said.

"Well, okay," Hanley said, "but I'm going to start looking for a jacket."

He went out of the gun turret to search for a life jacket and Adams began looking for Captain McVay. The captain had to know that no message had been sent. It might save lives that would be lost by waiting too long for relief that wasn't coming.

Adams came to the ensign who had tried to stop him from entering the light-lock hatch. "Sir," Adams said quickly, "where can I find McVay?"

The ensign glared at Adams. "It's Captain McVay, sailor."

"Okay, okay! It's Captain McVay. Where can I find him, sir? It's urgent."

"Just because we have received enemy torpedoes does not mean that naval protocol has been abrogated. You had better remember that, sailor."

"Yes, sir," Adams said impatiently. "I'll remember it. Where can I find Captain McVay? Sir?"

"How would I know in this confusion?"

Adams looked with incredulity at the ensign. "You wise-ass clown," he said through clenched teeth.

He turned away and looked out over the sloping deck. "I'll put you on report for calling an officer of the United States Navy a disrespectful name," the ensign screamed. "I'll have you confined to the brig. I'll—"

Adams was already terribly harried. The screaming ensign pushed his discretion over the brink. He turned back toward the ensign. "Fuck you," he said.

The ensign stood there, mouth gaping. That foul-mouth sailor . . . he'd have him court-martialed.

Adams had resumed his search for Captain McVay. He came to a group of men who were trying with their hands to pull open a jammed hatch on a deck locker. Through its four-inch opening Adams saw the scared, scorched faces of men trapped by the explosion-twisted hatch.

He heard their screams. He saw the flames that were licking at them and that would soon kill them if that damn stuck hatch couldn't be opened. "There's a dog wrench on the bulkhead forward," Adams said. "Maybe you can pry the hatch open enough to get those guys out."

A coxswain ran aft to get the dog wrench and Adams went on aft. He came to a lieutenant junior grade. "Do you know where I can find the captain?" he asked.

"Hell, how would I know?" the lieutenant said. He held out an inflatable life preserver. "Blow this up!"

"I can't, sir," Adams said. "I've got to find the captain. It's about his message to CinCPac."

"I'm giving you a direct order, sailor."

"I can't take the time," Adams explained. "I've got to find Captain McVay."

He turned toward the sinking ship's aft area and started toward it. The officer grabbed him and spun him around. "Blow it up, damn you," he bellowed.

Adams slammed a fist into the lieutenant's belly, broke away, and scurried aft along the canting deck.

Moments later a chief yeoman told him he had seen Captain McVay in an aft gun turret. "I don't remember which one. He might not be there now, anyway. He's been all over the place."

Adams hurried toward the aft gun turrets, frequently falling because of the deck's list, getting up as fast as he could, and going on again.

He came to a section of the tilted deck that had been greased by fuel oil geysered through a rent in the deck plate. Oil from this rent flowed down the deck and under the starboard rail.

The ship canted abruptly. Four men who were on the greased portion of the deck began to slide toward the starboard rail. They reached out for something, anything, to keep them from sliding off the deck. There was nothing to grab. They slid, screaming, under the starboard rail and into the sea.

Adams had been just above the greased area when the big cruiser lurched. He grabbed a hawser. It kept him from being thrown onto the grease and then sliding down the sharply sloping deck and under its rail.

He pulled himself to his feet. "Jesus . . ." he croaked. It had been close, that time.

He worked his way past the greased area, then hurried toward the aft gun turrets. He could see the fantail now. A hundred men, at least, were on this rearmost part of the big old cruiser. Some had life jackets. Some had inflatable life belts. Men were on all sides of a floater net. Each man was clutching the net, wanting to be sure he would have a place on it when the order came to abandon.

Confusion was everywhere. An officer ordered a group of enlisted men to go down the lifelines. Another officer forbade them to abandon the dying old girl.

Adams came to the aft gun turrets. He saw Captain McVay in an eight-inch turret. He climbed up to him. "Sir," he said, breathing hard, "radio could not send a distress except by key—and there is no assurance about that."

"Are they still trying?"

"No, sir. Radio One is flooded. Radio Two was zombied by one of the gook torpedoes."

The ensign whom Adams had insulted and who had been all this time catching up to Adams, floundered up into the turret. He pointed a shaking finger at Adams. "Captain McVay," he gasped, "I want this man confined to the brig to await trial, at which time I shall appear as a witness. He called me a wise-ass clown. Then he said, 'Fuck you.' He said that to me, Captain, an officer of the United States Navy. 'Fuck you,' he said. Right to my face."

The captain looked at the ensign with scorn he made no attempt to mask. "The Navy," he said, "can't condemn a man because of his talent for character analysis."

The ensign stared with flushed-cheeks astonishment at the captain. "Get out on the fantail," McVay said, "and help those men prepare to abandon."

"Yes, sir. But what about this man's insubordination, sir? And his obscenity? Can I depend upon you to—"

"Shove off and carry out your orders," McVay bellowed.

The ensign, mumbling to himself, went onto the fantail and McVay put a hand on Adams' shoulder. "Get a life jacket, Adams," he said. "Get it right away."

The captain picked up a bull horn. "Now hear this," he shouted. "Abandon ship! Abandon ship!"

5

ADAMS HAD BEEN ISSUED A pneumatic life belt. He had kept it suspended from a toggle in the navigation bridge where he could get at it quickly if he needed it. So what did I do when I needed it, he reflected while he plodded toward the navigation bridge, I left it there on the toggle; I didn't even think of it, I was so damn disoriented after we got hit.

Is that belt still dangling from the toggle? Someone might have taken it, so I'd better try to find another pneumatic or a kapok life jacket while I'm on my way to the navigation bridge. I damn sure want some kind of floater when I jump into that big ocean.

He came to the navigation bridge. His life belt was still on the toggle on the port bulkhead. He put it around his waist, several inches above his belt. Put it on too low, he reflected, and it will hold my ass above water instead of my head.

While he secured the life belt's buckle, he looked at Larry Keefer's body. The steel splinter was still sticking out of him, half on each side of the dead chief quartermaster.

"So long, Larry," Adams said, his eyes misting. It was a tough break the big chief had gotten; he'd been in the wrong place at the wrong time.

Adams went out of the navigation bridge and toward the men who were hustling a raft toward the starboard side of the sharply canted deck. Maybe he could get aboard that raft. He hoped he could. His chances of survival would be greater than if he had to depend on the pneumatic life belt, especially since rescue might be a long time coming.

He came to the raft. Chief Boatswain's Mate Mike McCurdy, a burly carrot top, was holding a flashlight while he guided the men with the raft.

The lieutenant who had ordered Adams to inflate his life preserver came, slipping and stumbling, up the sloping deck to the men with the raft. "Put out that flashlight, you idiot," he bellowed to McCurdy. "An enemy submarine might see it."

McCurdy looked at the lieutenant with absolute incredulity. "You gotta be kidding," he said. "These fires"—he swept an arm to indicate the flames that darted up from the dying cruiser in a dozen places—"can be seen long before anybody can see this little old flashlight. Besides which, no Jap sub is going to waste a torpedo on us. They've already given us the bananas. Clear up to our fuckin' ears."

"Consider yourself under arrest," the officer said.

He turned to Adams. "You're under arrest, too, sailor. The penalty for striking an officer—"

"Oh, for chrissake," McCurdy said.

He swooped up the suddenly startled lieutenant and flung him, screaming, off the bow. Then the big chief looked at Adams. "You hit that sumbitch?"

"I sure did," Adams said.

"Well, hooray," the chief said.

"Chief," Adams said, looking at the raft, "what's the chance of me—"

The *Indianapolis* made a great lurch to starboard, going over to more than sixty degrees. Adams and Chief McCurdy, the other men, and the raft plummeted off the deck and into the sea.

Adams sunk deeply into the water. Got to remember to press the plunger on my life belt, he said to himself. Then he reflected, Christ, man, right now is when you do it or you're never going to do it.

His head popped up out of the sea. He looked around. He

couldn't see the raft. "Where's the raft?" he yelled to a sailor with a kapok jacket.

"I wish I knew," the sailor said.

Other men were in the water. Adams didn't see Chief McCurdy or the raft. It was dark down here on the sea's rolling surface. The moon didn't do much good. The *Indy*, though, was lit up like a bonfire. Adams looked up at her. The way she was listing, almost on her starboard flank, she'd go any moment now.

Adams began to swim away from the doomed ship. Others who had been catapulted into the sea were already swimming as fast as they could. Some didn't have kapoks or belts. One of these unfortunates, a yeoman from Communications, kept screaming he couldn't keep it up much longer. "Somebody help me . . . please," he begged.

It was piteous. Without help he would soon be dead. Adams swam around him. It was a terrible thing to do, Adams reflected, but I can't help him. I'd be killing myself. We'd both be sucked into the *Indy*'s terrible vortex.

Adams could hear shouts from the *Indianapolis*. He looked over his shoulder. Men were still on the sinking ship. Some were jumping off. Some had life preservers. Some did not.

The wounded old cruiser began to sink, bow first. Adams and the others in the sea beside him could hear screams of men trapped inside. It was a hard thing to hear.

The sinking ship's hull raised straight up, her four screws exposed.

She seemed to stand there, her stern high in the air.

"We'd better get farther away," a floater near Adams said. "If she falls on us . . ."

He didn't say the rest of it. The old girl slid straight down. Very slowly. Adams and the others stared, mesmerized, until her screws disappeared into the rolling tropic sea.

Bubbles, debris, and bodies came to the surface all around the floating men. One of the items that came up was a life-jacket bag. Adams and others who saw the bag swam toward it as fast as they could. Adams was one of the four who got there first.

They began to ride the swells, each of the four holding on to a side of the bag. No one said anything. Each man held firmly on to his side of the bag and thought his own sad thoughts. Did Joe make it? Or Paul? Or Nick or Gary or Pete or Fats or Charlie?

How many had survived the torpedoing and sinking of the *Indianapolis*? One thousand, one hundred and ninety-five men had been aboard her when the torpedoes came. Many had been killed when the torpedoes exploded. Others had died in fires and explosions of the *Indy*'s depth charges and ammunition lockers. Some had been trapped below decks and drowned when the wounded old cruiser's lower decks filled with water. Others were drowning now. Right down there below us, trapped in steel-wall compartments and passageways.

Storekeeper Second Class Steve McKellip, still wearing his glasses, holding on to the bag opposite Adams, broke the silence. "It's going to be a long night," he said. "These swells got my guts churned up already. How long do you guys think it'll be before help gets here?"

Ralph Eggert, electrician's mate third class, on Adams' right, said, "I heard McVay got word to CinCPac the first thing. Which means Air-Sea Rescue seaplanes will be here from Saipan by dawn. So all we gotta do is just take it easy. Not anybody get scared or anything."

The other man was Charlie Moore, gunner's mate first class. He was forty-one. Twenty-two years on the blue. Regular Navy, not Reserve like these boot-camp quickies. He was a tough man, hard faced, tattoos on both arms and most of his chest. But he was decent and a practitioner of the fair shake.

"The way I put it together," he said, "we're five hundred miles from Guam. At thirty-five knots, that's what surface rescue craft can do if you kick 'em in the ass, they'll be here before noon."

"I got news for you guys," Adams said. "I don't think the distress got sent."

"Yeah?" Moore said. "How the hell do you know?"

"McVay sent me to Radio One with the distress. Right after we took that third torp. All they had going down there was an emergency battery outfit. They didn't think they'd got anything out on it. At least they didn't get acknowledgment from anybody."

"Do you know that for a fact," Moore demanded, "or is it just scuttlebutt?"

"Well, I was down there and Chief McGinnes told me. In person. He also said Radio Two got it one hundred percent, including the guys in there, from the first torp. So naturally they didn't get anything on the air."

"If that ain't a crock," Moore said. "A pure goddamn eighteen-carat chickenshit crock!"

He looked at the others, their faces visible in the tropic moonlight, the moon being brighter now that the *Indy*'s fires no longer subordinated it. "Fellas," he said, "we have got our balls on the bob wire. This particular part of the blue is full of sharks. In fact, this is one of the sharkiest places in the whole fuckin' Pacific. Which means the longer we're here the bigger chance we got of being shark bait. I'm not trying to spook you guys, but you ought to know what we're up against."

"Jesus . . ." McKellip squeaked, conjuring up a vision of a shark biting off his feet.

"I don't think we're quite as bad off as you said, there, chief," Eggert said. "I admit there are sharks in this part of the Pacific, but you want to remember—we all want to remember, CinCPac keeps in constant communication with every warship. All the time. Twenty-four hours a day. Okay, they don't hear from us. They'll naturally wonder why. They'll try to communicate. Nothing happens. So what'll they do? They'll send a couple planes out here to see what's going on. Which means it'll be just a little longer before Air-Sea's dumbos and surface ships get here.

"Another thing we want to think about," Eggert continued, "there might be a couple U.S. submarines around here that could surface anytime. So we actually got nothing to worry about."

"Except the sharks while we're waiting," McKellip said uneasily.

"Yeah," Moore said, "except the sharks. You guys know what worries me about them? It's blood from the guys that got wounded. The wounded ones that got off the *Indy* before she sank. Sharks can smell blood Christ knows how far away. So they'll be here, if they're not here already."

"Then we got nothing to worry about, do we?" McKellip said. "I mean us four guys. None of us got any wounds, have we?"

"All I got is this cut on my forehead," Adams said. "Which isn't bleeding anymore, anyway. Besides not being in the water."

McKellip looked at the others. Each said he had no wounds.

"That don't mean we're a hundred percent in the clear," Moore said. "If a shark is down there and he's hungry and he sees leg meat dangling right there in front of him, well, there you are."

"Do you have to talk about it all the goddamn time?" Adams said. "Christ, it's going to be bad enough without worrying about sharks."

"All right, I'm sorry I mentioned it," Moore said. "But I thought you guys would want to know, in case something bites off your leg, what bit it off."

"Why don't you knock it off, you morbid old bastard," Eggert said.

"Kid," Moore said, "you want to know what happened to the last guy called me a bastard? I'll tell you what happened to the son of a bitch. We were in this tavern on Market Street and this slob came up to where I was—"

McKellip shrieked. Horror swept over his face. "Something bit my leg," he babbled.

He felt down with his right hand, his left hand clinging to the life-jacket bag.

He pulled up his right hand. Absolute terror was on his face. "My God, something bit my leg clear off! Right below my knee."

He looked at the others. "Help me, please . . . you guys gotta help me."

Moore slammed a fist into McKellip's jaw. McKellip jerked back, releasing his grip on the life-jacket bag. He slid below the surface, dazed from the chief's hard blow.

"Everybody start swimming north, toward them stars," Moore said excitedly. "We gotta get away! His blood'll draw a million sharks!"

Adams, the chief, and Eggert, clinging to the life-jacket bag, swam northward as fast as they could.

"Look back," Moore said. "But keep goin'."

They looked back. Sharks were churning the sea. "They

call it a frenzy," Moore said. "Each of them wants to get the most he can. Keep goin'!"

A few yards farther Moore, who had been looking back at the frenzy while he swam, said, "Everybody quit swimming. Keep your feet perfectly still."

The frenzy was nearly over, he explained. "They'll be looking to see what else there is to eat around here. So don't attract them by moving anything. Feet, legs, your ass, anything!"

"Jesus . . ." Eggert squeaked, his voice shrill. "Do you think they'll come over here?"

"I'd bet on it," Moore said, "but if everybody is perfectly still, not moving the least little bit, they might think our legs are kelp or something."

"What if they don't?" Eggert worried. "What if they catch on it's human legs and feet?"

"Don't talk about it," Adams said.

"I'd rather have got it back on the *Indy*," Eggert said.

"Shut up! You're spookin' yourself," Moore said. "Just keep calm. Think about something else."

No one spoke for several tense minutes. Meanwhile they rode the swells, up and down, up and down. "We made it," Moore said. "They're gone by now. Or we'd know it!"

"Can we start swimming again?" Eggert asked.

"Just where the hell would we swim to?" Moore said. "We'll be better off right here. There'll be someone here in the morning. Before noon at the latest. We go wandering away, they might not see us."

"I wouldn't bet on anybody coming," Adams said.

"If you ain't a cheerful little son of a bitch," Moore said.

"I'm just trying to be realistic. I don't think CinCPac got the word about us."

"All I got to say is, if they didn't we're up the fuckin' creek."

"For chrissake," Eggert said, "can't you guys think of anything to talk about except sharks and nobody coming?"

"You got something there," Moore said. "Neither one is what anybody could call a cheerful subject."

"I keep thinking about McKellip," Eggert said. "I used to think being burned to death was the worst possible way to die. Not now, though. Being eaten alive by sharks is a thousand times worse."

"Not if you don't know it," Moore said. "Which is one of the reasons I busted that poor guy on the chin. So he would be unconscious when they bit into his guts. The other reason being so he would let loose and we could get away.

"He was the same as dead, anyway, and there was no use of the rest of us going, too, which would have happened if those devils had ate him right under us."

"We understand why you did what you did," Adams said. "Nobody's blaming you."

"God . . . being eaten by sharks," Eggert said. "While he was still alive. Even if he was unconscious, he was still alive."

"You better start thinking about something else," Moore said, "or you're going to worry yourself into a Section Eight case."

"Something just brushed against my feet," Eggert croaked.

"Everybody don't move," Moore said quickly.

Interminable minutes passed. "You're barefoot, ain't you?" Moore said.

"I took my shoes off when the captain said to abandon. I thought I could swim better without my shoes."

"You dumb stupid idiot," Moore said. "Bare feet attract sharks."

6

THE FIRST LIGHT OF DAWN broke the gloom, and some of the despair, of the endless night. Moore, Adams, and Eggert were still hanging on to the life-jacket bag. None had slept. Each was afraid, if he fell asleep, he'd lose his grip on the life-jacket bag and slip down into the sea.

But a worse fear had been that a shark might suddenly bite off a dangling foot. Or a leg. "Maybe sharks don't prowl around at night," Eggert had said.

"They do," Moore said. "They prowl as much at night as in the daytime. They're constantly looking for something to eat."

"What makes you such a specialist on sharks?"

"Listen, kid," the tough old gunner's mate said, "I've been in the United States Navy for twenty-two fuckin' years. I would of retired two years ago if it hadn't been for the war. You gotta stay in, they said, for the duration. But look at the bright side of it, this chickenshit officer said. You'll get a bigger pension.

"But getting back to sharks, the reason I happen to know a few things about sharks is because I have been in the Pacific warm waters a million times, which is where we are now—on the north side of the real warm part, which is also where the most sharks live.

"I've fished for sharks off fantails of different ships. I've shot the bastards with oh-three Springfields from whaleboats in lagoons. I've blasted 'em with ships' twenty-millimeter AA rifles. So don't ask me if I know anything about sharks. I happen to know quite a bit about them and one of the main things I know is, they're mean bastards. And I mean mean."

Eggert's face was grim. What Moore had been saying about sharks did nothing to relieve his fear that one of them might bite off a leg before rescue came. "I guess the most consoling thing we've got to think about is that Air-Sea Rescue ought to be here before noon. So all we've got to do is not get shark-eaten in the meantime."

"Don't count too strong on Air-Sea Rescue," Adams said.

"You still don't think they got a message off that we got torpedoed, do you?" Eggert said.

"I sure don't. Like I told you guys before, I was down there in Radio One. I talked to Chief McGinnes personally. If any word got out, McGinnes said, it was on the emergency battery outfit. But he wasn't sure it was working because there was no response."

"Maybe they could send but not receive," Eggert said. "There's always that chance, isn't there?"

"I suppose so," Adams said.

"Well, anyway," Eggert said, "CinCPac keeps in constant communication with warships. They'll send somebody out to see why they haven't heard from the *Indy*."

"I wouldn't bet on that," Moore said. "If there's any possible way to fuck up a situation the Navy'll do it. How long you been in the Navy?"

"A little over two years."

"Then you're the same as still in boot camp. In the twenty-two years I've been in I've seen snafus you wouldn't believe. I wouldn't be surprised if this turns out to be another one. Meaning, even if they got the message, some stupid-ass yeoman will file it instead of telling somebody. Or if he actually delivers it, some know-it-all officer will say that it's absolutely impossible, that somebody got their wires crossed. There's no gook subs this side of the north chop line or we'd be the first to know.

"However, he'll give that communication to the commander's yeoman. If the commander wants to send rescue craft out there, okay, but he doesn't want the responsibility. Christ, if he ordered planes and ships out there with no more to go on than that message, which doesn't add up just right because the closest gook submarine is a thousand miles from there, he'd be the laughingstock of the U.S. Navy."

Eggert said dispiritedly, "You can make a guy feel great. I'll give you credit for that."

"Listen, kid," Moore said. "I'm not trying to demoralize you. For chrissake, we're all in this together. What I was saying is, if anybody don't think the Navy can fuck up a situation, they don't know the U.S. Navy. You want to remember I've been a member of the club for twenty-two years and I've seen more fuck-ups than you can count."

Eggert's face became even more glum. "Just the same. I'm going to keep thinking the message got through and Air-Sea Rescue planes are on their way here. And also that some sub or surface ship that was around here close will show up. You got to admit that could actually happen."

"I'll bet you still believe in Sandy Claus," Moore said.

"All right," Eggert said, "suppose you two crepe-hangers are right. Suppose the message never got sent. Or if it did, it got screwed up. Then what are we going to do? Hang on to this life-jacket bag until somebody eventually comes?"

"What we're going to do," Adams said, "is hope you're right and me and Moore are both wrong. And in the meantime look for a raft or a floater net."

Moore said Adams was right, the thing to do was find something big enough to get on, or into. "Once we get our feet out of the water we won't constantly be in danger of being some shark's breakfast."

The sun was rising over the eastern horizon. "That's a pretty sight from down here in the water," Eggert said. "It looks different than from a ship."

"Nothing looks pretty to me," Moore said, "and it won't, either, until we get our feet out of this fuckin' water."

He looked around, in all directions. "It's still too dark, but it'll be light enough in a couple minutes to see what we're looking for."

"I wish I'd joined the Army," Eggert said. "I could have. They said at the induction station I could have either one."

"Soldiers get their balls in the gears, too," Moore said. "At least until we got torpedoed you had it pretty damn good compared to the Army."

"Well, it's not what I'd call good now," Eggert said.

"I hope we find a raft," Adams said. "We'll all feel better if we did."

"Even a floater net would be better than what we got," Eggert said.

"Not much, it wouldn't," Moore said. "You'd just have more to hang on to, is all. You'd still have your feet and legs in the water."

While these men and more than eight hundred other survivors of the torpedoed cruiser were floating on the Pacific's rolling seas, not far away—in fact, very close—Captain Mochitsura Hashimoto, Executive Officer Haruko Yomura, Navigation Officer Soyei Miyamoto, and several lesser officers were in the periscope compartment of the Japanese submarine that had sunk the *Indianapolis*.

Hashimoto looked, again, at his watch. His grim face was taut. He turned toward a hatch. He looked at his watch another time. What was taking his hydrophone officer so damn long? If enemy ships or aircraft were nearby, the *Nakapo* ought to be diving, not lurking just below the sea's surface.

Hydrophone Officer Seiho Yamashita came through the hatch. Hashimoto glared at him. "Make your report," he said. "Don't just look at me."

"Yes, sir," the little Japanese naval officer said. "I have found no indication of American submarines or surface ships."

Hashimoto, clearly, was nervous. He kept licking his lips. It would be a bitter stab of fate to be sunk before he could even report his victory, his sinking of the big American warship, to Fleet Headquarters in Tokyo. "Are you absolutely certain?" he demanded of his hydrophone officer.

"Sir," Yamashita said, "I have listened without even a moment's respite. Ever since we sunk the American ship, I have not depended upon my men, as capable as they are. I, personally, have listened to our instruments. There has been no indication either of enemy ships, surface or undersea, or of aircraft."

Hashimoto's brow furrowed. "Is it possible that surfaced American submarines or surface ships are lurking up there, waiting for us to reveal ourselves?"

"I don't think so, sir," Yamashita said.

"But you don't know for a certainty?"

"No, sir, I don't. I don't see how they could be up there without our detection. But it is not impossible. Americans are clever. They have invented a way of deceiving us by irregular patterns of their surface ships' screws. They may also have invented some kind of submarine silencing device or technique we don't know about."

Hashimoto glared at the hydrophone officer. "Yamashita," he said acidly, "with your capability for evasive replies you should have been in the diplomatic service."

Hashimoto waved the hydrophone officer toward the hatch. He turned to the other officers. He was not going to ask them what they thought he ought to do. A commanding officer of the Imperial Japanese Navy does not practice collegiality with his subordinates. He strode toward the sea periscope. Petty Officer Nokamura, who had been on scope duty before the attack, had remained beside the lowered scope. If Hashimoto or some other officer wanted it raised, it would be his duty to raise it.

"Up day scope," Captain Hashimoto said.

"Yes, sir," Nokamura said. He raised the scope and stepped aside.

Hashimoto looked into it. He swung it 360 degrees. No surface ships. But there might be a submerged submarine, maybe even a flotilla, or aircraft.

Nothing visible, though, except survivors of the big American cruiser. He swung the scope toward Moore and the others who were clinging to the life-jacket bag. They were very close—so close that the scope's magnifying lenses enabled him to see them as clearly as if they were in this compartment. He smiled. An idea had come to him. It would involve those three Americans.

He turned to Nokamura. "Up the sky scope," he said.

His face became grim. Sometimes an attack scope couldn't be seen, but a sky scope made a wake that was visible to aircraft a mile away. It was dangerous to use the sky scope. But it would be more dangerous, even foolhardy, not to use it and surface when, waiting like a flock of vultures, American planes could swoop down on the *Nakapo*. Long before the big submarine could be put into emergency dive, she would be destroyed by American bombs.

Nokamura raised the sky scope. Hashimoto, who had been waiting beside it, looked into it. He swung it 360 degrees, back again, then twice more. No aircraft.

Considerably relieved, he turned to the officers. "We're going to surface," he said.

"But, sir," Executive Officer Yomura said, "what if the silence is bait for some kind of trap? Such as a flotilla of American submarines, or just one or two, suddenly surfacing and shelling the hell out of us before we could even man our deck guns?"

"If they just shot off our conning tower," Navigation Officer Miyamoto said worriedly, "we would be doomed."

There was no more helpless war machine, he said, than a submarine without its conning tower. It couldn't submerge. It could only cruise on the sea's surface, an easy target for enemy aircraft who could take all the time they wanted getting to it.

"Sir," Yomura said to Hashimoto, "what is the point of risking this costly submarine, one of the few the Imperial Navy has left, when no real gain could come from it?"

Captain Hashimoto's face flushed in anger. Stupid damn riceheads. The obvious had escaped them. "I have decided I want definite proof that we sank the American ship."

"But, sir," Yomura said, "I will confirm its sinking. And so will Lieutenant Miyamoto. We both saw the American after three of our torpedoes made contact. Each of them, sir, striking at forty-two knots with twelve hundred ten pounds of explosives. There is no way—"

Hashimoto angrily interrupted his executive officer. "What you men saw you saw through a night attack periscope. We will surface so we can take photographs of the survivors. And to retrieve flotsam that is undeniably from the American ship."

Hashimoto's deep-set black eyes went from one of his officers to the others. "I want, and I will get, credit for a sure kill. There must be no doubt whatever at Fleet Headquarters."

Hashimoto went to the navigation desk and picked up the voice pipe's tube. "Surface," he said.

He turned to his officers. "The sinking of the American warship will not make one iota of difference in the final outcome of the war. We are already defeated. But it will make me a hero. Very likely this will be the last American ship to be sunk . . . and what a magnificent sinking it is. A major man-of-war, not some inconsequential supply craft."

Hashimoto's face beamed. "I will be recorded in the annals of heroism."

Hashimoto turned back to the voice pipe. He picked up its tube. "Gun crews, prepare to man your stations."

He looked again at his officers. "I want both of you to go onto the sea deck with me, with your cameras. I want photos of the survivors, several photos from various angles showing our conning tower in each of them to verify their positions in relation to ours. Similarly, I want photos of the flotsam."

Moore and his colleagues, unaware that they were about to play another part in the drama of the torpedoing of the cruiser *Indianapolis,* were looking in all directions for a raft. The *Indianapolis* had thirty-five rafts and twenty-four floater nets, the latter in baskets designed to float out of the baskets when they were on the sea. At least one of the rafts, they reasoned, should be somewhere around here and, hopefully, not occupied by so many men that they couldn't take three more aboard.

"It would be a hell of a thing," Eggert said, "to be eaten by a shark and a couple minutes later a rescue ship or plane showed up."

"The guy who got ate," Adams said, "wouldn't know it. So what difference would it make if the shark ate him one minute or one hour before rescue got here?"

"It wouldn't make any difference to the guy," Eggert said, "except the irony of the situation. Just the difference of one minute, or whatever time it might be, and the guy can be either in some shark's gut or rescued, in which case he'd have his whole life ahead of him."

"You got sharks on the brain," Moore said. "Quit thinking about them."

"How can I quit thinking about them when I saw a guy eaten alive practically right in front of us."

"You didn't actually see it. All you saw was, the guy said his leg had been bit off. Then I hit him and he sank like a brick. Down there, where nobody saw him, is where he got ate."

"Why don't we concentrate on looking for a raft," Adams said, "instead of talking about sharks."

"I second the motion," Moore said, "providing we can get Junior here to keep his fucking mouth shut."

"I won't say another word if that'll make you happy," Eggert said, his face showing his anger. "I won't even say anything if a shark bites off my balls. I'll just keep my mouth shut."

"Why don't you start practicing right now instead of waiting for a shark to bite your balls off," Moore said. "You're getting on my nerves, in case you never noticed."

"Hey, you guys . . . look!" Adams said excitedly.

Moore and Eggert turned to look in the direction Adams was looking. A submarine was rising out of the sea.

"I knew Air-Sea Rescue would get something here right away," Eggert said excitedly.

"You stupid jerk," Moore said, "that's not one of our subs. That's a gook sub. See the number on the conning? I-Fifty-eight. Notice how they've got the I. The top part slanted forty-five degrees to port. That's the way the Japs do it. I'll bet that's the sub that torpedoed us."

Eggert, suddenly terribly scared, said, "What are they gonna do to us? Kill us?"

"I wouldn't be surprised," Moore said, his face grim.

"I'm never going to see my little boy," Adams said, tears welling in his eyes. "Son of a bitchin' goddamn Japs!"

"Maybe we can swim away," Eggert croaked. "It's stupid, just doing nothing. Just waiting for them to kill us."

"Pull yourself together," Moore said. "Don't let the bastards think we're chicken."

"I'm going to swim somewhere even if you guys aren't," Eggert blubbered.

"Don't be an ass hole," Moore said. "You can't swim farther than those deck guns can reach."

Adams didn't say anything. He was thinking about the little boy he would never see.

The *Nakapo*'s platform rose above the surface. Her hatch opened. The six helmet-wearing men of her gun crew poured out of the conning tower, ran to the big submarine's deck-mounted rifles and machine guns, and quickly began to remove the watertights from them and from their deck-attached steel munitions boxes.

Four Japanese with combat helmets and Nambu machine rifles followed the gunners onto the *Nakapo*'s sea-dripping platform. Their eyes darted over the surrounding seas, making sure that no Americans were armed, looking especially at Moore and the other men who were clutching the life-jacket bag and who were so close to the big submarine they could spit on it. Then three of the Nambu men darted to equidistant positions on the submarine's long platform.

The one who remained near the Americans kept looking down at them, the Nambu in his hand, its murderous muzzle pointed toward them. Meanwhile Captain Hashimoto and the officers with cameras climbed up the conning's aluminum ladder and went out onto its sea deck.

"Start taking photos," Hashimoto said, looking all around and into the skies. "We're not going to spend the day up here."

Hashimoto went down the platform toward the Nambu man who was watching the Americans.

"That monkey-face little creep is probably the captain," Moore said. "The son of a bitch who ordered the torpedoing."

"Don't talk so loud," Adams said nervously. "Maybe he understands English. A lot of them do."

"What difference does it make?" Eggert croaked. "They're going to kill us anyway."

"Jesus, that's a big submarine," Moore said. "I never knew there was such a big one."

"Who gives a fuck how big it is," Adams said, his tongue flicking over his lips. "We won't be around to tell anybody."

The Americans' eyes went from Hashimoto, who was coming toward them, to the petty officer with the combat helmet and the Nambu machine rifle, a Japanese version of a tommy gun.

The gunner, burly Iko Tanaka, a former Kyushu fish-cannery foreman, never took his glinting Oriental eyes from the Americans. He wished he had orders to kill them. He despised Americans. American soldiers had killed two of his brothers at Saipan.

Maybe, he hoped, Captain Hashimoto would let him hose these Americans after the captain did whatever he intended to do with them. He'd stitch them with bursts from his Nambu, back and forth, back and forth. Chop them like meat in a grinder. Damn American murderers!

Hashimoto came to the end of the platform. He leaned on its rail and looked down at the Americans. "Do not be so terrible afraids," he said in understandable English. "I will not shoots you. Japanese officer does not shoots helpless peoples."

"Bullshit," Moore said.

"Cool it, for chrissake," Adams said quickly. "Maybe he won't . . . if you keep your mouth shut!"

7

"YOU LIKE FOODS AND WATERS?" Captain Hashimoto said, looking down at the three American Navy men who were clutching the life-jacket bag on the rolling morning sea beside the big submarine's starboard bow. "I give you foods and waters."

Hashimoto turned toward Executive Officer Yomura, who had been photographing the Americans, and other more distant survivors who were off the surfaced submarine's bow. "I want a canister of water, canned food, and fish. And a medical kit. The one in the officers' compartment."

Astonishment swept over Lieutenant Commander Yomura's intelligent, fine-featured face. "Are you going to give them to those Americans? Sir, our food and water are in short supply. We will barely have enough for our return to Japan. May I suggest—"

"Bring the food and water," Hashimoto said harshly. "And the medical kit. Immediately!"

Yomura, his lips tight, saluted Captain Hashimoto. Orders in the Imperial Japanese Navy were absolute. He turned and ran down the platform toward the conning-tower hatch.

"What's that all about?" Adams muttered.

"How the hell would I know?" Moore said. "Do I look like I speak Japanese?"

"That slopehead with the gun acts like he can't wait to zap us," Eggert said, his eyes on Tanaka, whose Nambu machine rifle was aimed at the men on the water. "He's a mean-looking bastard if I ever saw one."

Executive Officer Yomura and a glasses-wearing enlisted man came out of the conning onto the platform. The enlisted man was carrying seven cans of food and a canister of water. Yomura held the strap of a small chest with a Red Cross insignia on its sides, the camera in his other hand.

They came down the platform to Captain Hashimoto. "For chrissake," Moore muttered, "they're not going to give us those goodies, are they?"

"I can't imagine what the hell else they got them for," Adams said, keeping his voice low so Hashimoto couldn't hear what he was saying.

Hashimoto turned toward the other officer with the camera, Lieutenant Miyamoto, who was on the platform's stern photographing survivors and flotsam. "Miyamoto," the captain yelled, "I want you and Yomura to take photos of what I am about to do."

Lieutenant Miyamoto ran to the platform's bow. He bowed. "My camera is ready, sir," he said.

"Take good photos, both of you. Get everything focused just right," Hashimoto said, "and be sure that my face will be clearly identifiable."

He took the Red Cross chest from Yomura, got to his knees, and handed it down to the Americans. "Here is medicines for peoples who got hurted," he said.

"I'll be a two-head mule," Moore said, reaching up for the medical chest.

At the same time, still clutching the little chest, Hashimoto looked up at his officers and barked, "Take photos now."

He smiled and the officers got very nice pictures of their smiling officer presenting the three ragtag American survivors with a medical kit, clearly identifiable by the Red Cross on its flank which, by no coincidence, was toward the photographers.

"I don't believe it," Adams said. "I'm dreaming."

"They want the photos for propaganda purposes," Moore said.

"Who gives a damn what they want them for as long as we got the goodies?" Adams replied.

"They're going to give us some food now," Eggert said. "I'll bet there's water in that big can. Jesus, that's gonna be great. I never been so thirsty."

"There's something funny about this," Moore said, reaching up for the first of the seven cans of food that Hashimoto was to hand down to him.

Moore put each of the cans on the life-jacket bag, in its middle. "Watch they don't roll off," he said to the others.

"Don't worry about that," Adams said, looking hungrily at a can whose colorful label indicated that it contained plums. He liked plums. They had always been his favorite fruit.

The seven cans were on the life-jacket bag now. "Hold medicines this way, please," Hashimoto said to Moore, motioning that he wanted the little chest's Red Cross toward the submarine.

Hashimoto, still on his knees, looked up at his officers. "More photos. And be damn sure they include everything. The cans of food, all of the Americans, and my face."

He smiled, his gold teeth showing, and Yomura and Miyamoto took several photographs.

Hashimoto picked up the canister of water, which the glasses-wearing enlisted man had put on the platform beside the kneeling officer. "Be special carefuls," Hashimoto said, handing the canister down to Moore. "Do not let falls in ocean."

"Don't worry, Charlie," Moore said, carefully gripping the canister. "Water is the one thing we need the most."

Hashimoto looked at the Americans. "Make smiles, please," he said.

The Americans didn't have to force put-ons. It was easy to smile in appreciation of gifts that would surely keep them alive until rescue planes and ships arrived.

Hashimoto said to the cameramen, "These will be the last photos and they better be good. I want everything showing clearly, especially myself."

He smiled broadly, turning his head so that he would be semiprofiled against the smiling Americans and their gifts.

The photographers snapped their cameras. Each three times. "We got them, sir, just like you wanted. Everything perfectly framed," Miyamoto said.

Hashimoto's smile faded. He said something to Tanaka, the enlisted man with the combat helmet and the Nambu machine rifle. Tanaka became even more alert, gripping the Nambu tightly, his eyes darting from one American to another, a murderous look on his stern face.

Hashimoto turned to the Americans. "Thank you, please. Now give back the waters. And do not drop in ocean or you be shooted."

Moore's face became taut. "I knew it was too good to be for real," he mumbled to the others.

"Hurry, please, or I not be so nice," Hashimoto said, extending a hand down toward the Americans.

"Give it to him," Adams said. "Or fart-face up there will give us the treatment."

"He probably will, anyway," Moore said, his lips tight.

He held the canister of water up toward Captain Hashimoto. "Here you are, you mother-fuckin' slant-eyed son of a bitch," he said.

Hashimoto put the canister on the platform. "Now the foods, please," he said, reaching down again.

After he put the last of the seven cans of food on the platform beside the canister, he reached down for the Red Cross chest.

"After he gets this," Moore said quietly to the other floaters, "we'll get ours."

He looked quickly at Eggert. "Don't cry, goddammit! Don't give those gooks a chance for a photo they can laugh at. Take it like a man!"

He handed the Red Cross chest up to Hashimoto. After the Japanese put it on the platform he stood up and motioned for the glasses-wearing enlisted man to take the chest and the other items below. Then he looked down at the Americans. "Thank you, please," he said. "I hope you not die."

Hashimoto turned to his officers. "You thought I was actually going to give those things to the Americans, didn't you?"

"Yes, sir," Miyamoto and Yomura said in unison.

"It is little wonder," Hashimoto said, "that you men do not

have commands. A commanding officer must be able to turn each situation into an advantage."

"Yes, sir," the officers said.

"Think how these photos will look to the world. We will appear to be charitable and humane men and this will react favorably upon the terms of the surrender that Japan must soon negotiate."

Executive Officer Yomura said, bowing, "You are very intelligent, sir, and most perceptive."

"It is a gift," Lieutenant Miyamoto said, also bowing slightly.

"I am quite aware of these traits," Hashimoto said. "Now order everyone below, Yomura."

Yomura bellowed to the men on the big submarine's platform. Tanaka and the other Nambu men ran to the conning tower and vanished into its hatch. The gun crews began to secure their weapons and munitions boxes with watertights and soon everyone was inside the submarine and a boatswain's mate was turning the conning tower's heavy steel hatch lock.

The *Nakapo*'s conning tower began to disappear in a swirl of frothy sea as the huge submarine went below the surface. The Americans who were clutching the life-jacket bag watched it until there was no more swirling sea.

"Nobody'll believe it when we tell them," Moore said. "In fact, I don't believe it myself. I had to be dreaming."

"I thought for a minute there we had some water," Eggert said. "I wish I'd taken a drink when we had the chance. God, I'm thirsty."

"You're no thirstier than everybody else," Moore said. "Quit thinking about it."

Adams was still staring at the site of the *Nakapo*'s disappearance. "I thought sure they'd lace us after they got the photos. But they didn't, and that gook CO even said he hoped we wouldn't die."

"He wasn't a total son of a bitch," Moore said.

"When it comes to Japs," Adams said, "I guess you can't figure them."

"Well, I'm not complaining," Moore said. "At least we're still all in one piece."

He looked out over the sea. "I suppose what we'd better do

is what we were doing before that gook sub showed up. Which is find us a raft."

"There's one," Adams said, pointing.

The others looked. It was a half-mile away, perhaps farther; distances for men bobbling on the sea's surface are difficult to determine. Several men were on the raft. "I count seven," Moore said. "There'll be plenty of room for us."

"There's nine guys on it,' Eggert said. "I counted them twice."

"So there's nine," Moore said. "There's still room for us."

"What if they won't let us on?" Eggert said. "Maybe they'll think there's just enough emergency rations for themselves. I've read about people acting like that."

"If that's the case," Moore said, looking at the raft again, "somebody is going to get their fucking neck busted. Let's get going. If the drift is working against us, we're wasting time."

They began to swim toward the raft, hanging on to the life-jacket bag. They swam past debris from the *Indianapolis:* ammo cans, clothing, blankets, an occasional book, sheets of paper, shoes, jagged pieces of food, letters, photographs—just about everything floatable that had been in the big cruiser.

They came upon a floater net that had popped out of its basket. "Maybe we ought to use it to hang on to instead of what we've got," Adams said.

The life-jacket bag was becoming waterlogged. It wouldn't last until nightfall, if that long.

Moore looked at the floater net for several pensive moments. "Son of a bitch," he said, biting his lips. "If we latch on to that net we'll have something that'll stay afloat till hell freezes over. But if we do, we won't make it to that raft. Three guys won't be able to keep up with the drift, let alone gain on that raft."

The floater net's wide flat surface would be hard to propel through the water whereas the life-jacket bag offered almost no resistance, he explained. But the bag would soon be useless. "Then where in hell will we be if we haven't come to the raft. I'll tell you where we'll be. We'll be up the fucking crick without a paddle."

The thing to do, he said, was vote on it. The floater net and forget the raft. Or the life-jacket bag and a chance to get to the raft before the bag became so waterlogged it would no longer sustain the three men.

"The way I look at it," Adams said, "if we take the floater net we've still got the risk of sharks biting off our legs. Plus the floater net has got no emergency rations.

"But if we can get to the raft—and there's no guarantee we will—we'd be up out of the sea and we'd have water to drink and something to eat."

"What if we decide on the raft and we can't make it on account of the drift or something?" Eggert said.

"I already said where we'd be," Moore explained. "We'd be screwed, blued, and tattoed."

"Let's vote on it," Adams said. "That floater net is already drifting away. If we fuck around much longer, there won't be any point even thinking about it."

"All right," Moore said. "We will now take an official vote. I vote we try for the raft."

"Me, too," Adams said.

"I can't make up my mind," Eggert said. "Jesus, either one can be the wrong thing to do."

"Well, it's two out of three, anyway," Moore said. "Let's get going."

He and the others began to swim toward the raft, each of them clutching the life-jacket bag with one hand. They did not use their free hands to help them swim. Each man had a morbid fear of thrashing the sea with a hand. It might attract sharks. Better to have a leg bitten off than an arm.

It was illogical reasoning. Either way the victim would die. But they had an instinctive wish to preserve their hands. A hand is more versatile than a foot. A man can function without a foot. Without a hand he is inhibited.

They came to other floaters. Two were clutching a mattress already two-thirds waterlogged. It wouldn't last beyond noon. Two others were hanging on to opposite ends of a short thick log that still had bark on it. "Where the hell do you suppose that came from?" Adams said. "It sure wasn't a fireplace log from the *Indy*."

"Stuff from the islands floats all over the Pacific," Moore said. "I've seen coconuts almost to the arctic ice fields. One time, I was on a DD, we saw a kanaka canoe. We were halfway between the Marianas and Hawaii. That damn canoe had floated all the way from the Carolines because that's the only place where they make them like that one."

"We could use a kanaka canoe right now," Adams said. "Or any other kind."

"Nothing ever happens when you want it to," Eggert said. "I think we did the wrong thing, leaving that floater net. All these guys are going toward that raft, too. And there's a lot of guys closer than we are. By the time we get there, there might not be any spare room."

"Which means we've got to get there ahead of everybody else," Moore said. "So kick it in the ass, you guys. We can swim faster'n we been swimming."

They swam faster, keeping their hands on the life-jacket bag. The ocean's swells were rising. The rolling waves occasionally hid the raft, but when a crest raised the men, they could see it and the men who had climbed onto it. "There's nine guys on it," Moore said.

"That's what I said a little while ago," Eggert said. "You said there were only seven."

"Okay, so I said seven," Moore said. "You want to know something, Junior? You burn my ass."

"Listen, fellas," Adams said, "we've got more to worry about than if there's seven or nine guys on that raft. What we ought to be worrying about is, are we going to get there before everybody else does."

"You got something there," Moore said.

"I'm sorry I mentioned it," Eggert said. "I won't say another word. Every time I say anything, old gramps there gets ticked off."

"Watch who you're calling gramps, you stupid little piss ant," Moore said.

Adams was swimming between the others, on the opposite side of the life-jacket bag. "Why don't all of us quit talking," he said. "Arguing between ourselves is the stupidest thing we could possibly do.

"Besides, it says in the official U.S. Navy survival book—I was reading it just yesterday—that men afloat on the ocean should conserve their strength by refraining from singing, shouting, and excessive conversations among themselves."

"That part about singing must have been written by some desk jockey back in Washington," Moore said. "What the hell has anybody adrift on the sea got to sing about? Can you guys think of anything to sing about?"

"I'm not saying anything, remember?" Eggert said.

"Christ," Moore said. "Two million guys in the Navy and I have to get adrift with some half-baked kid that don't know his ass from a hole in the ground."

"I'm still not going to say anything, if that's what you're trying to make me do," Eggert said.

"For a guy that's not saying anything you keep saying an awful lot," Adams said. "Why don't we all shut up. Okay, Moore?"

"Okay," Moore said, "providing Junior there keeps his fucking trap shut."

"He will," Adams said. He looked over at Eggert. "Won't you, Eggert?"

"Absolutely," Eggert said, his jaw squared.

Perhaps thirty other survivors were swimming toward the raft. An accurate count was impossible. The swells were rolling higher. When some of the men were on a crest, others were in a trough. At no time could all of the swimming men be seen.

Most of them were sustained by kapok jackets. They were superior to the inflatable rubber belts that Moore and his colleagues were wearing. Their belts, inflated by two capsules, held their heads above the water, but just barely. A kapok jacket held a man's head and shoulders above the surface, an important difference in rolling seas.

"I wish we had jackets instead of what we've got," Moore said, breaking the little group's silence. "We could see where we're going a hell of a lot better than we can now."

They had been swimming past floating bodies, injured men who had not survived the night. Most of them were wearing thick blue-gray kapok vest jackets.

"We could take jackets off those floaters," Adams said. "They sure don't need them anymore."

"Here we go again," Moore said. "Should we or shouldn't we? Okay, we take time to take the jackets off those dead guys and put them on ourselves. The time we lost might mean when we get to the raft everybody else is already there. If we don't take the time, maybe everybody will be there anyway. In which case we're right where we are now. With a bag to hang on to that's getting waterlogged and life belts that have been known to develop leaks, meaning if they leak we have got nothing to keep us from deep-sixing. So what'll we do? Take another vote?"

"I vote we glom some kapoks," Adams said.

"Likewise," Moore said.

"Me, too," Eggert said. "I'm getting tired of water splashing in my face all the time. And getting up my nose."

Moore looked around. "There's a floater. Let's borrow his kapok."

They swam to the dead man. "I knew this guy," Adams said, looking at the corpse, which was floating faceup. "Shorty Kiernan. He was a radar first."

"I didn't know him, but I've seen him around," Moore said. "Well, let's get on with it."

It was a slow procedure, untying the knots of a kapok vest's water-soaked fabric thongs. Moore and Adams fumbled at it. "Let me do it," Eggert said. "I've got smaller fingers."

Eggert, dexterous with his fingers, soon untied the swollen thongs. Moore pulled the jacket from under the floating corpse and it sank quickly, feetfirst.

"Jesus," Adams said. "He was looking right at me when he went under."

"He wasn't seeing you," Moore said. "They all got their eyes open. Their mouths, too. Take this jacket, kid," he added, holding it out to Eggert. "I'll hold the bag while you're putting it on. Better help him, Adams, so he don't sink while he's doing it."

Soon Eggert was wearing the dead radarman's kapok. He and the others swam to another floater. "I knew him, too," Adams said, his lips tight. "Rollie Thomassen, Alabam, we called him. He was a yeoman third in Communications."

"I knew him from a personal point of view," Eggert said. "We went on the beach together there at Pearl that last time. We hung one on. We got us a couple women—his was some kinda gook—and a jug of Old Granddaddy and—"

"Big fucking deal," Moore interrupted. "Take his jacket, Adams. I'll take the next one."

They swam to another dead man. "Well, goddamn, if it isn't that loud-mouth chickenshit gunnery lieutenant that was always riding us number-one-turret guys," Moore said.

"Pardon me, lieutenant, sir, for not saluting you, you son of a bitch," Moore continued, "but us lowly peons have got a little something else to do at the present time."

The lieutenant's jacket was swiftly untied. "Good-bye, son of a bitch," Moore said.

He pulled the jacket from under the corpse. Immediately it sunk beneath the sea's rolling surface.

"I despised that prick," Moore said, putting on the dead officer's jacket. "He was a twenty-four-karat creep. He caught some of us guys peeking in at a movie in the officers' wardroom a couple months ago. You know what he did? He put us on report. Just for watching a movie only officers were supposed to watch. You'd think it was something important, the way he carried on."

"There's officers like that," Eggert said. "There's also some good ones."

"There is?" Moore said, tying the jacket's thongs. "I'll be doggone. You learn something every day."

He looked at the others. "Jesus, it feels good having a guy's face up out of the water. Well, let's get the show on the road."

He and the others began to swim toward the raft.

8

MOORE, ADAMS, AND EGGERT, THEIR faces and shoulders held above the sea by the kapok jackets they had removed from corpses they had come upon, swam steadily toward the raft, each of them gripping the life-jacket bag.

Other survivors of the big cruiser swam toward the raft, perhaps as many as thirty, though it was hard to tell in the midmorning swells, which were running at better than two feet.

The swimmers passed bodies of men who had died during the night or in the early-morning hours. Eggert avoided looking at these corpses, held afloat by kapok life jackets. Their mouths gaped. Their eyes were open. They seemed to be staring at him, accusing him that he had no right to be alive while they were not.

He knew many of them and this made it more difficult to look at them.

"They get to you, don't they, Junior?" Moore said. "Well, to tell you the truth, they get to me, too. You know what I think of every time we see one of them? I think how come he got it and I didn't. I've thought about that every time the *Indy* and the other ships I've been on have been in combat.

Some guys get it and some don't, and there's no understanding why.

"Twice I've been right beside guys that got it and I didn't even get a scratch. One of them, my beer-drinking buddy Charlie Karnopp, a gunner first on the can we were on—it was the *Foote,* ol' DD five-eleven—got it right in the face from a gook cruiser.

"It was at Empress Augusta Bay. The second of November in forty-three. I never will forget the date. That gook shell took off Charlie's whole fucking head. Nice and neat, like he'd been guillotined. And there I was, right next to him, loading the *Foote*'s forward rifle, and I don't even get a scratch.

"That's the way it goes, Junior. So don't take it too hard when you see guys you know. It isn't your fault they got aced, and there's nothing you can do about it."

Eggert had listened closely to the big craggy-faced gunner's mate. It made him feel a little better. Not quite so guilty. "I guess being in the Navy as long as you've been in makes a difference in how you look at things."

"You better believe it makes a difference," Moore said. "When I got in I was just barely eighteen and I still thought the moon was made out of green cheese. But not anymore. This old boy has learned quite a few things during them twenty-two years I've been in the United States Navy. The two main things I've learned is: take it as it comes, whatever it is, and don't try to figure the answers. The second thing is: don't ever question an order because nine times out of ten the guy who gave it to you don't know, either. He's just carrying out somebody else's orders. So I just say aye, aye, sir, and do whatever the son of a bitch tells me to do. That's the way to get along in the Navy, Junior."

"If you don't like it, how come you stayed in so damn long? You were in before I was even born."

"I didn't say I didn't like it. If I didn't like it, I'd of told them to stick it up their ass when my first enlistment ended. What I was saying is that there's ways to get along. And right now, in the situation we're in, one of them—take it as it comes—is coming in damn handy. Whatever happens to you, figure it won't last forever. Look at it that way and you can stand anything."

Adams had taken a second look at the floating corpse they had just passed. "You didn't notice that last dead guy," he said to Moore, "you were talking to Eggert. It's Ace McConnell. The guy ran the blackjack game. The squeaky bastard drew the wrong cards this time."

"He wasn't dealing, is the only reason," Moore said. "Where is he?"

"Aft and port a couple swells. I saw him real good. He was on a crest. It was him all right. There was only one guy with a nose like McConnell's. I'll bet he sent a hundred thousand back home, at least. His widow won't go hungry waiting for the government's ten thousand."

Moore wasn't listening. He was looking aft, and to the left. He saw the corpse, its head and shoulders sustained above the waves by a kapok jacket. "Listen, you guys," he said, "I'm going to go back and get his wallet. It'll only take a minute."

"Maybe he left it on the ship," Adams said.

"You trying to be funny? Ace McConnell wouldn't leave his money anywhere, anytime. He'd get it if it was the last thing he ever did. That guy worshiped money."

"What about the raft we're supposed to be swimming to?" Eggert asked.

"You guys keep swimming. I'll catch up with you."

Moore didn't wait for a reply. He loosed his hold on the life-jacket bag and began to swim, using his arms, toward the dead boatswain's mate's floating body.

He came to it and quickly he began to frisk it, feeling for a wallet like a cop frisks a suspect. "I knew you had it," he said to the bobbling corpse, pulling a wallet from a side pocket of the dead man's denim pants.

He opened the wallet. "Goddamn," he croaked. The wallet bulged. A hell of a lot of money, whatever it came to. But this, of course, was no place to count it. Moore worked the wallet into his left hip pocket. Then he said to the floating corpse, "Thanks, you bottom-dealing thief."

He hadn't liked McConnell. Nobody had liked the big boatswain's mate. But he always had a game going. It passed the time, and now and then somebody actually beat the fast-card dealer. But not Moore. In his last game, just three nights ago, he had dropped sixty dollars.

Well now, he reflected, swimming as fast as he could

toward Adams and Eggert, whom he could see whenever a swell lifted him, if they weren't in a trough, I got my sixty back plus the other money I've lost. Plus a little interest.

McConnell really had been a thief. He was the fastest dealer, fastest shuffler Moore had ever seen. Everybody suspected him of stacking a deck and bottom-dealing. He was so damn fast, though, you couldn't tell for sure. But he won more times than the law of averages said he should, and this meant something.

Moore caught up with the others. "I'll let you guys drive for a while," he gasped, grasping the life-jacket bag. "I gotta rest a couple minutes."

"Did you get the money?" Eggert asked.

"Naturally."

"How much, if it's any of my business?"

"Well, it's none of your business. But even if it was, how would I know? Back there wasn't exactly a place to count it."

He looked over the life-jacket bag at Adams. "If we get out of this mess," he said, "I'm throwing a party for you guys. In Honolulu. Frisco. L.A. Diego. Wherever we hit the beach. Two-inch-thick steaks, fried spuds, ice cream, choc'lit pie, and a case of champagne. Then afterward we'll get us some women."

"I'm married," Eggert said. "So I'll skip the woman part."

"Christ, everybody's married," Moore said. "What the hell has that got to do with it?"

"He hasn't been in the Navy very long," Adams explained with a wink.

"Junior," Moore said, "I'm going to tell you about women. When you're in the Navy and a war is going on, and maybe it's your last chance— Jesus Christ, look!"

He pointed with an outstretched arm. The others looked. A shark's dorsal fin was slicing the water. It was going toward a survivor who was swimming to the raft. He was George Caswell, who had been a radar-screen watch in Combat Intelligence Center.

Caswell didn't see the shark. He kept looking at the raft, which he could see every time a swell lifted him onto its crest, as if the raft would vanish if he didn't keep watching it.

"He doesn't see that shark," Eggert babbled.

"There's nothing he could do if he did," Moore said. "Goddamn . . . I like that guy. He's true-blue. He's got a family in L.A. Always showing you his kids' pictures. It's a son of a bitch what's going to happen to him."

"Why don't we yell at him?" Eggert said. "If we all yell together he might hear us."

"It wouldn't do any good. There isn't a fucking thing he could do; anyway, it's too late!"

The dorsal fin had disappeared. "He doesn't even know," Eggert croaked.

"It's better that way," Moore said. "I wouldn't want to know, if it was me. You couldn't do anything about it, if you did."

"Why's it got to be a guy like him," Adams said. "Jesus Christ, he's got four little kids. Just yesterday, there in the forward galley, he showed me—"

He didn't finish. Caswell had screamed. It was a terrible, shrill, haunting scream.

"Oh, God," Eggert said, staring, like the others, at the horrid tragedy of a shark killing a shipmate, a man they knew.

Caswell screamed again. He flailed his arms. His face turned toward the men who were clutching the life-jacket bag. It was a caricature of anguish, knowledge of his ghastly fate, and a plea for help, all of it blended into an unforgettable mask of sheer horror. "George," Moore said softly, "there ain't a damn thing I can do to help you . . . and, Jesus, I'm sorry."

Moore and the others kept watching the terrible scene.

"God, what a way to go," Adams said.

Then, suddenly, the shark pulled his agonized victim below the surface. "We gotta get out of here," Moore said. "There'll be a million sharks there in a minute."

They began to swim toward the raft. They kept looking back. If a shark was coming toward them, they wanted to know.

The water where Caswell had been began to thrash. It became red. Sharks' fins, tails, pointed heads, jutted out of the water, vanished below the surface, appeared again.

It was a feeding frenzy. Caswell was dying a death of indescribable horror. He was being dismembered bite by bite as his executioners bit off a foot or a leg, quickly swallowed, then attacked again to bite off another foot, or arm, gulped these gruesome morsels, then attacked to bite the flesh from their victim's buttocks.

The head of the victim of a sharks' feeding frenzy was almost always the last to be eaten. This was the way it was with George Caswell. His head bobbed up to the surface, spinning like a top in the reddened sea, its eyes distended, its mouth gaping as if he couldn't believe how horrible his death had been.

Suddenly a huge sixteen-foot shark, a great white, surfaced, its underslung jaw open. It swallowed Caswell's head and dived into the sea.

The orgy had ended. The sea became calm. "I'm sick. I've gotta puke," Eggert said. "That was terrible. Seeing his head, just his head, and a couple minutes ago he was just like us."

"Don't puke! Dammit, don't," Moore said. "It'll attract sharks. The ones that ate Caswell. They're real close anyway."

"I can't help it," Eggert said. He began to vomit.

"We've gotta get away from it," Moore said. "Everybody swim like crazy for ten strokes. Then stay still."

They swam from the vomit, then quit swimming and looked back. They saw a shark's dorsal fin coming quickly, in the peculiar straight line of an attacking shark. But was it coming to the vomit, or to the men whose legs were dangling below the sea's rolling surface?

It could be either. The men were on the opposite side of the vomit. The way the shark was coming he wouldn't have to change course to attack the floating men.

"Don't move, for God's sake," Moore said grimly, his face ashen. "Hold perfectly still."

The shark's dorsal fin sliced through the vomit. It came toward the men.

"He's going to attack us," Eggert screamed.

"Don't move, dammit," Moore said. "Sometimes they just sniff around, then go away."

No one, including Moore, believed the shark was coming to sniff. He was coming to eat. Who would be his victim? Which of the three, in another moment, would suffer a severed leg, then be pulled below the surface and dismembered and gutted?

"He's coming for me," Eggert said, choking. "My mom

said I wouldn't come home. She said it when I got on the train. She was crying."

"You don't know, Junior," Moore said, his teeth clenched. "None of us know. It can be any of us."

Adams didn't say anything. What was there to say? He hoped it wouldn't be him. He hoped it would be one of the others. A mean, selfish thought, but the same mean, selfish thought was coursing through the minds of the others. When it comes to the zero hour, doesn't any normal man hope if somebody has to get it, it'll be the other guy?

The dorsal fin went below the surface. "Whichever of us he doesn't hit," Moore said quickly, "stay perfectly still. Don't make the slightest little movement!"

Eggert shrieked. "Mom . . . Mom . . . Mom . . ." he screamed.

His mother couldn't help him. No one could but God, and God wasn't helping the big cruiser's survivors. At least that's what some of the survivors said later.

Moore and Adams, their hands clutching the life-jacket bag, stared at the anguished face of their doomed colleague. His eyes bulged. His mouth was opened so wide they could see into his throat. He was suffering the agony of an unanesthetized amputation plus the ghastly realization that within seconds the rest of him would be in a shark's belly.

The shark pulled the shrieking sailor beneath the surface. Then the pack came. They went into a feeding frenzy, their bodies thrashing against the legs of the men who were clutching the life-jacket bag.

Blood and gore surfaced. The sharks' wild thrashing splashed it onto Moore and Adams. "Don't wipe it off," Moore said. "Don't move, for God's sake."

Sharks in a feeding frenzy, particularly when the source of the frenzy is a human body, are one of the most horrible of all sights. When it was over, and Moore and Adams realized they had been spared similar deaths, they remained unmoving, their faces blanched.

Moore came out of it first. "Let's get to that raft. We've got to get our feet out of the water."

They looked toward the raft. A drift had swept it farther away. "Oh, Christ," Adams said.

"Well, we can't just stay here," Moore said. "Let's swim

toward it anyway. Maybe if we go a little faster we can catch up with it."

"I thought I was lucky, surviving the torpedoing, and the sinking," Adams said. "I'm not sure now. How long do you think a guy lives when a shark pulls him under?"

"Not very long," Moore said. "Those sharks don't fuck around. In a couple minutes they've got him one hundred percent eaten."

But the victim wouldn't be alive during all of those two minutes, Moore continued. "I'd say right after they bite off his other leg and bite into his guts, he'd become unconscious, not to mention he'd be drowning in the meantime. So most of the time they're eating him, he'd be either unconscious or else already dead."

The men began to swim toward the raft. "There's more guys on it now," Adams said. "There must have been guys a lot closer than we were."

"There'll be room for us," Moore said. "Keep going."

They swam until their chests were heaving.

"Gotta rest a little while," Adams wheezed.

He and Moore looked toward the raft. They could see it when they topped the swells. "We're not going to make it," Adams said. "It's farther away than it was."

"The drift is screwing us," Moore said. "A raft with all those guys naturally catches more drift than two guys low in the water."

He and Adams quit swimming. It was no use. They were exhausting themselves for nothing. They rested, holding on to the life-jacket bag, which by now was close to becoming so waterlogged it would be a burden to thrust through the water on their next foray, if it were a long one.

"I just thought of something," Adams said. "If the drift is moving that raft farther from us, why isn't there a chance the drift might be moving another raft closer toward us?"

"That's the smartest thing you've said all day," Moore said. "Let's look around."

They looked over the sea's debris-littered surface and were able, when they were lifted onto crests of the swells, to see fairly long distances.

There were no rafts, just floating men, alive and dead, and flotsam from the torpedoed cruiser.

"There's something over there," Adams said, pointing. "Maybe it's big enough to get on and get our feet out of the water."

Moore looked. "What do you think it is? I can't tell from here."

"Me neither," Adams said. "But it looks like something we at least ought to investigate."

Before they went off on another wild-goose chase, Moore said, he would calculate the drift as it related to their objective and their present position. He took a waterlogged pack of Camels from the pocket of his faded blue shirt. He worked a half-dozen cigarettes out of it and tossed them onto the sea.

They bobbled near the floaters. "Get going, you stupid little bastards," Moore said.

As if they understood, the cigarettes began to carry out their mission. They floated toward the raft, which was ninety degrees from the floating object the men wanted to investigate.

"It won't drift toward us, but not directly away either," Moore said. "So let's start our engines and hit the road."

They swam toward the floating object, stopping to rest briefly after several minutes, then resuming. They rested twice more. Then, while Moore was on the crest of a particularly large swell, he said excitedly, "It's a boat. One of them little rubber jobs."

The sea lifted Adams. "There's nobody in it," he said.

Both men, forgetting their fatigue, swam swiftly toward the little boat, which was bright yellow. "Gotta rest," Moore said gasping. "Guess I'm not as young as I used to be."

They rested. They could see the boat every time the sea crested them. It was a rubberized-fabric emergency boat—capacity, six men.

"There were four of them little jobs," Moore said. "They belonged to the marines we had aboard. Them dudes we took on at Pearl."

"Guess who that particular one belongs to now," Adams said, looking at the little yellow boat.

9

THE *Nakapo*, THE JAPANESE SUBMARINE that had torpedoed the *Indianapolis*, had reached a depth beyond which American aerial bombs or depth charges could harm it.

"Set a course, true, for Sasebo," Captain Hashimoto said to his navigator.

He was impatient to return to the big naval base. The *Nakapo*, provisioned and fueled for a fifteen-thousand-mile search for enemy ships had barely enough fuel, food, and water for its return to Japan when it sunk the American cruiser. In fact, it had been on the parabola of its swing toward Japan when the night periscope watch had sighted the *Indianapolis*.

Hashimoto was even more eager to return to Japan to report, in detail and with photographs, his sinking of the big American warship. It was a significant achievement for Japan. And, of course, for himself.

He went to the *Nakapo*'s Shinto shrine, which was aft in the big submarine, as were Shinto shrines in all Japanese attack submarines.

He knelt before the shrine and recited prayers. Then he offered thanks for the *Nakapo*'s great victory and for the preservation of his crew. He prayed for the emperor's continuing wisdom and for the welfare of his wife and four sons, for the men who had died in combat and for the miracle of a Japanese victory, though he did not know how this could be, at this late hour, even with divine guidance.

He rose to his feet, bowed before the shrine, and turned to go to his quarters. He was surprised to see several officers and enlisted men standing beside the bulkhead aft of the shrine.

"Those of us who are not at duty stations," Lieutenant Toshi Shiguro, the *Nakapo*'s damage-control officer, said, bowing and smiling, "have arranged a party in your honor, sir, to celebrate the sinking of the American warship."

Hashimoto was fatigued. The suspense, the excitement of it all had been wearying. He had intended to go to his quarters and lay on his cot. But he would not disappoint his crew. It was personally flattering, too; he hadn't known they'd thought enough of him to throw a party in his honor. He had been somewhat of a martinet. But then, he had always said, a tight ship requires strict discipline.

"Thank you," he said, bowing. "I will be most pleased."

The party was in the torpedo room. The *Nakapo*'s officers and men toasted their captain with sake, each man bowing when he raised his glass. "It was a great victory back there," Executive Officer Yomura said. "We made the Americans bleed."

"It will bring glory to Japan," Navigation Officer Miyamoto said. "And to our captain!"

He raised his glass. Everyone else raised their glasses. Together they bowed toward Hashimoto. He returned the bow, raised his glass, and everyone drank the toast.

"May the winds of victory always blow upon Captain Hashimoto," Chief Petty Officer Tashimake, the engines technician, said, raising a glass refilled with sake.

The officers and enlisted men joined in this toast. Hashimoto returned it, praising his crew for their diligence and competence. "You men are fortunate," he said, "to have me as your commanding officer, for all of you will share in the glory I have brought to Japan."

There were more toasts, more glasses refilled with sake. Hara Yamado, the *Nakapo*'s chief provisions officer, a dilettante of sake—a Japanese wine made from rice—had seen to it that provisions for the *Nakapo*'s most recent cruise had included ten liters of Shiratsuyu sake, Japan's finest, a decision that under certain other conditions might not have been considered discreet.

After several more toasts, including a lengthy one from Jinsu Koritu, the *Nakapo*'s chief medical officer, that the victory had been achieved without so much as a scratch on any of the crew, Captain Hashimoto began to feel the glow that fine sake brings to those who imbibe generously of it. His wife and sons, who lived in the beautiful shrine city of Kyoto, would share in the glory he had brought to the emperor and to Japan, he reflected. They would be proud of him as would his aged father and his uncles and cousins and their families.

He envisioned victory parades and public acclaim from military and civil dignitaries. His picture would be in the newspapers. His name would be on the radio. He would be the idol of the cadets in the Japanese Naval Academy, his alma mater.

Women would make themselves available to him. But first he would bed with his wife, Sitzu. It would be denigrating to Sitzu—in fact, a public humiliation, if he chose another woman first.

The party continued. The *Nakapo*'s radioman, little Nano Isokamamo, who was only four-feet-ten when he stood at attention, was the crew's comedian.

The little Japanese Navy man stripped down to his breech garment and performed the lewd Rooster Hop dance, pretending to be hopping onto geisha girls and sexing them, keeping a lively monologue going while he performed these lascivious fantasies.

Everyone laughed uproariously. Isokamamo was really a comic. He should have become a professional.

"One more toast," Hashimoto said, raising his glass, "to the honor and glory the sinking of the American warship will bring to Japan."

Everyone raised his glass, and when they were empty, Hashimoto said, "No more sake. The party is ended."

He would be derelict in his duties as commandant if he permitted these officers and enlisted men to become drunk, a situation to which they were already perilously close. A ship's crew must always be ready and able for combat, even though on the present cruise of the *Nakapo* a combat engagement was most unlikely.

"Thank you for honoring me," Hashimoto said. He bowed, turned on his heel, and went out of the torpedo room.

There was a small amount of sake remaining in one of the liter bottles. It was the responsibility of Chief Provisions Officer Yamado, who was unusually skinny for a man who had access to food when others did not, to put away the remaining bottles of sake.

"Hang around," he muttered to his friend, Chief Engine Technician Tashimake, "until the officers leave. Then let's finish the sake in this bottle that's already been opened."

It would be a shame, he said with a wink, to shelve it; as everyone knows, an opened bottle of sake soon spoils.

"I'll help Yamado clean up the mess," Tashimake said to the others.

This would present a credible excuse to hang around until the others were gone, whereupon he and Yamado would finish the sake, about four inches, in the opened bottle.

The officers and men began to file out of the little compartment. Lieutenant Shiguro was one of the last. He turned to Tashimake, "Your sudden interest in housekeeping wouldn't have anything to do with the sake that remains in that opened bottle, would it?" he said with a wink.

"Oh, no, sir," Tashimake said, grinning. "The thought never occurred to me."

"Damn you chiefs," Shiguro said, smiling, "you get away with things for which us gold-stripers would be hanged. I envy you," he added. He mocked an upraised glass. "Dedicate one of them to me, you sneaky devils."

He would need all the good luck he could get, he said, when his wife discovered he had impregnated another girl, this one in Kawatana, a small fishing village on the shore of Omura Bay, a girl whose father was some kind of prefect and who was not taking the matter lightly, having already, in fact, complained to the commandant at the Yokosuka Naval Base.

Lieutenant Shiguro, small of stature, witty and wiry, and frequently smiling, was the *Nakapo*'s most popular officer. His exploits with women were common knowledge on the *Nakapo*, and for that matter in the whole Imperial Submarine Navy. It was said, though probably with a great deal of exaggeration, that he had sired enough bastard sons to man the Combined Fleets during the next war.

He had a rapport with the *Nakapo*'s enlisted men, disregarding the regulations that forbade camaraderie with enlisted personnel. "Piss on the rules," he said. "We're all in this fucking war together. An enlisted man is going to bleed like an officer if he's wounded and he's going to be just as damn dead as an officer if he's killed."

A dozen times Captain Hashimoto had threatened to put Shiguro on report. But he hadn't done it. Shiguro was probably the best damage-control officer in the entire IJN. It was said he could swiftly and competently repair damage from depth charges and enemy shellfire with little more than his wrench and profanity, which, a flotilla commandant once said, intimidated the damaged plates back into place.

For another thing, while fraternization with enlisted men was a violation of the Officers' Code of Conduct, Hashimoto saw no real harm in it, especially on a submarine, where everyone was forced to live in cramped quarters, in intimacies unknown on surface ships. Besides, Shiguro's camaraderie with the enlisted men sustained their morale. The *Nakapo* was known as a "happy ship," one with unusual esprit de corps.

Much of this attitude was due to the affable little raconteur, Hashimoto realized, and while he had chastised him, threatening to report him to the chief of the Combined Fleets—an ominous threat—he had done nothing of the kind. His blusters were primarily because, as the *Nakapo*'s captain, they were expected of him.

The likable little officer brushed the others out of the torpedo room and closed the hatch, and Chief Yamado filled his own glass and Chief Tashimake's with sake from the opened bottle.

"Here's to the women we're going to bounce when we get home," he said, clicking his glass against Tashimake's. "May they be hot and durable and know all the tricks."

"And may we have the durability to last the night," Tashimake toasted.

"Night, hell," Yamado said, "make it our whole leave time."

They clicked their glasses on this ambitious aspiration and drank the wine, and Yamado poured what was left into their glasses.

While this revelry was going on, Captain Hashimoto was in his stateroom, which, because it was on a submarine—even one as large as the *Nagapo*—was of necessity quite small.

He sat at his desk for several minutes, his fingers drumming the desk. Then he lay on his bunk. A nice party, but without meaningful significance. Japan is done, he reflected, staring up at the overhead. The sinking of the big American cruiser won't alter the outcome of the war one damn iota. In reality, it will be merely an opiate to the morale of a sinking nation that needs an opiate badly.

But for Hashimoto personally and for his family, it was a beneficent achievement, the greatest of their lives. "I wish I'd sunk that American two or three years ago," Hashimoto said aloud.

It would have had enormous significance. He would have been appointed a flotilla commander. Then he could have become Japan's ace, the samurai whose wolfpack of submarines brought defeat to the Americans.

He closed his eyes. It wouldn't have turned out that way. Those damn Americans were continually increasing their capabilities for the war, forever inventing new devices and tactics that always seemed to work. The bastards had no end of resources, ingenuity, and temerity.

It had been a mistake, attacking Pearl Harbor and awakening that great sleeping colossus, the United States of North America.

The whole damn war had been frustrating, Hashimoto reflected. Like his personal career, it had begun with hopes and intentions that the Americans kept thwarting.

After he was graduated from the Japanese Naval Academy he served in waters off China's shores as an intern in submarines, a frigate, a mine layer, a mine sweeper, and a destroyer. Japan, at the time, had overrun Manchuria, and China was at war with Japan.

In 1938 Hashimoto, twenty-nine, and a junior-grade lieutenant, was assigned to the Imperial Navy Torpedo Training Program, and a year later he was sent to the IJN's Submarine Indoctrination Center.

In 1940 Lieutenant Hashimoto became contact officer on the *Masatake*, a new submarine of the I-24 class. The *Masatake* and three other I-24s were formed into a top-secret midget submarine attack flotilla. A two-man submarine was attached to the platform of each I-24, and after intensive indoctrination in the launching of the midget submarines from the I-24s, the flotilla became a unit of the Pearl Harbor Striking Force.

The day before the Japanese attack on Pearl Harbor, December 6, 1941, Lieutenant Hashimoto's submarine and the others of the midget-sub flotilla were in attack positions near Honolulu.

At 5:45 on December 7, after religious ceremonies before the *Masatake*'s Shinto shrine, its midget-submarine's captain, Sublieutenant Kazuo Sakamaki and his one-man crew, Coxswain Kyoji Inagaki, climbed into their tiny submarine and cast off. Their mission: to launch their little craft's single torpedo into the soft belly of any of the U.S. Navy warships in Pearl Harbor, below the steel-plate-armor level that a conventionally launched torpedo would strike.

The midget-submarine program was an embarrassing failure. Nothing was ever heard of the midgets from the other submarines of the flotilla. But a great deal was heard of the one from Hashimoto's submarine. Two days after the launching from the *Masatake,* an American coast patrol found Lieutenant Sakamaki sprawled on a beach near Bellows Field. His midget submarine was found caught on the rocks of a nearby reef. "We attacked a reef instead of a battleship," Sakamaki said. "We got confused."

The body of his crewman, Coxswain Inagaki, was never recovered, but Lieutenant Sakamaki achieved distinction and dishonor as the first Japanese prisoner of war to be captured by Americans.

After waiting another day for the return of the midget submarines, the I-24 flotilla, feeling a depression of unworthiness, began the long cruise back to Japan.

To Hashimoto's surprise, but not dismay, he was ordered to report to the Victory School at the Submarine Indoctrination Center. He was elated. This meant he would be given a command of his own submarine.

After he was graduated from the Victory School, he was ordered to command the *Hataka*, an ancient submarine assigned to coastal defense.

It was uninspiring, monotonous duty, and he begged the IJN Submarine Assignment Command for an attack submarine. "I want to help destroy the American Navy before none of it remains," he said.

He was assigned to a training submarine. Then to a research and new devices experimental submarine, an R-O class.

"Don't worry about not having a chance to sink an American ship," his colleagues told him. "The Americans are building ships faster than we can torpedo them. There will be plenty for you when you eventually get an attack command."

Hashimoto got an attack command in May 1944, when he was given command of the I-class submarine *Nakapo*, one of the most modern submarines in the world, superior even to the finest *Unterseebooten* of the Germans' vaunted U-Waffe.

Frustrations kept tormenting Hashimoto. He did not destroy so much as an American tugboat with his costly new submarine until by the sheerest of chances, he came upon the heavy cruiser *Indianapolis*.

So, at last, he had achieved a victory. But too late to help change the course of the war. The big and powerful Navy that had launched the Pacific war forty months ago, with every reasonable chance of victory, had been struck down on April 17, 1945, when 386 carrier-based Hellcat fighters and Avenger bombers of an American task force destroyed the Japanese Second Fleet and sunk the battleship *Yamato* in the sea between the Japanese main islands and Okinawa.

With the death of the *Yamato*, the world's most powerful battleship, the Imperial Japanese Navy was finished.

Hashimoto fell asleep wondering if the Americans, when the war finally ended, would hang officers of the Imperial Japanese armed forces. No, that wouldn't be the American way, the efficient way. They would probably line up a hundred officers at a time beside a trench grave, then machine-gun them.

The Americans would do something like that, no doubt of it. Americans were barbarians. A mongrel species derived from the scum of Europe. Not a people of tradition and culture like the Japanese.

My sons will know that I died for Japan, Hashimoto reflected, and for this they will be proud.

10

ADAMS AND MOORE SWAM TOWARD the little yellow rubber boat as fast as they could. They swam with desperation. It was important to get to it before the drift or a sudden wind could sweep it out of their reach.

It would be the means of saving their lives. It would enable them to get out of this shark-infested sea. The constant worry of a shark biting off a foot or an entire leg was harrowing.

"Keep going," Moore said. "We're damn near there."

Damn the swells. When the swimmers were in their troughs they couldn't see the little boat. They wanted to see it every moment. It made the swimming easier, even though their lungs were agonized.

Suddenly, on the other side of a swell, they were beside the boat. They grabbed its starboard gunwale and pulled it down far enough to look inside.

"Jesus," Adams said. Two horribly burned dead men were sprawled on the deck of the little survival boat. Their eyes stared at the sky. Their mouths gaped.

Another man was in the boat. He was alive, though—apparently, just barely. His head lolled against the gunwale opposite Moore and Adams; none of it was above the gunwale, not even his tousled blond hair, so that to the swimmers the boat had appeared to be unoccupied.

Blood oozed from a bone-exposing gash on his left shoulder. He moaned piteously. His eyes were glazed slits. His face was contorted, indicating that his pain was intense. He was unconscious, or very near it.

"He's the new marine CO we took on at Pearl," Adams said, looking over at Moore. "Chandler, I think his name is. A lieutenant. I don't recognize those dead guys, the way they're burned."

Moore said he knew the little one. "Jim García. He was a striker in the forward engine room. Motor Mouth, everybody called him. Always talking. You never saw him when he wasn't. A nice guy. You couldn't help liking him even if he was a Mexican."

"Well, he's done his last talking," Adams said. "Jesus, did he get burned!" He looked at the other dead man. "He got it even worse. Look at those ribs. Flesh burned right off of them. Jesus, that must have hurt, all that raw flesh and salty water splashing on it."

Moore looked nervously out at the sea, in all directions. There were no dorsal fins cutting the water. But, he realized, that didn't mean sharks weren't in the vicinity, perhaps coming toward them at this very moment.

"We'd better get aboard," Moore said, still gasping from the exertion of his fast, prolonged swim toward the little survival boat. "I'll help you, then you help me. Then we'll throw those dead guys out."

"Maybe we ought to pull them out first," Adams said. "We're going to pull this gunwale awful low getting in, with them in there."

"You're not thinking it through," Moore said. "Put those blood-oozers into the water and every fucking shark in the Pacific will be here before we could get aboard. Move over here and I'll push up on your ass. Then grab my arms and pull me in."

"Okay," Adams said. He looked at the bodies and the agonized marine. He'd sprawl on them, getting in. He'd try not to roll onto the marine.

"Come on, dammit," Moore said. "I want to get in there with all my legs."

Adams, sliding his hands on the gunwale, went beside the big gunner. Moore grabbed the seat of his pants. "On the ho," he said. "Heave, ho!"

Adams lunged and Moore shoved and Adams flopped out of the water into the boat. Immediately he reached over the gunwale and grabbed Moore's hands.

"On the ho," Moore said. "Heave, ho!" He shoved with his feet, Adams pulled on his hands, and he came over the gunwale into the little boat.

The boat careened to port, shipping water over its port gunwale.

It rocked to starboard, then back to port. Then, its gunwales just inches above the sea, it became steady.

Moore and Adams looked at the interior of the little rubber survival boat. Beside the two dead men and the injured marine officer there was a paddle. "There's supposed to be a survival kit with water and food and flares and fishing gear," Adams said. "And two paddles. I've seen all that stuff in the boats there on the *Indy*."

"Quit your bitchin', man," Moore said. "Good God a'mighty, we're out of the water and we got a paddle. Which means we're one thousand percent better off than we were a couple minutes ago."

"You've got something there, all right," Adams said. "We got a real break getting out of that damn sharky water with all our parts. It would have been nice, though, if a survival kit had been in here. I never been so damn thirsty."

Moore had been looking at the little boat's slight freeboard. "We've got to get those dead guys out of here and also the water that shipped in when I came aboard. If we don't and a sea comes up, with the little freeboard we've got we're screwed."

Adams looked at the water that sloshed around the bodies. His lips became tight. Getting rid of that water would not be a pleasant task. It would have to be scooped out with their hands and it wasn't just seawater. Blood and gore from the corpses and the injured marine were mixed with it.

"Let's take García first," Moore said, "and throw him facedown." He didn't want to look at his face, he said. "When you know a guy it makes a difference."

Moore and Adams, on their knees, one forward, the other

aft of the little engine-room striker, grasped his feet and shoulders and lifted him over the port gunwale.

He was on his back. Moore flipped him onto his belly with the paddle. Then he and Adams lifted the other corpse out of the boat. Moore pushed it away with the paddle, giving it a hard shove, doing the same to García's corpse, and a lesser shove to the life-jacket bag to which he and Adams had clung for so long.

Very quickly, as fast as he could, Moore began to paddle the boat away from the floating bodies. "The middle of a shark feeding frenzy is the last place we want to be."

He didn't quit paddling until he was exhausted. "I don't want to see those devils eat García," he said, his face grim.

Adams, who was examining the moaning lieutenant, said, "At least he'll already be dead when the sharks hit him. It won't be like he's still alive."

"He had a family," Moore said. "He showed me their pictures the last time we played poker. There in the forward galley, last Friday night. His wife's a real looker and I don't mean for a Mexican. I mean for anybody. They had two little kids. The poor little bastards won't ever know their dad."

"That gook sub made sure there'd be a bunch of widows and kids that won't ever see their dads again," Adams said, looking at the lieutenant's eyes, which were barely open. "That shoulder cut isn't all he got. He's got a cut in his high guts. A real deep one. You can see it when I pull his shirt back." He pulled back the marine's shirt.

Moore, who had quit paddling, looked at the injured man. "That's a mean one. Worse than his shoulder. Anytime your guts get cut you're in trouble."

"He hasn't got hardly any pulse, either. In fact, you can hardly tell if he's got one."

"He's hurting, even if he is unconscious," Moore said. "Look at the way he keeps moaning."

"Seawater probably got into that cut in his belly when we piled in," Adams said. "I'll bet that salty water on his cut guts is pure hell."

"He was carrying on like this before we came aboard," Moore said. "So it isn't just the seawater. Anyway, there's nothing we can do for the poor bastard. We better get that juice out of here before we wish we had."

Kneeling on the little boat's rubberized bottom, which depressed it at the points of contact, he and Adams began to scoop up the smelly fluid with cupped hands and toss it overboard.

"I wish we had an ammo can," Adams said after he had scooped countless times. "There was one floated past us just before we got here. I shoulda grabbed it. We don't get much more than a cupful at a time this way."

"I saw that ammo can, too, but who'd ever thought we could use it," Moore said. He looked over the sea, all directions. "It's long gone now."

He resumed scooping the water out of the little boat. "If you take it by tens it don't seem like it's such an everlastin' job. That's the way I've been doing it. Ten times, then ten more. It gives you something to think about."

Adams began to count his scoops. "One . . . two . . . three. . . it does make it easier," he said. "Five . . . six. . . ."

They stopped to rest a little later. "We've got it down more than halfway," Moore said. He looked at the lieutenant. "Think he'll make it?"

"I'd hate to bet more than a million dollars on it," Adams said.

"We couldn't do anything for him even if we had a medic kit," Moore said.

"We could if we knew what we were doing," Adams said. "A corpsman could probably do something. He'd know what he was supposed to do."

"Let's get the rest of this fucking water out of here and then see if we can find a raft with a corpsman."

"I thought you hated officers."

"I wasn't just thinking of him," Moore said. "They'd have water and food for us, too, on the raft."

They scooped up the bloodied water, cupping their hands and counting the scoops to ten, then beginning again.

In less than an hour they finished their tiring, unpleasant task.

"He don't seem any worse than he was," Moore said, indicating the lieutenant.

"He also don't look any better," Adams said. "Personally, I think he's about as close to kicking off as you can get. He's just barely breathing."

"Steady me," Moore said. "I'm going to stand up and see where that raft is we've been chasing all over the Central Pacific."

Slowly, while Adams supported his legs, the big gunner rose to his feet. "Watch it on the swells," he said uneasily. "Here comes a big one."

The little boat, Moore standing upright, rode onto the crest of the swell. "It's still there," Moore said excitedly.

He looked at the sun and back at the raft. "Help me down," he said. Soon he was sitting in the little boat. "Taking the sun for a fix, it's sixty degrees to starboard."

"How far would you say, just guessing at it?"

"I can't even make an intelligent guess. It's pretty hard to estimate distances on the ocean. At least it always was for me. But it's quite a ways. I could see it when I stood up, but from here, even when we're on a crest, you can't see it."

Adams said that sounded like the raft was a hell of a distance from the boat.

"We won't get any closer to it just sitting here talking about it," Moore said, picking up the paddle. "We can make time now, now that we got rid of that water." He began to paddle in the direction of the raft.

"I wish we had another paddle," Adams said.

"If one guy paddles as hard as he can, and we change off," Moore said, "we ought to do pretty good even with just the one paddle. How's the marine?"

Adams examined the lieutenant. He looked up at Moore. "He's hanging on."

"That's a real professional answer," Moore said.

"Well, for chrissake, what do you want me to say? You want me to say his tacheoctomus needs a spizzerectomy?"

"You know something, Adams? You got the instincts of a smart ass. You know something else? I don't like smart asses."

"Fuck you," Adams said.

Neither man spoke for a long while. It had been stupid, what they had said. It was hard enough without animosities.

"I didn't mean what I said there a couple minutes ago," Moore said. "My nerves got the best of me, I guess."

"Me neither," Adams said. "My nerves aren't in the best shape, either."

"We got to get along, for chrissake. So why don't we both forget it."

"That's a deal," Adams said. "Want me to paddle for a while?"

"Not just yet. I'm good for a little longer."

"Is that raft we're heading toward the same one we were chasing when that shark got Eggert?"

"I think so. I wouldn't say for sure, though. I didn't have much time to look at it. It's a raft, though, and that's what's important. Man, I sure could use a drink of their water."

"What if they've already drank all of it?"

"That's a hell of a thing to even think about."

"I know it is, but it could happen."

Adams looked up at the sun. "I didn't realize it got so damn hot. You don't notice it on the ship."

"You ain't even noticing it here. Wait'll you start paddling."

The lieutenant moaned a long wail. Adams knelt beside him. He tore off a piece of the marine's tattered, bloody skivvy shirt and dipped it into the sea.

"That's a stupid thing you're doing there," Moore said. "One little shark bite and, zap, no hand!"

Adams jerked his hand and the water-dripping rag out of the sea. He looked over his shoulder at Moore. "I must have left my brains on the ship," he said shakily. "Thanks for reminding me."

"He ain't worth it. No officer is worth risking your hand for."

Adams folded the rag and put it on the lieutenant's brow. "I've known some good officers."

"You and me must have been in two different navies," Moore said. He looked at Adams, who was wiping the lieutenant's face with the wet rag. "If he knew some lowly enlisted joker was nursemaiding him he'd piss in his pants."

"You really hate officers, don't you?"

"You can say that again. They're ass holes. Every damn

one of them. This one is a double ass hole. Meaning he's not only an officer, he's also a marine."

Adams wiped the lieutenant's brow again. "What's the matter with marines?"

"You're talking like a man with a corncob up his ass."

"That's not answering the question."

Moore didn't reply and Adams looked up at him. Moore had quit paddling. He was staring forward.

"What are you looking at?" Adams asked uneasily.

Moore turned toward him. "What I was looking at when I was on that last crest is something I wish I hadn't seen. Between us and that fucking raft there's a bunch of guys. We're going to have to go right through them and every damn one of them is going to want us to take them aboard."

He and Adams had better, he added, decide what they were going to do about this situation before he paddled any farther. "What do you think we ought to do?"

"We can pick up three guys," Adams said. "These yachts can hold six people."

"It'll slow us down."

"I know it will. But, Jesus Christ, suppose it was us out there. It could have been if we hadn't found this boat."

"It's going to be tough, picking up just three. I'd bet there's forty guys there."

"We pick up the three most-worse-off guys."

"I don't think that's the right way to go. If they're not going to make it anyway, we'd be doing more good saving somebody else."

They talked on it. They decided to pick up three injured men, providing their injuries were not, apparently, going to be fatal.

"It'll be rough, making the decisions," Adams said, his lips tight. "Especially if we personally know some of those guys."

"Hell, I'll know a good ninety percent of them," Moore said, picking up the paddle.

"Suppose somebody tries climbing in and we don't want him in?"

Moore's face clouded. He hadn't thought of this possibility. He looked over his shoulder at Adams. "There's just one thing to do in that case. I'll give the son of a bitch a face full of this paddle."

"Suppose he's an officer and he demands we let him aboard?"

Moore turned toward Adams. "If that happens, you know what I'll do? I'll tell you in plain goddamn English what I'll do. I'll bust his fucking head for trying to pull rank."

"Well, don't bust the paddle busting his head," Adams said. "We've got to get to that raft."

11

THE SEAS HAD CALMED. THE men in the little rubber survival boat, except the unconscious marine lieutenant, could see the raft. It was southwest of the noon sun and it was a long way from the boat.

Moore tossed a soggy Camel into the sea and watched its drift. It went northward at almost ninety degrees. "Outside of glomming on to this boat," Moore said, "that's the best news we've had since we got torpedoed. What it means is, the drift will bring the raft closer to us."

If they kept paddling, he explained, at about thirty degrees southwest they would intersect the raft on its northward drift.

"The way the drift is, we could cut to starboard around those guys," Moore said, looking at the more than forty men who were bobbling in the sea, kept afloat by kapok life jackets and inflatable life belts.

"I thought we had decided we'd pick up three men," Adams said. "Nobody said anything about cutting out around them."

"Nobody's going to cut out around them," Moore said, paddling toward the floating men.

"Then why did you mention it?"

"I don't know. It just hit me all at once, after I saw the

drift. I couldn't actually do it, though. I couldn't say we got it made so fuck you guys. I'm just not that kinda guy." He continued to paddle the little yellow survival boat toward the floaters.

"It's going to be tough, deciding who we'll take," Adams said.

"You can say that again," Moore said. "What's going to be the worst part is knowing that some of the guys we leave probably won't make it. It's kinda like playing God and, Jesus Christ, I'm not a guy who ought to be doing that."

"It's like we've got a piece of destiny in our hands," Adams said. "The decisions we make, on what guys go with us, can change a whole lot of lives. The wives of the guys who won't make it, their kids. And their folks."

"We've got to get off this religious kick," Moore said, digging deeply into the sea with the paddle. "We've got to look at it from a cold-blood practical way. We can take three men. We can't take any more. That's all there is to it. It'll be like us coming onto this boat. Everybody didn't latch on to a boat. It's the same thing."

You're right, Adams reflected, looking at the floaters. The boat was almost close enough for them to recognize faces. But being right doesn't really make it right, either. Take myself. If I were one of them and I wasn't one of the three that got picked up, and I didn't survive for some reason or another—sharks, most likely—then the lives of my son, the kid I've never even seen, and my wife, and my mom and dad would be a whole lot different than if I came home from this fucking war. Same thing with those guys and their families.

But what can we do except what we're going to do? Take three and hope the others make it. That's all we can do. But still, no matter how you rationalize it, how you justify your actions, it's one hell of a decision.

Moore looked over his shoulder at the lieutenant, and then at Adams. "I've been thinking. If the lieutenant isn't going to make it, we'll be beating some other guy out of a chance, some guy who definitely would make it, if we keep things the way they are."

Adams said he'd had the same thoughts. "But I couldn't push him overboard, knowing for sure he wouldn't survive if we did. Could you?"

"No," Moore said, his face grim. "Not even a fuckin' officer, and a marine one besides. I'm just too goddamn much of a goody two shoes."

"That's not it. You're just basically a decent guy."

"Knock it off, Adams. I'm an eighteen-karat son of a bitch and I've got the papers to prove it."

Neither man spoke again until they were so close to the first of the floaters that they could be identified. "That guy over to starboard—not the closest one but the one back of him—is a personal friend," Moore said. "Chuck Nicholson. A metalsmith deuce."

"You going to want to take him aboard?"

"Not unless he's been hurt. We decided how we'd handle it, Adams. That's the way we're going to do it."

"Hey, Moore," Nicholson yelled to the men in the little yellow boat. "How about hitchin' a ride?" He waved to make sure Moore saw him and heard him.

Moore paddled toward him. "You got burned or cut by the explosions?" Moore said when he came to his floating friend.

"Uh-uh," Nicholson said. "I was lucky." He put a hand on the survival boat's gunwale. "How about helping me?" he said. "I don't want to bring any more water in than necessary."

"You're not coming," Moore said. "We're picking up three injured guys."

Astonishment swept over Nicholson's face. "You got it wrong, buddy," he said. "I'm comin' aboard."

"Take that hand off the gunwale," Moore said. "I told you what the deal is."

"Suppose I don't?"

"Then you get a face full of paddle."

Nicholson, who was wearing a kapok jacket, removed his hand. "Some friend you turned out to be," he said bitterly. "Let me tell you something, you son of a bitch, someday I'm going to meet you on the beach. Think about that, mother fucker."

Moore, his lips tight, paddled toward a straw-hair man whose contorted face indicated that he was in agony. He was Joe Gehringer, a seaman first class. "Take me, please," he begged. "I've gotta find a medic. I've got a busted leg. I can't hardly stand it."

While Gehringer was making this plea, several other survivors swam toward the little rubber boat. One kept shouting, "Wait for me!" Another yelled, "You gotta take me," repeating it again and again, his voice choking in pathetic sobs. Another screamed that he'd die if he wasn't picked up.

Others shouted and yelled too. Nicholson's embittered voice came through the others. He shouted obscenities and threats to Moore, and then he yelled that he hoped the little boat would sink, adding that if he had a knife he'd swim under it and slash its fragile rubberized-fabric keel.

"Some of you guys help Adams lift Gehringer in," Moore yelled.

A half-dozen men lifted Gehringer into the boat.

Everyone else wanted to be rescued, too, and soon survivors of the big U.S. Navy cruiser were on all sides of the little rubber boat, gripping its gunwales and begging to be taken aboard.

"We only got room for two more," Adams said, avoiding the eyes of the begging men. "We'll take the two—"

He didn't finish. Everyone tried to convince Adams that he should be one of the two to be taken aboard, each man trying to present his case louder than the others.

"Shut up, ever'body," Moore bellowed.

The big gunner's mate was a tough-looking man, and right now his craggy features were as grim as they had ever been. The men became silent, except for Chuck Nicholson, who kept up his tirade, and the men who were still swimming toward the little boat, each man shouting for the boat's crew to please, for God's sake, wait until he got there.

"All right," Adams said, "which of you guys got either burned or zombied by the explosions?"

Steve Connelly, a yeoman striker, said he had been badly burned. He bobbed up out of the water, to his waist, to show his burns. Flames had seared his belly. Only a thin wall shielded his guts. They were visible, purple and horrible, through this thin veil of seared flesh.

Adams looked over at Moore. "Uh-uh," Moore said. "He won't make it anyway."

"I'm sorry," Adams said. "We're only taking guys that aren't hurt very much."

"Oh, God . . . please," Connelly said, sobbing.

"No," Moore said.

Connelly released his grip on the gunwale. He began to cry.

"Jesus Christ," Adams said, his face ashen beneath its sun- and sea-reddened hue. His lips were tight. This was the worst thing he had ever done, the worst he hoped he'd ever have to do. It was bestial, telling that kid he couldn't come aboard. The poor little bastard.

"Anybody not hurt real bad?" he asked the others.

Jack Erickson said he had been burned. "But not near as bad as most of the guys. All I need is a medic and I'll be all right."

"Let's see where you got scorched," Moore said, gripping the paddle like a spear, warily watching to make sure no one tried to climb into the little boat.

Erickson lifted his kapok jacket. The flesh had been burned from several rows of ribs, exposing the ribs. "I got burned under my arms, too," Erickson, a seaman first class, said. "That's why I have to hold my arms out all the time. Jesus, it hurts under my arms. Please take me, fellas . . . please!"

Adams looked over at Moore. Moore nodded his head. "Give me both your hands," Adams said, "and when I pull, you kick."

A moment later Erickson was in the boat.

"One more," Moore said.

"I'll give you ten thousand dollars," a young ensign named Gary Cathers said. "My dad's a wholesale grocer in Cleveland. I'll tell him to give you the money just as soon as we—"

"You just blew it, Moneybags," Moore said. "Get your fucking hands off that gunwale and go for a walk."

"Fifty thousand! Dad can afford it. You'll get the money—"

He didn't finish it. Moore had put the blade of his paddle under the ensign's chin and shoved on it. Cathers released his grip on the gunwale and slid, backward, a whaleboat's length on the rolling sea. Moore, it was obvious, had pushed hard.

"Okay, one more guy," Adams said, looking out at Cathers, who was choking and gasping and clutching his throat, his mouth gaping, his eyes distended. I wonder, Adams thought, if Moore squashed his larynx when he gave him that shove.

Ocie Justin, a handsome black youth who had been a messboy in the senior officers' wardroom, said, "I got a cut on my high belly. I can feel my guts when I reach in. Take me, please. A doc can fix it up."

"Let's look at it," Moore said.

"Lift him up, a couple of you guys," Adams said.

"Why should we?" a radarman said.

"Because I'm telling you, you son of a bitch," Moore said, gripping the paddle as though he intended to decapitate the radarman.

The radarman and a storekeeper first class, Harold McCurry, lifted Justin up out of the sea.

"He's hurt pretty bad," Moore said, looking at Adams. "What do you think?"

"Let's take him," Adams replied.

"Okay, you two that lifted him," Moore shouted, "help him in."

"Fuck you, you nigger-loving freak," the radarman said. Quickly he swam out of Moore's reach.

"You . . . and you," Moore bellowed, pointing the paddle at McCurry and at Joe Marinelli, a machinist's mate. "Help him in."

They lifted Justin into the boat, Adams gripping his wrists. "That's it, fellas," Moore said. "That's all we got room for. So ever'body take your hands off the gunwale!"

"You got room for me," a coxswain named Eberhardt said, "and I'm coming in!"

He began to climb into the boat, pulling the port gunwale almost to the sea's level.

"Let loose and go back," Moore shouted.

Eberhardt didn't reply. He kept trying to climb into the little rubber boat. Moore reversed the paddle, gripping its blade. He swung its handle onto Eberhardt, striking him above his left ear.

The blow knocked Eberhardt unconscious. His numbed fingers released their grips on the gunwale. His head fell forward onto the gunwale. Adams extended a leg and shoved his head off the gunwale. He began to float, his mouth gaping, his eyes opened.

"Ever'body else back off our bow," Moore yelled. "We're shovin' off."

"You nigger-lovin' bastard," a floater who had released his grip on the gunwale screamed. "Why'd you take a nigger when there's white guys?" He turned toward the floaters who were near him. "Hey, you guys! Let's roll 'em over, the nigger-lovin' sons a bitches!"

"Wait for me," Nicholson yelled. "I want to help." Nicholson swam toward the boat.

"The rest of you guys help, too," the man who had started it yelled. He put a hand on the starboard gunwale, near the little boat's bow.

Moore swung the paddle. Its handle smashed the bigot's nose. He took his hand from the gunwale and clasped his agonized face. "You nigger-lovin' sons a bitches," he screamed. "I'll get you someday, goddamn you! I'll get you if it takes a million fuckin' years."

Moore began to paddle the boat toward the raft. "Get out of the way," he bellowed to the men foward of the bow. They swam aside and Moore, paddling as fast as he could, propelled the now heavily laden boat past them.

Taunts, obscenities, threats, and pleas followed the men in the boat.

"Thanks, Adams," Gehringer said. "I never would have made it."

"I owe you guys," Erickson said. "God, I hope they got a corpsman on that raft. I can't hardly stand it under my arms. When that salty water gets on it, like when I got in this boat, it feels like somebody with a blowtorch is—" He quit in mid-sentence, his mouth open. "Jesus Christ, look," he screamed.

He pointed aft. The others looked. "Oh, God," Adams said. Dorsal fins, ten at least, were slicing the sea among the men who had been left behind.

One of the floaters screamed for the men in the boat to come back and rescue them, a physical and realistic impossibility. Then a floater shrieked. His head vanished below the sea. So did the sharks' dorsal fins.

A second man screamed and was pulled below the surface. A moment later a third man vanished.

The sea churned with sharks and screaming men and blood and froth as the sharks went into a feasting frenzy.

The men in the little yellow survival boat stared at this horrid sight. Moore had quit paddling. He was staring, too.

Gehringer made the sign of the cross. Tears streamed down Erickson's cheeks. Most of those unfortunates had been his friends.

Justin rolled his head from side to side. "Sweet Jesus," the handsome young black said, repeating it again and again.

The orgy ended. The frothing, blood-flecked sea began to subside. "How many did they get?" Moore said, picking up his paddle.

"Four, at least," Adams said.

"They got five," Gehringer said. "Powell. Salazar. Ellis. Aldridge. Kruger."

He began to cry. Justin put an arm around him. "We couldn't of done anything if we'd been on a PT," he said. "There wasn't nothing anybody could of done."

"I know it," Gehringer said, sobbing. "But I knew every one of those guys. Three of them slept in my compartment. When you know a guy—"

"It was my fault," Moore cut in. "I shouldn't have hit that big guy so hard it drew blood. That got the sharks coming. They can smell blood a mile away."

"He asked for it," Adams said. "Don't blame yourself."

"He was pissed off because you took in a nigger," Erickson said. "It wouldn't have happened if you hadn't."

Justin began to sob. "Don't blame me . . . please," he choked. "I can't help being what I am. All my life people been throwing it at me. I wouldn't of hurt those guys for a million dollars."

"Don't lay it on yourself," Moore said. "The fault was that big peckerwood's. Being a bigot cost him his life."

"And four other guys, too," Erickson said.

"We all know how many other guys," Moore said, his jaw squared. "It was my fault. It was Justin's fault for being born black. It was that big flap-jaw's fault. It was the gook sub's fault for torpedoing us in the first place. Take your fucking choice. But shut up about it. The next guy says anything I'll bust his fuckin' head. That goes double for you, Erickson."

"I didn't mean I don't like blacks," Erickson said. "What I meant was—"

"Shut your goddamn mouth!" Moore said.

He began to paddle and the little yellow rubber boat wallowed toward the raft.

12

NO ATTACK OF ONE SPECIES upon another is more horrible to witness, or more terrifying to its victims, than a shark's attack upon a human. It has an almost deranging effect upon witnesses; the sheer terror and ferocity of its attack are frequently more than the human brain can withstand.

But its most horrendous terror is experienced by its victims. The sheer horror and physical agony of a suddenly bitten-off foot or hand, or a whole leg or arm, or of the sudden slicing off of the flesh from buttocks, or of a ripped-open belly—its victim remaining alive while the voracious shark quickly swallows the first morsel and comes for another—are torture of the utmost degree.

Sometimes before death ends the victim's agony, a shark will nibble him to an agonized, shrieking caricature without hands or feet, devouring his intestines while he watches and screams for help that will not come, nor could it save him if it did.

The sharks that attacked the survivors of the U.S. Navy cruiser *Indianapolis* were great white sharks, known to biologists as *Carcharodon carcharias* and to natives and sailors of the Pacific warm waters as man-eaters.

The great white shark's appetite is unbelievable. He spends most of his life searching for food. He cruises at about four miles an hour, his head turning from side to side, until he smells something edible. Then he swims toward it as straight as a torpedo, and almost as fast.

With four to six rows of razor-sharp, pointed teeth, he can snip off a leg with the tidiness of a surgeon. His stomach walls are tough as leather, and his digestive juices are so strong that a single drop will blister human flesh.

Even baby sharks are to be feared. They are born hungry, with a full set of teeth and the savage instincts of their species.

They have an incredible sense of smell. They can detect and zero in on a scene as dilute as one part of blood to fifty million parts of water.

Their noses are homing devices of fantastic efficiency. When a scent comes stronger in one nostril, the shark turns in that direction. Sharks are also acutely sensitive to vibrations in the sea. Irregular, erratic motions attract them.

Sharks have been the tigers of the seas for 350 million years; they are contemporary beasts of the predinosaur age. Having developed so many years ago and surviving to this day, they are an intriguing combination of prehistoric primitiveness and barbarity, and superb adaption.

The effect of their attack and feasting frenzy upon the men in the little rubber survival boat was stupefying. They thought of nothing else while Moore paddled toward the raft. Even Moore, his paddling requiring no concentration, kept thinking about the horrid sight he had witnessed. "That's the worst way to die in the whole damn world," he mumbled.

The sound of an airplane mitigated everyone's thoughts about the sharks' attack. They looked into the sky. The noise of the plane indicated that it was approaching.

Adams saw it first. It was a twin-engine bomber. It was almost directly overhead and flying very high. The men in the little rubber boat cheered and whistled and waved to the high-flying plane. So did the survivors of the sharks' attack, the men on rafts and other survivors of the big warship; though the drifts had dispersed them over a wide area, all of these men could see and hear the big bomber.

The plane made no sign of recognition. It kept going.

"They don't see us," Adams said. "I wish we had a signal mirror."

"They saw us," Moore said. "That was a scout they sent out from Guam. Right now I'll bet they're talking to Headquarters. Giving them our location. Which means rescue will be here in no time at all."

"Who'll they send first?" Gehringer asked.

"Air-Sea Rescue Catalina seaplanes," Moore said. "They'll have a corpsman in each one and they'll take you injured guys first."

The men in the crowded little rubber boat, except the unconscious marine officer and Adams, shouted happily.

Everyone looked at Adams. "You still think that wasn't a scout, don't you?" Moore said.

"It wasn't a scout. They wouldn't have sent a bomber. Besides, which, it was too high to see us."

"You're hanging on that no message got sent, aren't you?"

"Yes, I am. And I hope to God I'm wrong."

"You're wrong, man. That plane was a scout. I'd lay a month's pay on it."

"I hope you're right. But I don't think you are. I was down there in Radio, remember, just before we abandoned. Nothing got out. Nothing."

"Well, Christ, Adams, suppose nothing got out. Wouldn't somebody wonder why all at once nobody's hearing a single fucking word from the *Indianapolis* and send a plane out to see what's going on?"

"I hope so," Adams said.

"If they don't, I've had it," Gehringer said morosely. "I'll get gangrene in this leg. If you don't take care of gangrene right away, it spreads through your whole body."

Adams put an arm around the depressed young man's shoulders. "You're not going to get gangrene," he said. "We're going to get to that raft. There'll be first-aid equipment there and maybe even a corpsman. Maybe Doc Haynes himself."

Moore looked over his shoulder at Adams. "Speaking of that raft made me suddenly realize I've been paddling this yacht for the last couple hundred miles. How about changing off with me, Adams?"

"I don't know how to operate a paddle," Adams said, winking at the others.

"You put the flat part in the water," Moore said, "then you push, after which you take the flat part out of the water and put it forward of where it was."

"What do you do then?" Adams said, winking again at the others.

"Get up here and start paddling," Moore bellowed.

Adams, who had been leaning against the aft gunwale, got up and, steadying himself with a hand on the starboard gunwale, went toward Moore.

"Take a look at him first," Moore said, indicating the marine lieutenant.

Adams bent over Lieutenant Chandler. Then he looked up at Moore. "He doesn't look any different than he was."

"I can't hardly tell he's breathing," Erickson said. "I'll bet he won't make it unless a rescue plane comes right away."

"What the hell would you know about it?" Moore said.

He didn't like Erickson. He hadn't liked the remarks he'd made about the racial situation after the sharks attacked the floating men they'd had to leave.

"I don't know anything about it," Erickson said. "I just mentioned you can't hardly tell he's breathing. You don't like me, do you? You wish you'd left me back there and got somebody else, don't you?"

"You're a mind-reader," Moore said, handing the paddle to Adams and getting up from his place on the gunwale.

Erickson began to cry.

Moore put a hand on his shoulder. "I didn't mean it, kid. It's just that you're always saying something that gets on my nerves. Take it easy. We'll be on that raft in a little while and then everybody's nerves will settle down."

"I'm sorry," Erickson said.

Moore patted his shoulder and went back to the bow, where Adams had been. "Don't wear yourself out," he said to Adams. "Let me know when you're too tired to keep it up." Meanwhile, he said, he'd try to sleep for a little while. "It don't take a whole lot of paddling to get to you in this fucking heat."

A floating Navy towel caught his attention. "Hey, Adams," he yelled. "Spear that towel!"

Adams reached out with the paddle. He pulled the towel to the boat and tossed it back to Moore.

Moore folded the water-dripping towel and wrapped it around his head. "Goddamn," he said, "that feels good."

He lay back and closed his eyes.

"You look like a Arab sheikh," Erickson said.

"Shut up," Moore said, his eyes closed.

"Don't get mad at me again. All I said was, you look like a Arab sheikh with that white towel around your head."

Moore looked at the garrulous young sailor. "One more word out of you and you're gonna walk the plank."

Erickson wanted to know what walking the plank meant.

"It means," Adams said, looking over at Erickson, "you'd better not say anything more to Moore."

"More to Moore," Erickson said. "That sounds funny."

"Hey, funny man," Gehringer said, "why don't you button it up? You're bugging me, too."

"I'm just trying to be friendly," Erickson said, pouting. "I don't know why everybody gets mad at me for that. I suppose if I didn't say anything and acted grouchy, then everybody'd be happy."

"How'd you know?" Moore said. He closed his eyes and lay his head back against the gunwale.

Twice he alternated paddling with Adams, each time dipping the towel into the sea then wrapping it around his head again. "It feels cool," he said.

"That saltwater will peel the skin off after a couple days," Adams said.

"I don't plan on being here a couple days," Moore said.

A little later Moore paddled the little rubber boat beside the raft. It held an almost unbelievable number of men. "It looks like everybody else got here first," Moore said, looking over at Adams. "But if they'll give us a drink and some food, and a first-aid kit, we can make it to some other raft."

Chief Petty Officer Pete Kramer, who had been oil king on the *Indianapolis*—the enlisted man who had charge of the big ship's fuel—had apparently appointed himself king of the raft. He stood on the side of the raft nearest the boat, his legs spread, his hands on his hips. "Keep right on going, Moore," he said. "We already got a full house."

Moore's eyes swept over the men on the raft. They were a

sorry lot. They seemed dejected and miserable. Some of them waved at the men in the boat. For the others, the effort was just too much.

"We've got some bad-hurt guys, Kramer," Moore said. "Including a marine officer who's playing footsie with the Man in the Sky. You got a corpsman over there?"

"Hell, no! But we sure could use one ourselves. We got burns, two shark bites, shrapnel from the torpedoes, the whole fuckin' bit."

Adams said, "How about letting us borrow your medic kit, chief? We'll give it right back."

"We don't have one, Mac."

Anger swept over Adams' face. "The hell you don't! Every raft's got a medic kit. And water. We need a drink, too!"

Kramer, who had a short fuse even when things were going his way, bellowed, "Listen, wise guy. We're on the bottom of this fuckin' raft. The bastard fell off the ship upside down. All that stuff that's supposed to keep us well and happy is underneath. And we need a drink, too, in case you're interested."

Adams' eyes met Moore's. "We did a hell of a lot of hard paddling for nothing," Moore said. "Besides making a hospital ship out of this boat."

"I don't see where it's as tough as that big jackass says," Adams replied, not saying it loud enough for Kramer to hear. "If that stuff is underneath the raft like he says, it hadn't ought to be hard to get."

"You got something there," Moore said, his lips tight.

He turned toward Kramer, whose raft was about ten feet from the boat. "How about sending somebody underneath to get those goodies?"

"That's a real stupid idea you just come up with, Moore," Kramer said. "You think I've just been sitting on my ass? For your information, Moore, I already sent a guy underneath. Sharks got him. They damn near tore the raft apart eating him right there under us. I sent another guy. He got the water can loose before the sharks got him. So we lost our water. I saw that fucking can sink outta sight and nobody could dive down after it on account of the sharks."

Moore's face became taut. This was bad luck in spades. Four gallons of delicious pure distilled water down there,

God knows how far, and it might as well be on the moon as far as recovering it. "Shit," he said through clenched teeth. "Just plain shit!"

Justin, like the other injured men in the little rubber boat, had been listening to the dialogue between Kramer and the men in the boat. "Chief," he yelled over to Kramer, "is the medic kit still there?"

"It could be, Sambo, but I wouldn't bet on it. The chances are all that action from the sharks worked it loose."

"It would float if it came loose," Adams said.

Kramer got angry all over again. "I know they float. I didn't just get out of boot camp. But that doesn't mean it would conveniently float where we could get it. It might be floating up against the raft. Right under us."

Recognition swept over the chief's face. "Say, ain't you a quartermaster one? You didn't happen to be on duty and quit zigzag just before we got torpedoed, did you? If you're the one, mother-fucker, and I'll find out, you can bet your bottom dollar I'll find out, I'll tear you apart, you son of a bitch."

"Cool it," Moore said. "He was on duty, but securing from zigzag wasn't his idea. It was an order from the Man. McVay himself."

Kramer turned his attention back to Adams. "Is that the true facts?"

"That's the way it was. I didn't want to secure. I thought it was the stupidest thing we could possibly do. But the Man said secure, so I secured."

"That idiot," Kramer said bitterly.

"It wasn't his idea," Adams said. "He told me he'd got the word from CinCPac."

"That figures," Kramer said, his thick liver lips tight. "I'll find out who the horse's ass is that gave that order and I may be busted to seaman deuce and get a big dime at the Portsmouth brig, but I'm going to paste that son of a bitch on the wall."

"Chief," Justin said, "if you think that medic kit might still be under your raft I'm going to try to get it."

"You gotta be a Section Eight, Sambo," Kramer said. "That is unless you know something I don't know. Which is, sharks don't like dark meat."

"That's enough of that racial shit," Moore said. "And his name's not Sambo."

"Sorry, Reverend Moore," Kramer said. "I didn't know you were carrying the torch for our pore, mistreated little black brothers. But it's still a stupid idea. He wouldn't make it."

"I'm going to at least try," Justin said.

Moore looked over at the handsome young black. "You gotta be kidding. For chrissake, Justin, that stuff that's oozing out of that hole in your guts will draw sharks like flies at a picnic."

"That's right, Justin," Adams said. "And even if a shark didn't get you, you're too weak. If you came up under that raft you might not have the strength to swim out."

Determination came over Justin's features. "I won't make it unless I can get some sulpha in that hole in my guts. So what have I got to lose? Besides, if I can get that kit I won't be the only one who benefits."

Kramer, still standing on the port side of the raft, his hands on his hips, had been taking it in. "I wouldn't advise it, kid," he said. "You'll just be killing yourself."

Very quickly, so fast that Moore and Adams didn't realize what he was doing, Justin dived over the side of the little rubber boat. Moore grabbed for his ankles, and missed. "That crazy little bastard," he said, watching Justin swim the short distance to the raft.

Everyone else was watching him, too. Then, suddenly, he vanished under the raft. "Anybody want to lay a little money on him?" Kramer said. "I'm laying five to one he don't make it."

Adams, his eyes on the sea that flanked the raft, the point at which Justin had swam under the raft, said, "You goddamn ghoul . . . you're not even a human being!"

This sentiment had swept over the men on the raft. "You money-grubbin' creep," one of them said. "That little nigger's got guts where you've got nothin'."

"You're wrong, Mac," another man on the raft said. "Our big heroic chief here hasn't got nothin'. He's got a big fuckin' mouth."

"Up yours," Kramer said, glaring at the men.

They didn't keep it going. They were watching the sea

beside the raft. So were the others. The men on the side of the raft facing the boat dropped to their knees and looked down at the sea. Their faces were grim. Their hands were outstretched and barely above the water. Their intention was clear. The moment Justin appeared they would grab him and jerk him aboard.

Someone screamed, "A shark's coming!"

He pointed. A dorsal fin was slicing toward the raft. "Oh, Jesus Christ," Adams croaked.

"The poor little guy," Moore said.

The kneeling men on the raft were tense. One of them licked his lips. Another's mouth was gaping. A third man's lips were very tight. All of them had their fingers outstretched, ready to grab Justin and, if they possibly could, swoop him up out of the shark's reach.

"I'm not a praying man," Adams muttered, "but I'm praying."

"He won't make it," Moore said softly. "He ain't got a chance."

13

THE SHARK'S DORSAL FIN SLICED the sea's surface as it sped toward the wounded man who was trying to recover the medic kit from the underside of the raft.

"He can still make it," Moore said, "if he comes out before that fucking shark gets under there."

"He won't know the shark's coming," Adams said, "until it's too late."

The kneeling men on the edge of the raft were still holding out their hands, each man ready to grab Justin and jerk him onto the raft if he were lucky enough to get out from under the raft before the shark bit off a leg or an arm.

The dorsal fin submerged just before it came to the raft. "Oh God," Adams said, clenching his fists.

The shark was under the raft now. Justin wouldn't have a chance of surviving its voracious attack.

The raft tremored. The shark had slammed into it, on its underside.

"There goes your hero," Kramer said, balancing himself on the quivering raft.

Moore opened his mouth to tell the chief he could at least show a little respect for Justin, but before he got it started, the little black darted out from under the raft so swiftly that the kneeling men couldn't grab him.

He swam desperately, terror on his face, toward the little yellow boat. The shark emerged from under the raft. It pursued Justin.

Adams dropped to his knees, steadied his left hand on the survival boat's port gunwale, and reached toward the swimming man with his right hand.

Moore had swooped up his paddle. He was gripping it like a spear, a feeble weapon with which to repel a shark, but it was all he had. "Kick her in the ass, Justin," Moore muttered, his eyes on the swimming youth and the shark behind him. If Justin could swim a little faster, or if the boat was closer, or if the shark was a little farther back, the poor kid might make it.

Justin was very near the boat now. While the men on the raft watched this macabre race, some muttering prayers for the little black, Adams reached out as far as he could toward the swimming man and Moore gripped the paddle a little tighter.

Justin had been watching the men on the boat. He reached out with his right hand. Adams grabbed it and rolled himself onto the bottom of the little boat, flipping Justin out of the water.

At the same time Moore shoved the end of the paddle onto the shark's nose, which deterred its course just enough to keep it from clamping its gaping jaws onto Justin's feet.

The shark swerved back toward Justin. He wasn't quite fast enough. His jaws clamped together with a horrible clicking sound just as Justin flopped into the boat, his feet only inches from amputation.

"Hooray!" everyone on the raft, including Kramer, shouted. Then, suddenly, they became quiet. The frustrated shark wasn't swimming away to seek a meal elsewhere. The big sea monster was circling the little yellow survival boat. He was so near the surface that everyone could see his murderous little eyes. "Jesus," someone on the raft croaked.

No one else said anything. It was a time of enormous peril for the men in the boat. The shark, a great white at least sixteen feet in length, was capable of capsizing it in any of several ways. He could ram it. He could surface under it. He could rip its fragile rubberized keel with his terrible razor-sharp teeth.

He kept circling the boat. Its occupants kept turning to watch him. A single thought coursed through each man's brain: if the shark capsized the boat, perhaps he would be able to swim to the raft. The shark couldn't eat all of them. Not at the same time.

Suddenly the shark's dorsal fin vanished below the surface of the gently rolling blue sea. "He's either going away," Moore said, his tongue flicking over his lips, "or he's going to come up under us."

The shark had gone away. "Sambo," Kramer shouted from the raft, "what'd you find?"

"You son of a bitch," Moore said. "The kid just barely makes it and all you give a damn about is what did he find under your raft."

Moore turned to Justin, who was sitting on the deck of the little raft, his head lolling against a gunwale. He was breathing heavily. "Flap-jaw, over there," Moore said, "wants to know what you found under his raft. Besides that shark."

"I heard him," Justin said.

He sat up and looked toward the raft. "There wasn't a medic kit," he said. "The ration kit was there, though. I got it loose and then I saw that shark coming. I shoved the kit in his mouth. He swerved off and tried to eat it before he spit it out and came after me."

Moore, his eyes on the big chief, was grinning. "You owe me, Kramer. Fifty bucks on the ten-buck five-to-one he wouldn't make it."

Chief Kramer looked at Moore like he couldn't believe his ears. "Are you nuts? You didn't call the bet. You got off on some kind of nigger do-goody. Or are you trying to give me the shaft? You know what I think, Moore, I think that's it . . . you got your little nigger back and now you're trying to give me the shaft. Well, up your ass!"

"He called you on that bet, chief," Adams said. "I personally heard him."

Erickson, leaning against the gunwale, his broken leg causing continuous pain, got in on it, too. "That's a true fact, chief. I heard him call you, too. Ten bucks, and you gave him five to one."

The men on the raft began to grin. This was an opportunity to needle the big-mouth, arrogant chief petty officer who had been treating them with considerably less than respect. "I heard him, too," one of the men on the raft said.

"So did I," another man yelled.

"Me, too," a third man said.

"We all heard it," someone else yelled.

The chief, standing there with his hands on his hips, a stance he always used when he was the *Indy*'s oil king and was telling some enlisted man what he'd done wrong, glared at the grinning men on the raft. "You mothers didn't hear any such fucking goddamn thing," he bellowed. "You're giving me the shaft."

"Why, chief," a yeoman, Tom Neders, said, a smile creasing his long angular face, "we wouldn't give you the shaft under any circumstances. Would we, fellas?"

"Of course not," Coxswain Andy Johnson said, grinning. "We like you, chief."

"That's right," another man on the raft said. "We just dearly love you, Mr. Kramer."

"Fuck you sons a bitches," the chief said, his teeth clenched. He turned toward Moore. "All right, wise guy, I owe you. First payday after we're on the beach you get the fifty bucks you screwed me out of."

Moore's smile split his craggy face. "See you, sucker," he said.

He picked up the paddle and took the boat away from the raft. In the distance he could see another raft. Maybe it would have water and food and a medic kit.

He had paddled about fifteen minutes when Adams said, "A shark's following us."

Moore looked aft. "I noticed him a couple minutes ago," Adams said. "I didn't think anything special about it at first. Then I caught on he's following us."

"Maybe it just looks like he is," Moore said, his eyes on the dorsal fin of a very large shark.

The fin came toward them. "My God, I believe he is," Moore said.

He quit paddling. "There's a way to tell. If he goes on past it's just a coincidence."

"I think it's that same shark," Adams said. "The one that

tried to get Justin, then circled us like we were a covered wagon and he was a bunch of Indians."

"I don't know how you figure it's the same shark," Moore said. "You've seen one you've seen 'em all."

"That one back there had a notch on his fin. Like it had been bitten."

"That's a fact," Gehringer said. "I noticed that notch, too."

"If he's the same one," Erickson said shakily, "what'll he do, do you think?"

"First, we find out if he's the same one," Moore said, looking at the approaching dorsal fin, "before we start worrying about it. There's a million sharks around here, remember."

"Suppose he is the same one?" Erickson said.

"Shut up, kid," Moore said, his eyes on the oncoming dorsal fin. "We got more to worry about than some stupid question." Moore, it was obvious from the way he kept looking at the dorsal fin and biting his lips, was apprehensive. That shark, if it was the same one, was a big bastard. He could capsize the boat any damn time he wanted to. And now there was no nearby raft to try to reach.

The shark was close to the boat. "It's the same one," Adams said. "See that notch in his fin?"

"I can see it," Moore said. "I ain't blind."

The shark began to circle the boat. "Kick my ass for not getting my forty-five before we abandoned," Moore said, his eyes following the shark's, and looking at the shark's unblinking eyes.

"It wouldn't do any good if you had," Erickson said. "The ammo would have got wet."

"Shut up, goddammit," Moore said.

"He'll eat us, won't he," Erickson said, "when he gets through playing cat and mouse?"

"Button it up, Erickson," Adams said, his eyes on the circling shark.

"Okay! Okay," Erickson said. "But you guys want to remember, I'm in this just as much as you."

"Goddamn you, you flap-jawin' little freak," Moore snapped. "One more word and I'll shove this paddle into your mouth and clear down to your balls."

"Don't talk anymore," Adams advised the young sailor. "You're making all of us nervous."

"All right," Erickson said. "If that's everybody's attitude."

"Christ," Moore muttered, watching the shark.

"What's he up to, do you think?" Adams said.

"I don't know. But I sure as hell don't like it," Moore said.

The dorsal fin vanished. No one said anything. They would know, in a moment, if the shark would attack the boat under its fragile keel.

Nothing happened. Moore picked up the paddle and inched the little boat toward the raft.

"He's following us again," Adams said a little later.

"What are we going to do?" Erickson said uneasily, looking back at the shark.

"We're going to keep paddling toward that raft," Moore said. "What the hell else can we do?"

Justin was watching the shark. "You know what scares me the most? It's what he might do after night comes. I think he's waiting for it to become dark before he attacks us."

Moore said he doubted that nightfall would make any difference. But he conceded that it might. "When it comes to sharks, I don't think anybody can figure what they'll do."

"Are we going to get to the raft before it gets dark?" Gehringer asked, looking toward the raft.

"I'm sure as hell going to try," Moore said.

No one spoke for almost an hour. Then Moore, exhausted and dripping sweat, quit paddling. "I'm not making any hay," he said. "That fucking raft is farther away than it was."

A ten-knot wind was drifting the torpedoed cruiser's rafts. It was drifting the floating men and the little rubber survival boat at about one knot.

Moore took the towel from his head and flipped it into the sea. He wrapped the newly wetted towel around his head. "Goddamn," he said, "that feels good." He turned toward Adams. "How about running the engine for a while?"

Before Adams could say he'd take over with the paddle, the sound of an approaching aircraft came to the men in the little boat. Everyone looked toward the sky, in all directions.

Adams saw it first. It was very high, so high that it looked like a tiny silvery moth. It was too distant, too close to the sun, to identify. It kept going and soon it faded from the watchers' sight, though they could still hear the noise of its engine.

"I wish we'd had an emergency signal mirror," Adams said.

"I wish we had a whole lot of things," Gehringer said. His broken leg had become agonizing. He kept clenching his fists and biting his lips, which had become raw and bloody.

Moore was looking in the direction into which the plane had faded. "Maybe they saw us. The way we're scattered, there's a good chance of it. Maybe right now they're radioing our position to Air-Sea Rescue."

"I hope so," Adams said. "Well, I suppose I might as well start paddling."

He looked at the sun. "Four more hours of this frigging heat," he said.

"Take a peek at the lieutenant while you're coming over here," Moore said. "He's been awful quiet lately."

Adams felt for the pulse of the marine lieutenant. There was no pulse. He looked into his eyes. They were glazed. He wasn't breathing. "He's dead," Adams said, looking up at Moore. "It must have been for quite a while. He's stiff."

"We'll all be dead pretty soon," Gehringer said.

"Knock off that kind of talk," Moore said.

"It's the truth," Erickson said.

"I never saw anybody who had all the answers, no matter what we're talking about, any more than you," Moore said, getting to his knees beside the dead officer. He began to search the dead man's pockets.

"There's a name for people that steal from dead bodies," Erickson said. "I don't remember what it is, but it's a special word."

"It's ghoul," Justin said. "G-h-o-u-l is the way it's spelled. And Moore isn't being a ghoul. He's just looking for identifications, aren't you, Mr. Moore?"

"You got it, Justin," Moore said. "I'll turn whatever I find over to somebody, someday."

"Maybe you will," Erickson said. "We have to make it first or you won't."

"Listen, kid," Moore said, glaring at the garrulous young man. "This is tough enough without you. Now shut your fuckin' mouth."

There were no papers in the lieutenant's pockets. Just a wallet. Moore opened it. It contained several identifications, photos of a blond woman and a little girl about two, and seventeen dollars.

Moore tossed the wallet to Adams. "When we get to a raft with an officer, give it to him. Minus the money, naturally."

It wouldn't be stealing the dead lieutenant's seventeen dollars, he explained to the injured men. "That money would never get to his widow. Somebody along the line would steal it, so it might as well be us."

"Don't bother looking for any money on me if I kick off," Erickson said. "I don't have any."

"In that case," Moore said, "we'll just toss you to the sharks as is."

"I'll bet you would, too," Erickson said.

"If you don't quit yapping all the damn time," Moore said, "I won't wait until you're dead. Now go forward so we can pitch Lieutenant Chandler overboard."

Adams and Moore jockeyed the body of the dead marine officer over the port gunwale of the little survival boat. The drift floated it from the boat. It was grotesque. It had rigor-mortised in a sitting position. It floated in this position, as if the dead man were sitting on an under-surface seat.

"It'll be easier paddling now," Moore said. "Every guy makes a difference."

"I'll get us as far from the body as I can," Adams said, picking up the paddle, "before our friend back there starts nibbling on it and his buddies come to help."

Soon Chandler's body was floating between the boat and the shark that had been following the boat. The shark seemed disinterested. "If I'd had a knife," Moore said, "I'd have cut Chandler in a couple places. Got him bleeding so that shark would smell his blood. Maybe after he ate him he'd quit following us."

The shark circled the floating body. Then its dorsal fin disappeared. A moment later the lieutenant's body vanished.

"Scratch one marine," Moore said.

"That's a terrible thing to say," Erickson said, "even if you don't like marines."

"Wouldn't you rather I said that instead of scratch one stupid little seaman first class that talks all the fucking time, which I'm going to do if that particular seaman first class don't start keeping his mouth shut?" Moore said.

Erickson's eyes became wide. Fear swept over his face. Moore might actually throw him out of the boat. He was a big mean guy. It didn't seem to bother him when somebody died and sharks ate his body.

Erickson decided he wouldn't say anything further. That is, unless something important came up. He looked over at Gehringer and Justin. Gehringer's face was red. He was running a fever. His busted leg must be hurting him terrible, the way he kept chewing his lips.

Justin was in pain, too. He kept holding a hand over the hole in his guts and some kind of smelly stuff kept oozing out of it and sliding down onto his belly from under his hand.

Erickson wondered what had made that hole in the little black's guts. A piece of metal from one of the Japanese torpedoes, probably. Or maybe a fragment of metal from the *Indianapolis* that a torpedo's explosion had blown off and hurtled into Justin's guts.

I got off better than those guys, Erickson reflected. All I got are burns. They're pretty bad and the ones under my arms hurt all the time, but they're better than a busted leg or a hole in my belly.

"I'd like to kill the son of a bitch who invented these boats," Adams said, taking the paddle from the water to rest from the effort of propelling the little boat. "He ought to have been made to stay in one of them for at least a day in this damn heat, and try paddling the bastard. Then you can bet he'd have made some changes."

"He was probably some desk jockey that never even saw an ocean," Moore said. "Man, if your ass is as sore as my ass, you have got one sore ass."

"I don't know how sore your ass is," Adams said, "but mine is sure hurting."

The rounded gunwales and seats in the little survival boats chafed their occupants' buttocks. "You get a wet ass from this fucking seawater," Moore said, "and while you're paddling, it grinds back and forth on those roundy gunwales and then there you are, an ass with no skin."

"I hate this fucking sea," Adams said, dipping into it with the paddle. "Goddamn, I hate it. If I never get my feet on dry land they're going to stay there."

"I'd sign up again, if my enlistment was up," Moore said.

"You can't blame the ocean for what happened. You want to blame the gooks on the sub that torpedoed us. They're the ones that put us here."

"Guess what's following us again," Erickson said.

Moore looked aft. So did Adams and Justin. Gehringer didn't look. He was too feverish to comprehend. Besides, he didn't care anymore.

"I'll bet when it gets dark he'll attack us," Erickson said. "He'll jump right in this little boat and grab one of us."

"Guess which one I hope he grabs," Moore said.

Erickson began to cry. He'd be the one the shark grabbed. He knew he would. He didn't need Moore telling him.

A little later Moore began to paddle. Then Adams, and Moore again. Neither man could paddle very long. They had developed blisters. The blisters had broken. Salty seawater had gotten into these raw places. The pain was continuous.

In the last light of dusk the men in the little survival boat could see that it wasn't a single raft they had hoped to reach, but two rafts with a floater net between them.

"We're drifting at the same speed now," Moore said. "If it keeps on this way we can get to them early tomorrow morning."

"If that shark don't eat us first," Erickson said.

Moore looked aft. The shark was pacing them.

The big gunner's face became grim. There was something to what that flap-jaw kid had said. This could be one hell of a night.

14

THE IMPERIAL JAPANESE NAVY'S TANAPAG Seaplane Base was on the west coast of Saipan, Mariana Islands, on the shore of the placid palm-fringed lagoon north of the sugar refinery town of Tanapag.

The Japanese seaplane operations were headquartered in a reinforced-concrete building with four-foot walls. Hundreds of tons of earth had been rounded over the sturdy little concrete building and red hibiscus shrubs had been planted on this great mound to prevent erosion from the frequent tropic rains; the mound, because of the flowers, resembled the upper half of a huge red ball.

On June 15, 1944, U.S. forces attacked Saipan. The Japanese resisted desperately. Saipan was one of the most important Japanese military bastions in the Central Pacific. It was a focal point for control of the Central Pacific and a shield for the southern approaches to Japan.

It was a fueling and supply station for the Imperial Japanese Navy and a principal seaplane base. Islito Airfield, on its southern tip, was a fighter and bomber base and an air-ferry stop. The island itself was a staging, rest, and replacement center for External Challenge Forces of the Imperial Japanese Army.

The American invasion was inexorable and soon the seaplanes at the Tanapag base were destroyed by aircraft and naval shells of the invading Americans. No amount of pounding, though, could even dent the earth-mounded Headquarters building. "All we did," said Commodore Vernon F. Grant, USN, who was to become Saipan's deputy island commander and commander of naval air bases, "was blast off the Japs' pretty red flowers."

When U.S. marines stormed ashore, Japanese technicians were still operating communications and signal equipment in the mound-sheltered reinforced-concrete building.

A twenty-man marine fire team with flamethrowers and an antitank rocket launcher demolished the building's door-protection baffles, then burst its heavy steel door with antitank rockets.

Immediately the marines with flamethrowers doused the interior of the impregnable structure with their terrible flames, barbecuing the forty-two Japs inside.

Seabees of the 117th Battalion removed the charred corpses and the now-useless Japanese communications equipment, painted the interior of the building, and installed electric lights and power.

U.S. communications equipment was brought into the renovated structure, which now became the Headquarters, Air-Sea Rescue, Marianas.

Even before the Stars and Stripes was raised on Saipan's 1,554-foot Mount Tapotchau on July 9, 1944, hundreds of B-29s took off almost daily from Army-operated Isley Field, the former Japanese Islito Airfield, for offenses against Japan.

Air-Sea Rescue Catalina seaplanes made daily forays rescuing airmen whose big bombers had been damaged by Japanese flak and who were unable to make the long flight back to Saipan, ditching in the Pacific's shark-infested waters.

A year later there was little for the pilots and crews of Air-Sea Rescue's Catalinas to do. The great armadas of B-29s no longer bombed Japanese cities and military installations with high explosives and incendiaries. Only minor flights were made, and sometimes the planes dropped leaflets urging surrender, pointing out the futility of further resistance, instead of HEs and fire bombs.

Only occasionally was one of these planes damaged by

Japanese AA fire and forced to ditch on the sea. As a consequence Air-Sea Rescue had little to do except wait for the forthcoming invasion of the Japanese main islands, which would be late in 1945.

On July 30, 1945, while Moore and Adams and other survivors of the *Indianapolis* waited thirsty and hungry, in need of medical care and in constant peril of sharks, for Air-Sea Rescue's planes to come, the pilots and crews who could save their lives were lolling in the cool earth-covered concrete building, unaware that just five hundred miles from Saipan the greatest sea disaster in the history of the U.S. Navy had occurred. Some of them were playing cards along with U.S. Navy Correspondent David Stafford who had been assigned by CinCPac several weeks earlier to write stories about Air-Sea Rescue's operation for U.S. newspapers and magazines.

It had been a dull assignment. Except for several flights over the coastal waters and lagoons of the Caroline Islands searching for Americans who might have been shot down by Truk-based Japanese aircraft—though none had been reported, the flights being merely something to do and to show the correspondent Air-Sea Rescue's modus operandi—there had been no action at Air-Sea Rescue, Marianas.

No message had been received from the *Indianapolis*, or from CinCPac or anyone else. No one knew of the terrible plight of the big warship's survivors. As a consequence, the pilots and crews of Air-Sea Rescue whiled away their time with countless poker games in the earth-covered Japanese-built concrete building whose interior offered solace from the remorseless tropic July sun.

"I'm going out of my mind with nothing to do anymore," Aviation Chief Radioman Ralph Kaley said to the others in a stud-poker game.

"I don't wish any of our guys any hard luck," Pharmacist's Mate Bruce Lorton replied, "but I sure could stand a little action like we used to have."

Lieutenant Michael Canaris laid his hole card on the table, faceup. It was a queen. He already had two queens showing. "Anybody beat these three ladies?" he said.

"Hell, no," Kaley said.

Kaley and the others tossed their cards in front of the man who would deal the next hand and Lieutenant Canaris raked in the pot he had just won. "We might as well be realistic," he said, "we're all through being heroes. There aren't going to be any more rescues of men from torpedoed ships or of flyboys who ditched their zinged-up planes in the beautiful blue Pacific."

Kurt Vaughn, a machinist's mate, picked up the cards and shuffled them. "I wish they'd at least send us on a search mission."

"They won't," Lieutenant Canaris said, putting a match to a soggy Camel. "What the hell would we search for?"

While these men played another game of stud, then another and another, Moore quit paddling the little yellow rubber survival boat. Night had fallen on the survivors of the *Indianapolis*. "What a fucking climate," Moore said, shivering. "It's just as cold at night as it is hot during the day."

"It's not really all that cold," Adams said. "It just seems cold compared to what it was a couple hours ago."

"Well, I feel cold. Don't you?"

"I sure do," Erickson said. "I got goose pimples all over."

"Shut up, kid, and get some sleep," Moore said. "We've all got to get some sleep or we won't be in shape for tomorrow."

"Is that shark still following us?" Erickson said. "I can't sleep if he is."

"He disappeared a little while after I quit paddling," Moore said.

"Maybe he's down under us getting ready to bite through the boat where our feet push the bottom down."

"You can think of the nicest things," Moore said. "Now knock it off. There's nothing we can do about that shark and we've got to get some sleep."

Moore lay his head on the gunwale, the paddle in his hand. He fell asleep quickly. He was fatigued. Paddling in the remorseless sun had been exhausting.

Soon all of the men in the little boat were sleeping. About midnight Gehringer said, "I'm going to buy everybody Cokes. Great big ones. With chipped ice."

This awakened Adams and Moore. Adams felt the delirious man's cheek. "He's hotter than a firecracker," Adams said.

"I've got a date afterward," Gehringer said. "I'm taking Ann to the movies."

Justin had awakened. He put a hand on Gehringer's arm. "Go back to sleep," he said gently.

"I'm gonna get a Coke first," Gehringer said.

His eyes were partially open. The moon was bright enough to show that they were glazed. There was nothing anyone could do and soon the men were sleeping again.

A little after midnight something bumped against the boat. Adams and Moore awakened. "What the hell was that?" Moore said softly.

"God . . . look!" Adams croaked.

A corpse, sustained by its kapok life jacket, had banged against the starboard gunwale, inches from Adams' head.

The corpse seemed to be staring at the men in the boat. Its eyes were open. Its lips were parted. In the moonlight it was an eerie, macabre sight.

"That's Louie Paulino," Moore said. "A water tender. He slept in my compartment. Two aft, same row."

Moore extended the paddle to Adams. "Push him away so he don't keep bobbling against the boat. The drift will take him somewhere else."

Adams put the paddle's blade against the dead man's chest and shoved on it. The corpse glided away from the boat.

It bobbled for a while, then the drift began to move it. Moore and Adams watched it until it had gone past the little boat's stern.

"If that isn't something to wake up to," Adams said. "I turned around to see what had hit us and, Jesus, his face wasn't six inches from mine."

"It was spooky, all right," Moore said. "Why don't we see how Gehringer is before we hit the sack again?"

Gehringer's mouth was open. His eyes seemed to be staring at the moon. Adams felt his brow. Then his cheeks. "He's dead," Adams said.

Moore knelt beside Gehringer and tried to feel a pulse. There was none. Further, rigor mortis had begun. "We'd better get rid of him before Justin and Erickson wake up," Moore said quietly. "They've got it rough enough without watching us deep-six this poor bastard."

"He must have been in worse shape than he looked when

we picked him up," Adams said. "He didn't look too bad to me, then."

"Me neither," Moore said. "It's hard to tell unless you're a corpsman and know what to look for."

He looked over at Justin, who was sleeping. "You know something, Adams? Unless rescue comes tomorrow, that kid won't make it either."

"I know it," Adams said. "I've been watching him. He's in worse shape than he lets on."

"A hole in your guts is the worst thing that can happen," Moore said. "That stuff that's oozing out of his hole is starting to stink. At first it was just blood and some kinda white slimy stuff. Now it looks like shit."

Adams said, "It's too high up to be shit. It's some kind of infection."

"Whatever it is, it don't look good to me," Moore said. "Grab hold of Gehringer's shoulders. I'll take his ass."

They lifted the dead man out of the boat and laid him on the sea on the little boat's drift flank. Moore picked up his paddle and pushed the body out as far as he could. The drift caught it and soon it faded into the gloom.

Adams and Moore laid their heads back against the gunwale. "If we don't get some water pretty damn soon," Adams said, "none of us are going to make it."

"I can't believe somebody won't come for us tomorrow," Moore said. "Jesus Christ, Adams, the *Indy* was the flag of Fifth Fleet. It wasn't some fucking little old supply boat."

"I can't figure it," Adams said. "Even if no message got out, which I know it didn't, they ought to be wondering by now what's going on."

"Something is sure fucked up," Moore said. "Why don't we knock off the yakking and get a little more sleep. It'll be hotter than hell in a couple hours."

"You got something there," Adams said. He closed his eyes and soon he was sleeping.

A little later, still asleep, he flung his right arm over the gunwale and rolled his head onto his forearm.

The tips of his fingers dangled in the sea.

A shark, attracted by the disturbance they made on the sea, swam swiftly toward them.

15

THE SHARK SWAM TOWARD ADAMS' dangling hand. Before he got to it, the big killer's nostrils detected the odor of blood. He swerved under the boat and swam swiftly toward Gehringer's body. A little later Adams, sleeping restlessly, turned his head the other way and pulled his hand into the boat.

He would never know how close he had come to amputation.

Erickson awakened in the first light of dawn. He sat up, rubbing his eyes. He saw that Gehringer wasn't in the little boat. He grabbed Moore and shook him awake. "Gehringer isn't here," he shouted. "He must of fallen overboard."

The shouting awakened the others. "He died during the night," Adams explained.

Erickson looked from Adams to Moore, then again. "You guys tossed him overboard, didn't you?"

"We didn't have a shovel," Moore said, "so we couldn't dig a grave."

Horror swept over the young seaman's face. "I'll bet sharks ate him. You'd throw me overboard, too, if I died, wouldn't you?"

"Like I mentioned yesterday," Moore said, "I might not wait until you're dead. Listen, kid, your constant yakking bugs the living shit out of me. I want you to keep that flap-jaw shut from now on. Got it?"

"I suppose so," Erickson said.

"You'd better do better than suppose," Moore said.

Adams had been looking at the sea, in all directions. "I don't see the shark that followed us yesterday."

The others looked. "I'll bet he's out there, though, even if we can't see him," Erickson said.

Moore's jaw firmed. His lips became tight. "Kid, you weren't listening just a little while ago, were you?"

"You mean about not talking all the time?"

"By God, you were listening. Now hear this, you mouthy little freak, keep that fucking trap shut, starting right now. We're going to have a rough enough time today if rescue doesn't show up, or even until it does, and what we don't need is some stupid-ass kid bugging us."

"If he won't throw you overboard, I will," Adams said.

"Well, all right," Erickson said. "I won't say anything. Even if the boat gets a leak I won't even mention it. I'll just keep my mouth shut."

"Hooray," Moore said. He picked up the paddle. "I might as well get started," he said.

He looked every direction. He put the paddle down again. The predawn fog hadn't lifted. It was impossible to see more than a hundred feet from the boat. "It's no use paddling," he said, "until we can see where we're going."

His eyes fell on Justin, who was staring blankly at the sea. "You all right, kid?"

"I'm so thirsty I can't hardly stand it," Justin croaked.

"Well, soon as that fucking fog lifts we're heading toward those rafts we saw last night. The ones with the floater net between them. They're bound to have some water."

"I'm all on fire inside," Justin said.

Adams put a hand on his shoulder. "Keep yourself together, Justin. We'll be at those rafts before noon. Besides, rescue might get here before we got to the rafts. Either way, you're going to get a drink."

Justin grimaced from the agony of the perforation in his guts. "I'm so thirsty . . . and so hot inside. It hurts, too. All the time. It didn't hurt very much at first, there on the *Indy*'s weather deck. It just felt kind of bubbly."

Adams put a hand on the agonized black youth's head. "Don't think about it, Justin. Keep thinking you're going to get a nice big drink of water before too long. And don't give up."

"You pay attention to that last part," Moore said. "Don't give up."

Suddenly the hot tropic sun burned off the fog. "Oh, Jesus Christ," Moore said bitterly, looking at the rafts.

They were barely visible. "That goddamn drift," Moore said, "screwed us deluxe." His eyes met Adams' eyes. "Well, there's just one thing to do. Start paddling."

"Don't overdo it," Adams said. "We better change off every half-hour. Erickson's got a watch, so we can tell when to change."

"You'll have to ask somebody else when it's time," Erickson said. "I'm not supposed to say anything, remember?"

Moore had picked up the paddle. The muscles in his cheeks twitched while he restrained himself. "You piss ant," he muttered through clenched teeth. "You goddamn stupid piss ant."

He put the paddle's blade in the water and began to paddle.

"He was going to hit me, wasn't he?" Erickson said, looking at Adams.

Adams, his lips tight, backhanded the garrulous young seaman. It was a hard blow. It knocked Erickson off his seat and sprawled him, dazed, on the bottom of the little boat.

"Thanks," Moore said, looking back over his shoulder. "I wouldn't have just hit him. I'd have killed him."

Adams bent over the dazed seaman and slid the watch off his wrist and put it on his own wrist. "I shouldn't have done it," he said, looking up at Moore, "but, God, he was driving me crazy."

"Maybe he's got the message this time," Moore said. "I wonder if I'm even keeping up with the drift, much less gaining on the son of a bitch."

Adams took a soggy paper from his shirt pocket, tore off a piece, and tossed it into the sea. "We're gaining," he said a little later, looking at the paper, which was astern of the little boat.

Then, aft of the floating paper, he saw the dorsal fin of a shark. He watched it for several moments. It was pacing the boat and it was notched.

"Moore," Adams said, "take a peek aft."

Moore looked aft. "That's all we need," he said. "Is it the same one?"

Adams said there was no doubt of it.

Moore resumed paddling. "For the first time in twenty-two years," he said, "I'm beginning to wonder if I shouldn't have been an Army man."

"It's enough to make a guy wonder," Adams said, looking at the shark again.

Justin said, "I wish I had a drink."

Moore turned to the little black. His head was lolling against the port gunwale. His mouth was open and his lips were parted. Moore took the towel from his head and dipped it into the sea and tossed it to Adams. "Put it around his head. It'll cool him a little bit."

Erickson got up onto his seat. "You better give me my watch back when we get to the raft. Or when a rescue plane comes," he said, glaring at Adams.

"I will," Adams said. "Don't worry about it. I just wish either of those situations were such that I could give it to you right now."

On the half-hour Adams began to paddle. A half-hour later, Moore, then Adams, and Moore again. "There's another bunch of guys," Moore said, pointing with the paddle.

Adams and the others looked. "That's going to be another rough one, going through those guys," Adams said.

"We're definitely not going to pick any of them up this time," Moore said.

"That's for sure," Adams said. "It's hard enough paddling with just us guys."

Moore kept paddling toward the floating men. His face was grim. It would be a hard, mean thing, to refuse to pick up any of them. It could be condemning them to death.

Adams looked back. The shark was still pacing the little boat. "Do you think we're doing the right thing, Moore, leading that shark into those guys?"

"Well, Jesus Christ, Adams," Moore said, "if we detour around them we might as well forget that fucking raft."

"I know it, and I'm not in favor of a detour. You know something, Moore. We're just like guys I've read about. At first you want to help everybody. Everybody's your buddy. We're all in this together and all that shit. Then you try to justify not helping them. You think of some excuse that juices your conscience. Then, later on, you don't give a damn. You just think about your own survival.

"So we really don't care if that shark eats some of those guys up ahead there, do we? In fact, subconsciously, we hope he will because if he eats enough of them maybe he'll quit following us."

Moore looked back at Adams. "Don't talk like that, for God's sake, man! I don't want to think about it. I can't think about it."

"It's the truth, though, isn't it?" Erickson said.

"Shut up, you son of a bitch," Moore said.

Soon the little boat was near the first of the floating men. "It looks to me," Moore said. "that a good half of them are dead. Or else awful close to it."

Suddenly Moore paddled sharply to starboard, toward a bobbling corpse that floated upright because of its kapok life jacket. "I thought I saw a knife on that guy's belt on that last swell," he explained.

"What the hell do you need a knife for?" Adams said.

"Nothing special," Moore said. "I'd just feel better with it, is all. We don't have any kind of weapon, except this stupid paddle."

He retrieved the knife and shoved it under his belt, then resumed his course toward the rafts.

He began to paddle through the floaters. Three were huddled together. One of them shouted weakly, "Hey, you guys . . . come here . . . please!"

Moore looked back at Adams. "What do you think? There's nothing we can do for them."

"Maybe we can give them a little moral support," Adams said. "It's a hell of a thing just to ignore the poor bastards."

Moore paddled slightly to port, toward the three men. They swam up beside the boat. The one who had shouted,

Gary Donelan, a ship's service laundryman, said, "You guys got a drink? Just a little bitty one is all we're askin' for."

"Man, we ain't got a drop," Moore said.

Another of the floaters, Cedric Pedregon, a turret captain, said, "You got water, Moore! All them survival boats got water. Please, for God's sake, give us just a couple swallows."

"Pete," Moore said, "this one didn't have anything in it except two dead guys, a zinged-up marine officer, and a paddle, and that's the pure gospel truth. We're so fucking thirsty ourselves we can't hardly keep going."

"Oh, Christ," Donelan said. He began a kind of choking sob.

"I'm sorry, kid," Moore said. "If I had any water I'd give you a drink. I honest to God would."

The third floater, Ray Traudt, a fire controlman, said, "You guys got some vaseline or some kind of salve? To put on my neck. Look . . ."

He raised his head so that the men in the boat could see his neck. His horse-collar kapok jacket had chafed his neck and underchin and the sea's salty water had inflamed these red, raw areas. "God, that hurts," he said. "You guys got no idea how it hurts. You got any kinda salve?"

"Mac," Moore said, "we ain't got anything. Especially salve. There'd probably be some in a medic kit, but we don't have a medic kit."

"How about taking me aboard, then?" Traudt said. "Them boats holds six guys and you only got four. You got room for me. And one other guy."

Moore looked over at Adams. "We already talked on it," Adams said quietly, his face grim. Moore looked back at Traudt. "Listen, Mac, we only got the one paddle. With six men aboard—I know what I'm talking about because we had six a while back—with six guys we'd never get to those rafts."

He pointed toward the distant rafts. "We've got to get there. We got two sick guys."

"Well, I ain't exactly in the best of health myself," Traudt said, looking at Justin and Erickson.

"We'd help you guys if we could," Moore said, "but we can't, so we're shovin' off."

Traudt put both hands on the gunwale. "Like hell you're

shovin' off. You're either takin' me or I'll tip this fuckin' boat."

"Let go of that gunwale," Moore said, "or I'll bust your stupid pumpkin head."

He picked up the paddle by its blade, intending to swing its butt onto Traudt if he tried to capsize the little boat.

Traudt pulled mightily on the gunwale, bringing it near the surface of the sea and very nearly rolling Justin and Erickson out of the little boat.

Adams grabbed Justin and jerked him back, then he grabbed Erickson's hair and pulled him back. The other floaters, frustrated and angered and wanting to strike out at somebody for their miserable plights, grabbed the gunwale and pulled on it, trying to overturn the little boat.

Adams, leaning against the opposite gunwale, kicked Pedregon in the face, flattening his nose, causing blood to gush from it. Meanwhile Moore swung the paddle's butt onto Traudt's head.

Quickly Donelan loosed his hold on the gunwale and swam away from the boat, out of reach of Moore's paddle.

Moore and Adams looked aft. The shark that had pursued them had smelled Pedregon's blood. Its dorsal fin cut a straight and very swift line toward Pedregon.

"Goddamn," Moore croaked. He reversed his paddle and dipped it into the sea and began to paddle as fast as he could. He didn't quit until he was winded. Then he looked back.

He closed his eyes and turned forward again. The sea where the boat and the floaters had been was a churning fury of splashing blood-reddened water, flailing sharks and human bodies.

"They asked for it," he said, his jaw squared. He turned to Adams. "Didn't they?"

"I would say they did," Erickson said.

Moore struck the garrulous seaman with a fist. "Goddamn you! I wasn't asking you!"

Erickson, knocked to the bottom of the little boat, got up, sat on his seat, and held his head in his hands and cried.

"It's my turn to paddle," Adams said. "Let's not stop beside anybody else. There's nothing we can do for them and it just torments us. And them."

Moore was looking aft. The frenzy had ended. "If we hadn't stopped beside those guys—"

He didn't finish it. He got up and changed places with Adams.

Adams began to paddle toward the rafts. "Is that shark following us?" he asked.

"Yup," Moore said. "The son of a bitch is right where he was. Fifty feet aft and holding true."

"It isn't because he's hungry and he thinks we're a meal," Adams said, his lips tight.

"That's what scares me," Moore said, looking aft at the shark again. "It's like he's got a personal grudge against us and he's just waiting for the right moment."

"The right moment for what?" Erickson said, lisping it because of his cut and rapidly swelling lips.

"Don't you ever get enough?" Moore said, glaring at Erickson.

"I've got a right to know, haven't I? Whatever that shark does to us, you want to remember I'm in on it, too."

"You got a point, I guess," Moore said. "That big devil's waiting for the right moment, but I don't know what for or when it'll be, any more than you do. Now shut up."

Adams began to paddle past a group of about thirty floaters. Ten, at least, were dead, held afloat by kapok jackets or pneumatic belts. He ignored the pleas and shouts and curses of the living floaters. There was nothing he or Moore could do for them. He paddled as fast as he could, not because he was trying to avoid them, which was their interpretation, but because he didn't want to bring the pursuing shark any closer to them than necessary.

He passed the last of the floaters. "Take over, Moore," he said, breathing hard. "I'm damn near dissolved."

The sun was remorseless. He looked at the watch on his wrist. "Three hours until night. If anybody's coming for us today they'd better be getting here."

Justin croaked, "Do you guys really think we'll be rescued? Gimme a straight honest answer."

"Sure we do," Moore said.

"They might not come today, though. Isn't that right?"

"That's right," Moore said. "We got no guarantee when they'll get here."

"How long can people go without water?"

Adams looked at the anguished young black. "A long time, Justin. A lot longer than you think. Take yourself, for instance. I'd bet that tomorrow at this same time, if we're still right here, which of course we won't be, you wouldn't be any thirstier than you are right now."

"A good ninety percent of it is in your head," Moore said. "You know what I mean . . . from thinking about it all the time."

"I hope so," Justin said, barely audibly. "I'm so thirsty. And I'm all on fire inside. My whole insides hurt now."

Moore motioned for Adams to give him the towel from Justin's head. He dipped it into the sea and extended it, dripping, from the end of the paddle to Adams, who wrapped it around Justin's head again.

"That feel better?" Moore asked.

"It sure does," Justin said. "Thanks. I sure appreciate what you guys are doing for me."

Adams looked forward, toward the rafts. "We're not going to make it before night, are we?"

"We might," Moore said. "The drift can always change and give us a kick in the ass. Better change off with me again."

Dusk came. The rafts were a half-mile from the little boat. "I thought for a while there we'd make it," Moore said. "We were gaining pretty steady. Well, we all might as well get some sleep. We can't paddle in the dark."

He looked aft. The shark's dorsal fin had vanished. "Every time we quit moving he deep-sixes. I wonder what that means?"

"I don't like to think what it could mean," Adams said, laying his head against the port gunwale.

Soon everyone, except Justin, was asleep.

Justin reached over the gunwale and cupped his hands and scooped up water from the sea. He drank it. Then he scooped up more, and still more.

He laid back against the gunwale. He felt better. He wasn't so hot inside.

Moments later his mouth gaped and his eyes protruded. His body tremored. He began to convulse. The others awakened. Moore and Adams scurried over to the agonized young black. "I drank some water," he gasped. "A whole bunch of it. And now, oh, God, I'm sick."

He went into convulsions. His feet beat a tattoo on the boat's flimsy rubberized fabric bottom. Terror swept over Adams' face. "For chrissake, he'll kick a hole in it."

Moore jerked the knife from his belt and shoved it to its hilt into Justin's chest, just under his ribs.

Justin died instantly and his head fell forward onto Moore's shoulder.

Moore pushed the dead sailor's head away and pulled the knife out of his chest. He wiped off its blood on Justin's pants. "I had to do it," he said. "He would have died in just a little while anyway, and if I hadn't stabbed him, he would have kicked a hole in the deck. Then we'd all been up the creek."

"Nobody's blaming you, Moore," Adams said. "But it was too damn bad he drank that seawater. He was a real nice kid. I was hoping he'd make it."

"I don't think he would have, even if he hadn't drank that water," Moore said, unwrapping the towel from the dead black's head. "He was slipping pretty fast."

Moore tossed the towel toward the little boat's bow and put the knife under his belt. "Throw him off our stern," he said, "but wait'll I start paddling. The way he's bleeding, he'll draw sharks like flies at a picnic and we better be long gone."

16

IT WAS AN INTERMINABLE NIGHT. Hope diminished at night. Rescue would never come, the men in the little yellow survival boat were convinced. Or if it did, it would be too late.

All manner of glum thoughts tormented Moore and Adams during the long cold dark hours; they slept only occasionally and restlessly. But Erickson didn't seem concerned about anything. He slept soundly.

He awoke at dawn. He sat up from the gunwale on which he had rested his head and shoulders. "I can't move my arms," he said. "They're froze where I got burned in my armpits!"

He stood up, wobbling. He looked grotesque, his arms sticking out like a scarecrow. "I can't piss and I gotta go," he said.

"It's all in your mind," Moore said. "We're all pissed out. When you don't have anything to drink for a couple days and you sweat all the time, you don't have anything to piss."

"That's what you think," Erickson said. "Well, I'm not going to do it here anyway. I'm going to the head."

He stepped up onto the aft gunwale.

"Hey, for chrissake," Moore said quickly. He lunged toward the deranged young sailor.

He wasn't fast enough. Erickson stepped off the boat. He sank immediately. He hadn't worn his life jacket for almost a day. It was too hot, he'd said.

Adams went to the stern gunwale and, leaning on it beside Moore, looked at the sea where Erickson had disappeared. Bubbles came up. They quit coming. Then several larger bubbles broke the sea's placid surface.

"I wish I hadn't been so rough on him," Moore said, staring into the sea. "But, Jesus, there was times I couldn't stand his everlastin' yakking."

"That isn't what made him go off his rocker," Adams said. "It was his burns. He must of been burned worse than we thought. Even worse than he realized himself. Besides, I was plenty hard on him, too. He had the kind of personality that grinds on a guy. And being cooped up here in this little boat, well, he got to you."

Moore turned around and sat on the stern seat. "It's just you and me now, Adams. Are we gonna make it?"

"We won't if help doesn't come," Adams said, sitting beside Moore. "Or unless we can get to a raft that's got water."

"God, why hasn't somebody come?" Moore said. "I just can't understand it."

"I don't get it either," Adams said.

"Something damn funny's going on," Moore said.

"There has to be," Adams replied. "But what the hell could it be?"

"I'll start paddling," Moore said. "Just sitting here talking on it won't get us a drink."

"Just take a little go at it," Adams said, "then I'll take over."

Moore hadn't paddled more than ten yards when a shark's dorsal fin surfaced astern of the little yellow boat. It was the mutilated fin of the shark that had been pacing them. "I wonder if he ate Erickson," Moore said, looking back. "He could have. He was around here someplace when Erickson jumped off."

"You know what we ought to call that bastard?" Adams said. "We ought to call him Tojo. Like that big-shot Jap warlord you hear about all the time. They're both persistent, mean SOBs."

"Since he seems to be the detached part of this ship's company," Moore said, "he ought to have a name, all right. And Tojo sounds like it fits him."

He looked aft again. "Tojo, you son of a bitch," he said, "if I had my forty-five I'd make you the deadest shark in the man-eating business."

What he would do, he told Adams, if he'd had the foresight to bring his Colt .45-caliber semiautomatic pistol, was lure Tojo close to the little boat's stern, then shoot him in one of his eyes.

"I'd put three quickies into him after which Mr. Tojo would no longer be in shape to follow anybody."

But since he had left his .45 in his locker on the *Indianapolis*, he said, he might as well forget about it and concentrate on paddling.

He and Adams paddled feebly toward the rafts that were connected by a floater net. They had little strength. They were dehydrated and dispirited.

"We can't make it," Moore said during his third turn at the paddle.

"We've got to keep trying," Adams said.

Moore quit paddling. He looked into the skies. There were no rescue planes. "God a'mighty, why don't they come for us?" he croaked. "Why are they ignoring us? Like we never even existed."

"I don't know the answers," Adams said, "but either keep paddling or let me do it. I've got a kid I've never seen and I'm going to see that little boy if there's any possible way . . . and getting a drink from that raft is absolutely necessary, because if I don't get a drink pretty damn soon I won't make it."

Moore looked back at Adams. Tears had welled in Moore's eyes. "You ain't the only one that's got somebody to hang on for," he said. "I promised my little girl I'd walk down the aisle with her and, God, Adams, I want to do that more than anything I ever wanted in my whole life."

He began to cry. "I love my daughter, Adams. Goddamn, you don't know how much I love her."

It seemed incongruous, a tough old salt like Charlie Moore,

gunner's mate first class, twenty-two years in the United States Navy, crying like a kid just out of boot. Adams stared at him like he couldn't believe it.

Here was a facet to the big Navy man's personality he hadn't seen, and very likely no one else had ever seen. Under his bark, Adams reflected, he's a sensitive man. I sincerely hope he'll be able to walk down the aisle at his daughter's wedding.

But self-sympathy is a bad thing. It diminishes a man's resolve. It reduces his abilities to do what must be done. "Hey, Charlie," Adams said, "I never supposed a big tough guy like you would toss in the sponge. Let's get the show on the road so you can take that walk. Give up now and for damn sure you never will."

Moore looked into Adams' sun- and sea-tanned face. He dried his tears with the backs of his hands. "I'm going to do it, by God! The wedding won't be until the last of August and I'm going to be there."

"Damn right you're going to be there," Adams said.

Moore picked up the paddle. "Let me know if Air-Sea Rescue shows up," he said, digging into the sea.

"I will if I haven't got anything better to do," Adams said, laying his head against the starboard gunwale and putting his arm over his eyes to shield them from the glaring tropic sun.

While these men and the other survivors of the *Indianapolis* suffered from thirst, the remorseless sun, and despair—their numbers reduced at the ghastly rate of a hundred a day by the Central Pacific's voracious sharks—the officers and enlisted men at Headquarters of the Philippine Sea Frontier went about their affairs as though the greatest sea disaster in the history of the U.S. Navy had not occurred.

Philippine Sea Frontier was at Tolosa on Leyte Island. It was in a large Quonset above whose main entrance a sign had been attached:

HEADQUARTERS
PHILIPPINE SEA FRONTIER

A little after 1700 hours Lieutenant Kenneth Odell went

into the office of Captain Frank Heberling, the base commandant.

"Sir," Lieutenant Odell said, standing in front of Captain Heberling's desk, "last Friday we received a dispatch from CinCPac of the departure from Guam at oh-nine-hundred Saturday of the cruiser *Indianapolis*, CA-three-five.

"The dispatch further stated, sir, that the *Indianapolis* would arrive in Leyte Gulf at eleven-hundred Tuesday. Which, as you know, is today. But it is—"

Lieutenant Odell looked at the watch on his wrist—"now more than six hours overdue. The moment I learned of this I checked with both Radio and Code. Neither has had word of explanation for the delay."

Captain Heberling took a cigar from his desk, put it between his teeth, and applied a lighter to it. He blew a smoke ring and then he said, "How long have you been on duty at this station, Lieutenant?"

"Three weeks, sir," Lieutenant Odell said.

"Were you in Communications elsewhere?"

"No, sir. But—"

The captain had blown another smoke ring. He watched it float toward the Quonset's ceiling while he interrupted the lieutenant. "I happen to have read the dispatch. It stated, and this is a point you seemed to have overlooked, that the *Indianapolis* would arrive at eleven-hundred today *unless diverted by CinCPac or other authority*."

The captain, tall, stern-faced, and Annapolis, sat straight in his chair and looked up at the uneasy lieutenant. "In time of war, Lieutenant, a combatant ship is frequently ordered to change destination."

"Yes, sir," Lieutenant Odell said.

"Your concern is appreciated, Odell. But unwarranted. The *Indianapolis* is quite capable of coping with any situation that might confront her."

"Yes, sir," Lieutenant Odell said. "Thank you, sir."

Embarrassed and wishing he hadn't brought up the subject of the *Indianapolis*, and hoping that it wouldn't tarnish his image with the commandant, Lieutenant Odell went back to his desk in Communications.

While Adams paddled feebly toward the rafts, he saw a potato floating on the rolling sea. Then he saw another, and a third. "For chrissake," he muttered.

He paddled toward the potatoes. "Hey, Moore," he said, "we're in the Central Pacific's produce department."

"I can't believe it," Moore said, looking at the potatoes.

He swooped up the nearest potato, then the others. "God-damn," he said, smiling.

He tossed two of the potatoes onto the bottom of the little boat, then took the knife from his belt and cut the third potato into slices, giving half to Adams, who had quit rowing.

Each man chewed a slice of the potato, swallowed its watery juice, then swallowed its pulp. "Goddamn," Moore babbled. "That tastes good."

They savored the potato, not eating it too swiftly because its juice, in their mouths, was too refreshing to swallow quickly. They talked on their good fortune, between slices, deciding that the potatoes had been part of the *Indianapolis'* food-locker supplies.

"I don't know how they got out," Moore said happily. "They kept that locker locked like a bank vault. But the important thing is they got out and, man, they taste better than Thanksgiving at Grandma's."

"I feel like we're going to make it now," Adams said, smiling.

"Fucking right we'll make it," Moore said. "Let's save those other two for later on. If we eat them all now we're liable to get sick in two different directions."

They looked out at the sea. There were no more potatoes.

"There was just about everything in the food locker," Moore said. "I wonder where it all went."

"Sharks probably ate it," Adams said.

"There's a million other kinds of fish, too," Moore said. "We're just lucky they don't like potatoes."

Moore reached down and picked up a potato. "I'm going to cut this little humpy part off," he said, "and tie it to a raveling from this towel I've got on my head and see if I can sucker a fish up close enough to stab with my knife."

He took the towel from his head and removed a long thread. Then he wet the towel in the sea, put it around his head again, and tied the thread around the little piece of potato.

He would dangle it off the boat's stern, he said, and if a fish came to investigate, he would try to impale it with his knife, which he would hold at the ready in his right hand, then flip the fish into the boat.

"The white part, where I cut it off the potato, ought to make them think it's something to eat. And it won't be big enough or make enough of a jiggle to attract a shark."

Adams said it would be a great idea if it worked.

"I think it will," Moore said. "I used to catch sunfish and crappies when I was a kid with just something flashy tied to a hook."

He looked into Adams' face. "I would have tried it before if I'd had anything to use for bait. You know something, George, I actually thought about biting a piece of meat from Gehringer after he died—I didn't have this knife then—and using it for bait like I'm going to use this little piece of potato. Then when Justin died, after I stabbed the poor little guy, I thought about cutting off a piece of him to use for bait. But I didn't. I just couldn't do it."

"Jesus Christ," Adams said, "I suppose you even thought about cutting them up and eating them."

"To tell you the truth," Moore said, "I actually did think about it with Justin. I didn't have the knife when Gehringer died. I thought about slicing some slices off of Justin's ass and drying them on the gunwale, which wouldn't take very long in this fucking sun. They'd be like jerky when they dried out. Like the pioneers used to make."

"Oh, God," Adams said. The thought of a cannibalistic meal was too hideous even to contemplate. "Let's talk about something else," he said. "How are we going to eat this fish you're going to catch? Raw fish doesn't sound like a gourmet meal to me, and we don't have any wood for the stove."

"I read somewhere about shipwrecked guys that sucked the juice out of raw fish and it kept them alive," Moore said. "However, I was thinking of jerkying most of it. Like I mentioned with Justin's ass."

There you go, talking about cannibalism again, Adams reflected. Now when he ate that jerkied fish he'd think about Justin. "At least it won't be him," he muttered.

"Won't be who?" Moore asked.

"Nobody in particular. I was just thinking out loud, I guess."

"Don't you go Section Eight on me," Moore said, "just when things are looking up. Watch when I flip a fish in and don't let him flop out."

Moore's scheme was an almost immediate success. A foot-long chunky silvery fish swam up to investigate the dangling potato.

"Get just a little closer, stupid," Moore muttered, his face tense. "Just a little bit more to starboard."

The fish came closer. Suddenly Moore stabbed it with his knife, flipping it into the boat with a continuation of the stab swing. Adams flopped onto it and soon each man was sucking on its firm watery flesh. "That's better'n the potato," Moore said happily, wiping the gore from his mouth. "Juicier, anyway."

A little later Moore said, "I'll slice up these parts we sucked the juice out of and jerky them, which won't take very long as hot as the gunwales and the sun both are. Meanwhile you row, Adams, and then I'll do it."

The men rowed toward the raft, alternating at fifteen-minute intervals. They rowed faster and with hope instead of despair.

"We got it made now," Moore said happily.

A little later, while Moore was paddling, they came upon a lone floater. He was Lieutenant Richard Hollens, the *Indianapolis'* forward gun captain, twenty-seventh officer in the big cruiser's chain of command, number one, as the ship's enlisted men had often said, in the cruiser's horse's-ass department. He had a Captain Bligh personality and a firm conviction that enlisted personnel were an inferior species.

"Get over here, you men," he bellowed.

"Well, doggone, look who's there," Moore said, glancing over his shoulder at Adams. "Our famous gunnery officer, the United States Navy's number-one creep."

"We'd better get over there, on the double," Adams said with a wink, "or we'll have our sore little asses in a sling."

"I'm proceeding at full speed," Moore said, returning the wink. "I wouldn't ignore that piss ant for a million dollars."

He paddled to starboard, beside—but not too close to

Lieutenant Hollens. "I'm commandeering your boat," the lieutenant said.

"No kidding?" Moore said. He looked over at Adams. "He's commandeering our boat. Which means we got to get out and walk."

"Heck," Adams said. "I was fixing to ride this boat right up the Missouri River to my house way back there in Omaha."

"You men are not amusing," Hollens said. "Now paddle over here beside me."

"Up your ass, sir," Moore said.

"Way up," Adams added.

"This is a direct order," Hollens bellowed.

"Them's the best kind," Moore said. "Mind if I ask you something? Sir?"

"What is it?"

"How come you're in such great shape after all this time in the drink? Or did you have the officers' mess boys bring your meals?"

"It is none of your concern, and a point of distinction between the mental processes of an officer and an enlisted man," the lieutenant said, "but when I saw that the *Indianapolis* was doomed, I had the foresight to requisition a canteen of water and a kit of rations before I abandoned. Now get over here and give me that boat."

"Fuck you, sir," Moore said. "But I'll tell you what we'll do. We'll—"

"You're going on report," the lieutenant interrupted. "For refusing to obey a direct order, thereby imperiling the life of an officer of the U.S. Navy! And for insubordination and obscene language. If you're lucky, you'll only get twenty years in the naval brig at Portsmouth. Now I'll give you one last, final chance, Moore and you, whatever your name is. Move that boat over here and get out of it."

"I'll tell you what I'll do," Moore said. "It's what I was going to say when you cut me off. What we'll do is, if you'll behave yourself, we'll take you aboard. But we are not, I repeat, not, going to give you this boat."

"You've got to be playing with a short deck to even think of such a stupid thing," Adams said.

"Damn you enlisted trash," the lieutenant screamed. "I'll see both of you in Portsmouth."

"We don't have to listen to this ass hole," Moore said, looking over at Adams, "so I'm ordering anchors aweigh, full speed ahead, and fuck the lieutenant."

"Suits me," Adams said.

Moore began to paddle the little boat toward the rafts. The lieutenant hurled curses, threats, obscenities.

"What nasty language," Moore said. "His mother should have washed his mouth out with soap."

"Uh-uh," Adams said. "She should have strangled him in the crib."

"He'll probably nail us to the cross," Adams continued. "It's too much to hope that Tojo would eat the son of a bitch."

"Sharks don't eat officers," Moore said. "They got too much self-respect."

They looked aft. Tojo was pacing the boat. He was ignoring Lieutenant Hollens.

"I wish he'd at least bite off his balls," Moore said.

17

MOORE DESPISED LIEUTENANT HOLLENS. AN incident several months earlier at Ulithi, the Navy's recreational island in the western Carolines, had done little to improve Hollens' image with Moore and the other enlisted men of the *Indianapolis* ship's company.

Before their attack on Okinawa the *Indianapolis* and other warships of the Third Fleet had anchored at Ulithi to permit their men to go ashore to enjoy its softball field, ship's service stores, and other facilities.

Moore had been in the starboard section of the *Indianapolis*, the big cruiser's second shore party on the little tropic island. "I decided the hell with softball," he said to Adams, who was paddling the little rubber survival boat. "Me and my buddies went for a walk. It felt great having a chance to walk on solid ground. Then we drank a couple beers, which was all each guy could have, after which we got in the line at a ship's service tent figuring to buy some M&Ms.

"You know how it is, Babe Ruths, Three Musketeers, and most other chocolate candy bars practically dissolve here in the tropics. You have to drink them. But those little round jobs, M&Ms, don't dissolve, so all of us guys decided to buy several packages apiece, everybody being hungry as hell for chocolate.

"We stand in line in that fucking heat for a solid hour, meanwhile working our way toward the tent. I'm within two guys of being able to buy my candy when along comes Lieutenant Hollens, the noble officer who is now floating in the drink aft of us.

"He requisitions all of the M&Ms they got left. We enlisted jokers can't even buy one package after standing in line all that time, in that goddamn heat.

"He walks away with four cartons of those goodies, meanwhile looking over at us and laughing like it was something funny. Well, I hope he enjoyed that candy. It'll give him something to think about now."

Adams quit paddling. It was Moore's turn. "I've seen other officers go to the head of the line," Adams said, "and requisition all the goodies there were. I saw a j.g. at Guam glom the beer us guys were supposed to get. Then he had the guts to order six of us guys to help him carry it to the Transient Officers Barracks.

"Another time, up at Saipan, after we stood in line like you did there at Ulithi, this baby-face ensign comes up and takes all the peanuts that were supposed to be for us enlisted guys, each guy being entitled on his chit to one little can of peanuts. So what Hollens did wasn't anything special."

"What he did special was sneer at us when he laughed, after he glommed the candy. Like it was real damn funny, us waiting in line for an hour and he just walks up with no waiting, because he's an officer, goes to the head of the line, and tells the enlisted guy who was buying to step aside. Then he bought them out. Every fucking package of that candy!"

Moore picked up the paddle and Adams stretched his arms and looked back at Lieutenant Hollens and then at the pacing shark's dorsal fin. "Tojo," Adams said, "I don't blame you for not eating that lieutenant. It would probably make you sick to your stomach. But it would have been a real nice thing if you'd done it."

Moore, who had begun to paddle, looked over his shoulder at Adams. "You know something, Adams? We've got our balls in the gears if Hollens survives."

"I've been thinking about it," Adams said. "He'll throw the book at us."

"I've got an idea. Why don't we go back and deep-six him? Just one good zonk on his head with the butt of this paddle would do the job. And nobody'd ever know what happened."

"That would make sure he wouldn't be able to give us the shaft, all right. But there's one big catch."

"Yeah?" Moore said. "What is it?"

"Neither you nor me could kill a guy in cold blood. Not even that son of a bitch. Not even knowing what he could do to us."

Moore smiled a little. "I know it. But it was a nice thought. Funny thing, I can lob a shell at a Japanese ship . . . mangle, burn a bunch of guys I don't have anything personal against, and it doesn't bother me. I don't even think about it. But when it comes to acing a guy I hate worse than any Jap, I'm chicken. Hollens will probably haul our ass into court and make it sound like we're a couple of pirates who ought to be busting rocks the rest of our lives."

He turned back so he could look aft, toward the lieutenant. "Goddamn you, Hollens, I hope—"

He didn't say the rest of it. Tojo's notched dorsal fin was slicing the water toward the floating officer.

"Hey, Adams . . . look," Moore said.

Adams faced aft.

"I'm beginning to like that shark," Moore said.

"I wonder," Adams said, "what made him suddenly decide to attack the lieutenant."

"The lieutenant did something to attract his attention. Probably wiggled his feet or something like that."

The lieutenant was staring in absolute horror at the approaching dorsal fin. "Hey, Hollens," Moore yelled, cupping his hands, "all you gotta do is pull rank."

The dorsal fin submerged. A moment later Lieutenant Hollens screamed his agony.

"God, what a way to go," Moore said, "even for him."

The lieutenant's scream became a shriek. He flailed his arms.

"Tojo must have bit off his other leg," Moore said.

The attack became a frenzy. Other great whites, smelling the lieutenant's blood, sped toward him and now each of the voracious beasts wanted as much of the doomed man as he could get.

Hollens disappeared. The site became a churning froth of frenzied sharks and bloodied water. Then, suddenly, it ended.

"Lieutenant Hollens," Moore said, "is now in numerous pieces."

"God, it was terrible," Adams said, shaken by the horror of the attack and the lieutenant's haunting shrieks.

"Funny thing," Moore said. "I couldn't have killed him. It would have bugged my conscience. But since a bunch of sharks did it, it doesn't do a damn thing to my conscience."

"He should have come with us. You gave him the chance."

"I'm glad I did. It makes me feel better. If I hadn't given him the opportunity I'd feel guilty. Like I was responsible for him being killed."

Adams picked up the paddle. He dipped its blade into the sea and the little boat moved in the direction of the rafts. "Tojo's manning his station," Moore said.

Adams looked aft. The big shark's dorsal fin was pacing the little rubber boat again.

"It gives a guy a funny feeling," Moore said, looking at the shark's mutilated fin, "knowing Hollens' legs, and probably some of the rest of him, are in that big devil's guts right there back of us a little way."

"You know who else's legs and other parts he'd like to have in his guts, don't you?"

It wasn't a nice thought, and Moore said, "Christ, why didn't I bring my forty-five? I had plenty of time to run down to my locker and get it after I saw we'd have to abandon. It would have only taken half a minute."

"You were in the water quite a while before we got this boat. That might have messed it up."

"I doubt it, not for any longer than that length of time. Anyway, I would have taken it apart and dried it in the sun here in the boat. It would have been just what we need to make that big devil quit following us."

A squall came up a little later. The skies began to swirl. The clouds blackened. "We're in for one hell of a storm," Moore said, "and we have got the wrong kind of boat. In fact, we couldn't have a worse kind of boat."

The storm came suddenly. It was a typical tropic summer

storm with drenching rains and violent winds. The little boat was tossed onto the summit of ten-foot crests, then flung into their troughs.

Moore sat on the paddle on the bottom of the little boat, the paddle parallel with his legs, and gripped the gunwales, port and starboard. Adams huddled at the stern, his hands clutching gunwales on both sides.

Great quantities of water washed into the boat, drenching its occupants. "Hang on, for God's sake," Moore shouted. "If we get washed out, we're dead."

They clutched the gunwales, riding great white-crested waves, plunging into deep troughs. Control of the little boat was impossible. It was terrifying. Then, as suddenly as the storm had arisen, it ended. The seas became calm and the sun came out.

"We lost our potatoes and the fish we were jerkying," Moore said, "but we were damn lucky the paddle didn't get away from us. Or punch a hole in the deck."

"We've got a hell of a bunch of water to scoop out," Adams said.

"I wish now we'd eaten at least one of those other potatoes," Moore said.

"We weren't thinking," Adams replied. "We should have each put a potato under our shirt."

"Losing our goodies isn't the only problem we've got," Moore said. "Those rafts have disappeared. The storm probably blew them halfway to hell and gone."

"It also blew another one over to port," Adams said.

Moore looked in this direction. "Well, I'll be doggone. You lose one, you gain one. And that baby's a whole lot closer than those twins we've been chasing. Plus which it looks to me like for once the drift is going to be on our side."

"Let's get to scooping this water," Adams said. "With the freeboard we've got now, it would take a diesel to get us moving."

For more than an hour they scooped water, with cupped hands, out of the little boat. The tropic sun bore down on them. It was hard, sweating work, and when they finished they were terribly thirsty. "I'll take the first shift," Moore said wearily, picking up the paddle.

He paddled slowly. Each dip of the paddle's blade into the sea, and the thrust on it, was an effort.

"Tojo's following us again," Adams said.

Moore looked back at the big shark's dorsal fin. It was in true line with the little boat's stern. "I don't like it," Adams said. "To tell you the truth, it scares me. He's up to something. There's some reason he's following us."

Moore resumed paddling. "The reason isn't hard to figure. He's following us because he thinks he's going to get a chance to eat us."

"You can make a guy feel real good," Adams said.

"Why else would he be following us? Can you think of any other reason? I can't."

"I can't either," Adams said. He looked into the sky. No sign of Air-Sea Rescue Catalinas. "That's got to be the biggest snafu there ever was," he said. "You know how far it is, flying time, from Saipan. Or from Peleliu?"

"I'd say they never got the word."

"I'm sure they didn't. In fact, I know they didn't. But, Jesus Christ, Moore, CinCPac keeps track of where every warship is every fucking minute.

"I've been in Operations there at CinCPac. On the hill there on Guam right above Agana. Two stories down in the ground is where Operations is. A bunch of marines guarding the place. They've got big boards with maps of all the oceans and little toy ships on them. Our ships, the Limeys', the Japs', everybody's. Guys pushing them around with sticks so they know, all the time, where every ship is.

"They've got the *Indianapolis* there. They've got all the U.S. big boys there. So are they just leaving the *Indy* on those charts where it was the last time they heard? In the same fucking place? Don't they wonder, for chrissake, where the *Indy* is now?"

"I don't get it, either," Moore said. "All I know is, something is sure as hell screwed up."

"And a hell of a lot of guys are dying because of it."

"I just hope we're not going to be two of them," Moore said, dipping the paddle into the sea. "Jesus, Adams, I wish we'd been able to keep those potatoes. I'm so goddamn thirsty my mouth's all dry inside."

Adams looked at the raft, then back at Moore. "Better let

me paddle for a while. We've both got to keep in shape or we won't make it. It's farther than it looks. Distances on the sea fool a guy."

They alternated twice more before they came to the edge of an oil slick . . . oil from the great tanks on the *Indianapolis*. "Son of a bitch," Moore said. "I knew we were going too fucking good for it to last."

The raft was on the other side of the slick, which had spread over a vast area. Moore, who had been paddling, said, "We're eight-balled now. If we go around it, we might never get to that raft. You can't trust the drift. But if we go through that oil we're taking one hell of a chance of the oil plus the sun rotting the rubber on this yacht. In which case Tojo will have a couple juicy meals."

"The ones he's been waiting for," Adams said. A tremor snaked down his spine. He could think of no more agonizing way to die than to be devoured by sharks.

"I wish we had a whaleboat," Moore said. "Oil wouldn't hurt a wooden-hull boat, so I'd take it into that slick. That would shortcut us to the raft, besides losing Tojo. He wouldn't go through that oil."

"Since we don't have a whaleboat," Adams said, "we've got to decide what we're going to do with what we've got."

He shielded his eyes while he looked out at the slick. "The sun's glare off that oil burns my eyes. And the way it stinks is giving my guts a bad time. Let's take the detour."

"If we do, we're gambling on the drift screwing us with that raft, and, man, if we don't get a drink from those guys I don't think we can make it much longer."

"On the other hand," Adams said, "if we go through that slick we're gambling a drink of water against the oil dissolving this little boat . . . and becoming a meal for Tojo."

It was a tough decision, a tremendous penalty for the wrong course. Moore's face furrowed. It could cost him his life if they went the wrong way. But which way was the wrong way?

"Okay," he said, his jaw squared, "let's take the detour."

He began to paddle parallel with the perimeter of the oil slick, keeping the little survival boat about twenty feet from the oil.

They came to seven live floaters. Adams looked back. Tojo

was there. "I don't think he'll bother those guys," Moore said. "Not the way they're covered with oil."

"I hope not," Adams said. "I'd hate to think we led him to the poor devils. Jesus, it must have been tough, being in that oil all this time."

They came closer to the floaters, who were just outside the slick. "Oh, God," Adams said. They were grotesquely piteous. The sun's glare on the oil had made little red balls of their eyes. It had blinded them. They were covered with thick black diesel fuel except for blotches of raw, red oozing flesh on their faces and foreheads.

"We can quit talking and go on past them," Adams said quietly, "and they won't know we've been here. Or we can talk to them . . . and maybe encourage them to hang on because rescue has got to come sometime."

"The sensible thing to do would be to keep going," Moore said. "But who ever said we had any sense. Besides, even if I had any brains, I couldn't do it. God, man, look at them and then look at us. We got a break. Jesus Christ, we got a break when we got this boat."

He paddled beside the floaters. They begged for water. "I'm sorry, fellas," Moore said, "we ain't got a drop and we're thirstier'n hell ourselves."

"Man, I wish you had some water," one of the floaters, Ralph Durks, aviation radio technician second class, said. "I never knew a guy could get so thirsty. But we're not as bad off, I guess, as we could be. There were twenty-two of us guys swam out of that slick. Four of them just gave up and died. The others, except us seven guys, died from having swallowed oil. They vomited until blood came up. Then sharks came. They ate those guys. God, it was terrible. The way they screamed."

"Keep your chin up, kid," Moore said. "Rescue'll be here in the morning."

"For sure?"

"Damn right," Moore said. "So hang on. Don't give up. Remember, you've stood it this long, so what's another night?"

"I'll hang on," Durks said, "now that I've got something to hang on for. God, I'm glad you told me about that rescue. What'll it be, planes or ships?"

"Both," Moore said.

He paddled away quickly, before Durks thought to ask how he knew about the rescue.

"That was a damn decent thing you did there," Adams said softly. "It gave that poor guy something to hold on to. And maybe rescue actually will come tomorrow."

Moore paddled beside another oil-covered floater, Jerry Medford, a yeoman striker. "Try to wash this fuckin' oil off your face or anywhere," Medford said, looking at the men in the boat with bright red unseeing eyes, "and your skin comes off with it. With the oil. Then the sun burns worse on where the skin was that came off because it's raw in those places. And when oil gets on those raw places, God, you wish you were dead.

"Please take me aboard. Please!"

Other floaters begged to be taken aboard the little boat. "We can't even think of it," Moore muttered to Adams, his face showing deep pity for his tortured shipmates. "The oil on those guys would rot this rubberized fabric in no time."

"I'm afraid of it, too," Adams said. "Why don't we just go on, not stop anymore. We're not doing anybody any good and it's ripping me apart looking at those guys. That kid, Medford . . . Jesus Christ, he always sat at my table in the forward galley."

Moore paddled on past the floaters. "It's a bitchin' thing, leaving those guys," he said. "But what the hell else could we do?"

"Nothing," Adams said, looking aft. "Not anything at all."

Tojo was following the little boat. "At least he didn't attack them," Adams said.

Moore looked back at the big shark's sea-slicing fin. "The oil that's killing those guys saved them from being killed by that shark and his buddies. How do you put that together?"

"I don't know," Adams said, looking at the oil-blackened, blinded floating men. "It's just one of those things nobody's got an answer for. Except maybe God, and I'm beginning to believe neither God or CinCPac knows the *Indy* got torpedoed."

18

SEVENTEEN MEN WERE ON THE raft. They saw Moore and Adams paddling around the north side of the oil slick. "If they're coming here and they think we're going to give them some of our water," Clyde Wittmer, chief boatswain's mate, said to the others, "they got another guess coming."

"We can't refuse them at least one little drink, if they haven't had any water," Tony Morales, fire controlman third class, said. "If it was us, we'd have a right to expect it."

"It ain't us! It's somebody else!" Wittmer, a burly six-footer, said to the little Mexican-American. "Look at it like you had some brains, Poncho. We only got what water we got, and if rescue don't come for another day, or maybe a couple days, we're going to need it ourselves."

"That's a damn selfish attitude," Ted Kipper, one of the ship's service barbers, said to Wittmer. "We've had water all the time and if those guys—"

"I'm not arguing it," Wittmer bellowed. "I said no water and I mean no water! Just remember I'm top rate on this raft and what I say goes."

"Damn right," someone said.

Another man said they couldn't be responsible for everybody else. "If everybody with water divided it with everybody else, then nobody would have enough and we might all die. What the hell kinda thinking would that be?"

"Just plain ass stupid," Wittmer said. "If those guys come here, I'll take care of it. Everybody else keep your fucking mouth shut! Okay?"

Everyone said okay except Morales and Kipper and a little yeoman who kept looking at Wittmer to see if he was watching who said okay.

Moore and Adams, alternating, paddled as fast as they could. They wanted to get to the raft before nightfall. The night drift might separate them further. Then, most likely, they would not have the strength to catch up to the raft.

"We're gonna make it," Moore said, digging into the sea with the paddle. "We're going to come out even with the daylight."

"Those guys look fat and happy," Adams said.

"Which means they've got food and water," Moore said. "Goddamn, a drink is going to taste great."

"Did you ever think how much water we used to waste taking a shower? And how many lives the water from just one guy's shower would save now?"

"I've thought more about that cold sweet wonderful water in the *Indy*'s scuttlebutts. Goddamn, all you had to do was push a little button and put your mouth down on that little stream of cold, cold water. You could drink all you damn well wanted. And come back any fucking time you wanted to.

"There's nothing better than that cold distilled water from those scuttlebutts. They're something we never gave a second thought to, either. Just took them for granted. But, God, right now wouldn't a drink from one of them be great?"

"You're torturing yourself even thinking about it," Adams said. "What you ought to think about is the water on that raft."

"You got something there," Moore said. "But, Jesus, if a guy couldn't think about other things, he couldn't make it. That's all that's kept me going—thinking about other things."

"Me, too," Adams said.

"What do you think about the most?"

"My wife. And my little boy I've never seen. I think about

him the most. I think about my dad and mom, too, and my kid sisters. About the job I used to have. What I'm going to do when this fucking war ends—if it ever ends. I think about just about everything, I guess. But lately I mostly think about just staying alive."

"I know what you mean," Moore said. "I've thought about the same things. Today, while I've been paddling, I've thought quite a bit about my grandpa. He's still alive, which is something, considering my age. Most guys my age, their grandparents are dead. But Gramps is still alive and the old guy writes to me all the time. I got a letter from him last mail call from the mail we took on there at Guam. Just before we started this pleasure cruise.

"He was a corporal in the First World War. 'Join the Navy,' he told me when I was just a kid. 'Don't ever get in the infantry. It's the shits from the word go.'

"Here lately I've been thinking Gramps had it ass backward. I never heard of anybody in the Army having to put up with what we've had to put up with."

"The Navy won't look so bad after we get that drink," Adams said, looking toward the raft.

"You're right," Moore said. "That drink is going to make a whole new world out of everything and, man, we're getting closer every minute."

Two paddling changes later Moore brought the little boat beside the raft. It was the first light of dusk and he and Adams were elated. At last they had reached a raft! Now, in just moments, they would have a drink of water.

"What can I do for you guys?" Wittmer said, standing on the side of the raft that flanked the boat.

"A little old drink of water will keep us hale and hearty," Moore said affably.

"You came to the wrong raft, Moore," Wittmer said. "We're holding on to what little water we got left."

Moore looked unbelievingly at Wittmer, whom he had known since he had joined the *Indy*'s ship's company. "For chrissake, man," he said. "We're not asking for a couple five-gallon jugs. All we want is just one drink for each of us."

"Move on, Moore," Wittmer said.

"Suppose we stay right here," Moore said, "and then suppose another suppose. Suppose I come aboard and bust a couple heads, including yours, you son of a bitch."

"Well, now, Moore," Wittmer said, grinning, "you don't look to me like you're in shape to bust anybody's head, especially since you'd have to bust quite a bunch of them, during which you would soon begin to look like a hamburger that hasn't been cooked. So if I were you, I'd pick up that paddle and start paddling."

Moore kept sitting on his paddle seat, glaring up at the big boatswain's mate.

"You got two seconds to start moving in," Wittmer said, "after which I'm going to slice that boat where it can't stand slicin'."

He took a survival knife from his belt and held it in his right hand. "Just one little cut, Moore, and you and what's his name, there, are not going to have a floatable boat. Now pick up that paddle and start paddling."

Moore picked up the paddle. He dug it deeply into the sea. His lips were tight. His craggy face was more grim than Adams had ever seen.

Neither man spoke until Moore had paddled well away from the raft. "I wouldn't have believed it," Adams said dispiritedly. "That sure puts us in a hell of a spot."

"I'm not holding still for that cute little caper," Moore said, his jaw squared. "Here's what we're going to do. After it gets dark, and let's hope it's a cloudy night, we're going to quiet-paddle up to Chief Chickenshit Wittmer's private personal raft. I'm going aboard and getting us some water. And if somebody gets hurt in the process, then somebody'll get hurt. But, by God, I'm getting some water."

"What do I do?" Adams said. "I want to do my share of it."

"What you'll do," Moore said, "is hang on to the raft while you're here in the boat. So I can toss a can of water into it, or anything else I can get my hands on, and then take off like a bird with a bee on its ass."

"Don't kill anybody," Adams said.

"I'm not fixin' to. But I guarantee I'll bust a few head bones if I have to, because it's not right they've got water and won't give us even one little drink of it. If something comes out of it later, well, I'd a damn sight rather be a live guy testifying than a dead guy that didn't get the drink he needed to keep him alive."

Adams looked up at the darkening sky. "There's some clouds. I hope they make it real pitch dark."

"It'll be better if they do," Moore said, "but if they don't, it'll be dark enough for the invasion of Charlie Moore, gunner's mate first class, United States Navy, because this sailor is not going to just sit on his ass and die from thirst."

A little after midnight Moore paddled, very slowly, very quietly, beside the near end of the raft. Floating clouds drifted in the dark tropic sky. The raft was barely perceptible in the gloom.

Its men were sleeping, except one. He sat on the raft's emergency rations box. He was, obviously, the sentry. His function, no doubt of it, would be to keep floaters and other survivors—Moore and Adams particularly—from stealing what was left of the raft's rations.

"Hold on to the raft," Moore whispered. "Don't let the boat drift away from it."

"Don't worry about it," Adams whispered. "Good luck, buddy."

Slowly and very carefully, so that his weight wouldn't cause a sudden dip of the big raft, Moore climbed onto the raft.

Crouched and gripping the paddle, he crept through the sleeping men toward the sentry on the rations box, who was George (Crackers) Graham, signalman second class. Graham began to turn to look at the other part of the raft. Moore dropped to the deck and laid unmoving, his eyes watching Graham, who was six-feet-two and muscled.

Graham turned back. He hadn't seen or heard anything suspicious. Moore got up. He gripped the paddle, butt end forward like a spear. He crept toward Graham, carefully watching to make sure he didn't step on a sleeper.

He was very close to Graham now, and aft of him about three feet. He jabbed the paddle forward, hitting the big signalman between his shoulders.

He had shoved hard. Graham grunted and fell forward, unconscious.

Moore went to him. He was wearing a Service .45. Moore took it from the unconscious man's belt and put it under his own belt. I hope I didn't bust the bastard's back, Moore reflected, but goddamn, I had to put him in dreamland with just one lick.

Moore had seen an emergency water can while he slunk toward Graham. It was in the middle of the raft. Moore crept toward it. His heart was beating rapidly. He had it made. Damn near, but not quite.

He wished Adams had the paddle now. It would be an impediment. He'd need both hands to carry the water can.

He came to the water can. He picked it up. Its contact with the paddle, which Moore held in his right hand, awoke the nearest sleeper, Ralph Behr, shipfitter first class, who was medium-size but stocky and good with his fists at shore socials that demanded fists.

Awareness came instantly to Behr. "Somebody's stealin' our water," he shouted. He started to get to his feet.

Moore jabbed him above his right ear with the butt of the paddle and he fell back onto the raft.

Wittmer leaped up along with several others. He lunged toward Moore. Moore put the water can on the deck and swung the paddle, gripping its blade. Its butt caught Wittmer on his left ear and broke the nose of another man.

Quickly, Moore took the .45 from his belt. He fired it toward, but not directly at, the two men who were lunging toward him. They stopped coming.

"Okay," Moore said. "Everybody stand back or I'll kill somebody else."

No one knew if he had actually killed anyone with that shot, or if he hadn't. It was too dark to tell. But not everybody was on his feet and maybe one of those who wasn't had taken that .45's bullet. So they cleared a path.

Moore, gripping the .45 in his right hand, his left arm around the water can and the paddle, went toward the little rubber survival boat. Adams reached up and took the paddle and the water can while Moore faced the men on the raft, the .45 in his hand. "Don't anybody even think about being a hero while we shove off," he said. "Or the first five guys, at least, are gonna suddenly become five dead guys."

He stepped into the boat and Adams swiftly began to paddle it away from the raft. "That's all the water we got," someone shouted. "You don't need it all."

"We'll take a bath with the part we don't need," Moore yelled.

Soon the gloom separated the raft and the boat. "Paddle ten more times," Moore said. "Then park it. We'll be far enough from those jokers we won't have to worry about anybody trying to find us. Then, old buddy, we're going to have us a drink."

A collapsible metal cup was attached to the emergency water can. Each man drank a half-cup, then another, savoring the second half, rolling it in his mouth before he swallowed it.

"We'd best not drink any more until morning," Moore said. "Too much when we haven't had any for so fucking long is liable to make us sick. Which we don't have time for because in the a. and m. I am going to make a deal with our waterless friends and I'm going to need all my marbles because I've got a hunch Chief Wittmer is not going to be in a very nice mood."

"Fuck that creep," Adams said.

"In spades," Moore said. "We better sack out because morning is going to come quicker'n we realize."

Dawn came. A haze covered the ocean in gently swirling wisps. Visibility was less than fifty feet. "Let's each drink a half-cup," Moore said, "and then another half-cup, like last night. And then we'll see what Wittmer has to say."

"He's liable to be a bastard," Adams said, holding the collapsible cup while, carefully and slowly, Moore filled it halfway to the top.

"He already is," Moore said.

The haze lifted suddenly, the morning tropic sun burning it off. The raft had drifted, but not very much. It was about a hundred yards from the boat.

"I'll take the first half," Moore said.

"Hell, no. I can handle that little bitty distance with one hand tied behind my back," Adams said. "You save your vitamins for Wittmer because he is going to be one pissed-off son of a bitch."

Adams paddled beside the raft, about twenty feet off its midflank. Wittmer had been waiting. He hurled obscenities to Moore that would curl the ears of a Missouri mule.

"When you get through," Moore said, "I've got a deal."

Wittmer said he wasn't interested in any deal.

"In that case," Moore said, "you and your pals are likely to get awful thirsty."

"All right," Wittmer said. "What's the big fucking deal?"

"The deal is, we'll give you two-thirds of this water we stole if you'll give us some of your food rations."

"No," Wittmer said. "But I'll tell you what you will get, if anybody ever gets around to rescue us. What you're gonna get, Moore and Adams, too—I found out your name, Adams—what you're both going to get is a charge of piracy plus assault on a ranking command, meaning you damn near tore off my ear, which I can hardly hear out of, when you assaulted me with that paddle. Plus firing a gun at two of my men. Which is going to put your balls in the gears, wise asses, for a very, very long time."

"Okay," Moore said. "When you fellas get thirsty enough, and if we're still in the neighborhood, you might think you really don't have to be thirsty." He turned to Adams. "Start paddling," he said softly. "Let's see if we bluffed 'em."

They had. Several men shouted for them to come back, that they'd make the trade if they had to deep-six Wittmer to do it.

Wittmer bellowed to these men. "I'm running this show. And I say no trade."

"You better think that over, chief," a tough little machinist's mate, Mike Griffin, said. "All it'll take is for some of us guys to give you the rush and the sharks got a breakfast."

"That's mutiny," Wittmer blustered. "You'll be sorry you even thought of it."

"Shut up, you mouthy blowhard," somebody yelled.

"You got the count of five to start talking deal," Griffin said, "and I'm starting with three . . . four . . . five. Okay, chief, it's been nice knowing you."

Griffin and eight others surged toward the big chief.

"Good God a'mighty," he croaked. They really would throw him overboard! "Okay! Okay," he bellowed. "I'll deal."

Griffin and the others stopped coming. Wittmer looked at them for an uneasy moment, his tongue gliding over his lips, then he turned toward the boat. "All right," he said, "what's the deal?"

"First, toss me the smaller of them two ammo cans," Moore said, "so we can put your share of the water in it."

"It's got flares in it," Wittmer said.

"Big fucking deal," Griffin said. He turned to one of his colleagues. "Empty the little can into the big one and toss it out to Moore."

"I'm the one that gives the orders," Wittmer said, glaring at Griffin. "When I need help I'll ask for it."

"Up yours," Griffin said. "Find out what food rations Moore wants."

The big chief, his teeth clenched, faced toward the boat again. "All right, you goddamn hijackers," he said, "what else?"

"What kind of rations have you got?" Moore said. "Hold them up where we can see them."

Griffin showed the men in the boat the raft's remaining emergency rations, holding up one item at a time. "Okay," Moore said. "We'll take one can of Spam, one tin of malted milk tablets, one package of that dried fruit, and two cans of them hard-rock biscuits."

"You realize there's only two of you and seventeen of us?" Wittmer said. "You're taking a whole lot more than your share."

"That's right," Moore said, "but you creeps been eating every day and we haven't. So the way I do my arithmetic, it's even Steven."

"Your day's coming, Moore," Graham, the sentry, said bitterly. "You damn near busted my back."

"Knock it off," Griffin said. "If you'd been doing your job, you wouldn't have a sore back." He turned toward the boat again. "The groceries comin' up," he said.

"Okay," Moore said. "We're going to pour two-thirds of the water into the ammo can. Then we're coming up alongside, and after we get the groceries, you get the water. And the first guy tries any funnies gets a forty-five hole where he don't need a hole."

The swap was going smoothly until Wittmer suddenly picked up the Very pistol that had been with the flares. He aimed it at Moore. "Give us everything back," he said, "including all the water, or you're suddenly going to have a gut full of pretty green fire. You ever saw a guy with a flare in his guts, Moore? I did. I put a flare in a gook's guts a couple years ago when I was on a shore patrol. He was the prettiest gook anybody ever saw. All bright red from his belly on down, those pretty flames burning off his tricks, which probably hurt quite a bit, too."

"I am not a gook on who you have got a sneak drop," Moore said, his face taut. "Before you fire that Very, ass hole, take a look at this forty-five in my right hand. It's looking at your chest. Right where your heart lives. You fire the Very, I'll fire the forty-five, so put the Very down and nobody gets hurt."

"Put it down, you blood-eatin' bastard," Griffin said.

"No," the chief said. "Not until he gives us back our water and eats."

Griffin chopped the chief's arm, coming up from its underside. The Very fired its flare into the sky, a bright, pretty green.

Griffin and Moore completed the swap and Adams paddled the boat away as fast as he could, out of the range of the Very pistol.

19

CHIEF BOATSWAIN'S MATE CLYDE WITTNER was infuriated by Moore's raid on his raft. His loss of face among the raft's other sixteen men angered him more than the water Moore and Adams had stolen. He was no longer accepted as captain of the raft.

The other men, except the few his dominant personality and fear of physical retribution intimidated, no longer obeyed him. They defied him. They laughed at him. They ridiculed him because of the raid.

Well, he'd show these louts they were fortunate that he was their ranking petty officer, even though their attitude was disrespectful, almost mutinous. He'd make them apologize for their insubordinations, their mockings of his capacities as a leader.

He had retrieved a forty-millimeter ammo can from the flotsam that drifted past the raft. He had ordered the men who wore rubberized pneumatic life belts to remove them and put them into the ammo can. "Next time we see a plane," he had said, "I'll fire a flare into that can. Maybe a red and green one, both. They'll set the rubber belts on fire. Everybody knows that burning rubber smokes like hell so a big cloud of heavy black smoke laced with green and red from the flares will come out of the can.

"The guys in the plane can't help but see it because, compared to the smoke from just a Very, which we have fired at the other three planes that flew over and nobody noticed, we'll have a smoke signal that's a smoke signal.

"Anybody seeing such a smoke coming up from the ocean is naturally going to investigate to see what the hell is going on. When they see us, they'll radio for Air-Sea Rescue and then *adiós* to this fucking raft."

"You stupids can laugh your guts out," Wittmer said after Moore's raid on his raft, "but when we're rescued because somebody saw this smoke signal that I personally invented, guess who's going to do the laughing then?"

Midmorning of the day after the raid the men on Wittmer's raft, the floaters, and the men on other rafts and those in little yellow survival boats heard the sound of an airplane.

Every survivor of the torpedoed cruiser looked toward the sky, hoping that this time it would be an Air-Sea Rescue plane, or at least a plane whose crew would see them and radio for help.

Adams and Moore, eating food they had bartered for return of part of the water they had stolen from Wittmer's raft, heard the approaching plane. "I wish I'd thought about making Wittmer give us that Very pistol and some flares," Moore said, looking up at the plane, which was so high it seemed no larger than an insect. "Our flares might be the one they'd see."

Flares went up from several rafts. They were more dispersed this time. The drifts had spread the survivors over a vast area.

Meanwhile Wittmer had fired a flare into the ammo can with the rubberized pneumatic life belts. It was a red flare. Immediately he fired a green flare into the can, which was already churning with concentrated fire and smoke from the first flare.

"In just a couple seconds, as soon as them rubber belts really start burning," he assured the other men on the raft, everyone watching the proceedings, "there'll be smoke coming out of that can the guys on that plane can't help seeing, even if they've gone quite a ways past us."

Soon great billows of black smoke intermixed with red and green, the fanciest smoke anyone on the raft had ever seen, poured up out of the can.

"That'll do the job," Wittmer said proudly.

It did the job, but not quite the one Wittmer was talking about. The sides and bottom of the can became red from the intense, trapped fires of the flares. Suddenly the smoking can fell into the sea through the hole the red-hot can had burned in the raft's fabric, creating an ammo-can-size hole almost in the middle of the raft.

Everyone turned to Wittmer.

"All right," he bellowed, "it burned a hole in our deck. You don't need to tell me. I can see it with my own eyeballs."

Not much smoke had gone skyward and it was quickly dissipated by the winds; most of the burning rubber that would have created the smoke had been extinguished by the water under the raft.

"Admiral," Mike Griffin, the tough little machinist's mate, said, "don't take it so hard. Look at it this way. We can catch fish from right here in the middle of the raft. That is, if we had anything to fish with."

"I know who I'd like to use for bait," someone said.

"Knock it off, you sons a bitches," Wittmer bellowed. "If you're all so fucking smart why didn't somebody mention them flares might burn a hole in the raft?"

"We could also use that hole for an indoor swimming pool," another man said. "You have to look at the bright side of things, Admiral."

Wittmer's humiliation was total. He was washed up as the little group's leader. "Wait'll we get on the beach," he blustered. "Just wait! I'll teach you comedians that people that bust a gut laughing at a chief petty officer of the U.S. Navy are liable to suddenly get a different face!"

While Moore and Adams listened to the fading sounds of the high-flying airplane's engines, Adams said, "I've thought of every way I can think of why nobody has come to rescue us guys, and none of them even begin to make sense. It's absolutely unreal that a major ship of the United States Navy could be torpedoed and nobody seems to know about it. If they knew, they'd send rescue planes and ships. So they don't know. But why don't they know? God, Moore, it's been four days."

It seemed incredible, but the facts were CinCPac did not know the *Indianapolis* had been torpedoed.

Neither did Philippine Sea Frontier, the big cruiser's destination.

Why didn't these commands know of the torpedoing, the greatest sea disaster in the history of the United States Navy?

There were several reasons and all of them, at the time, seemed reasonable. All of them came together in the complex jigsaw of wartime naval command.

Philippine Sea Frontier (PSF), a vast operation directed by 184 officers and 483 enlisted men headquartered in Quonsets in a swampy palm forest, was responsible for routing, dispatching, harbor operations, local naval operations, and area transportation, escort and salvage ships totaling more than two hundred.

But PSF had no control of, or responsibility for, combat ships that used its facilities, or that sailed on the waters within its administrative jurisdiction, which extended east from the Philippines to 130 degrees east longitude.

A fleet letter designated CinCPac 10-CL-45 clearly stated: "Arrival reports shall not be made for combat ships."

The reason was obvious and logical: Security.

Because of this directive there was amazement and confusion at PSF when CinCPac sent PSF the *Indianapolis*' departure and arrival times and dates.

The message went through PSF's chain of command, each officer passing it on to his superior, and eventually no further attention was paid to the matter because of fleet letter 10-CL-45, which later became the basis for PSF's disclaiming responsibility for failing to report the *Indianapolis* overdue.

There was, in incredible fact, no operational procedure for reporting a combat ship overdue.

As a consequence no one at PSF worried about the *Indianapolis*' failure to arrive on its scheduled date, even though after its arrival in Leyte Task Force 95 had been ordered to arrange seventeen days of special training by the Philippine Training Group for the big cruiser's crew.

The *Indianapolis*, the officers at Leyte who gave thought to its failure to arrive, might have gone off on any number of missions. Maybe it was hunting submarines that had suddenly showed up in the Central Pacific. Perhaps its orders had been changed by CinCPac and it was off to some other place. Maybe the weather had delayed the big cruiser. Or perhaps it was delayed by a breakdown. Or a midocean meet with other combat ships.

In any case, why worry about it? No concern of PSF.

As for CinCPac, who had dispatched the *Indianapolis* to Leyte and whose Supreme Operational Command worked in team with the Royal British Navy in the subterranean room at CinCPac's Headquarters at Guam, wouldn't they know where the *Indianapolis* was at any given moment?

It was supposed to be this way. The operational procedure of continual contact with combat ships traveling alone belonged totally to CinCPac.

What had gone wrong? Nothing. CinCPac was a victim of its own directive: Arrival reports shall not be made for combat ships.

No arrival report had been received because none was expected. No message of disaster had been received. Therefore the *Indianapolis* was out there somewhere on some kind of relevant activity. Nothing to worry about.

"Suppose rescue never shows up," Moore, who had been paddling the little rubber survival boat toward a group of three rafts, said to Adams.

"That's a stupid thing even to think of," Adams said. "Sometime somebody is going to realize they haven't heard from the *Indianapolis* in a hell of a long time. Then they'll get in a panic and send planes and ships to our last transmitted position to find out what's going on."

"We might be dead long before then," Moore said. "This water and groceries we got from Wittmer's raft won't last forever. In fact, except for some of the water, it'll be gone in another day."

He was concerned about the sores on his buttocks, he said. The constant chafing of the rubberized seats and gunwales of the little survival boat, compounded by the sea's salty water and the remorseless tropical sun, had formed large oozing sores. "I'm afraid they'll get infected, if they already aren't. I can stand the constant pain—every time I pull on the paddle it's like a blowtorch on my ass—but, Jesus, you get infection out here in the tropics and it can spread through your whole body in no time.

"I've seen it happen. On the beach, mostly. A guy gets a sore and don't take care of it, and then suddenly, he gets a fever and goes into a coma a little later. A doc told me once you go into that coma you're on your way to the Big Man's House in the Sky. Nothing, he said, can be done for you once you go into that coma."

"I've got sores on my ass, too," Adams said, "and on my hands where the blisters broke, and on my head, where I got zinged before I got off the *Indy,* but I'm not worrying. The way I look at it, we're so damn much better off than the guys who've been in the water all the time there's no comparison."

"I suppose if rescue ever comes they'll fly us to hospitals in Hawaii," Moore said. "Or maybe, if we're lucky, to the States. They've got a big navy hospital at Oakland. Across the bay from Frisco. I've seen it. I wouldn't mind being sent there."

"I'll bet guys with the least injuries stand a better chance of being sent there than to Hawaii," Adams said. "They'll send the worst ones to the closest hospitals. But you won't rate a hospital. Me, either. They'll shoot us with antibiotics and patch up our sores and say come back tomorrow at ten-hundred. We'll be there at ten-hundred and maybe three hours later some doc will get around to telling his corpsman to change our bandages."

Moore hadn't been listening. He was staring forward, and a little to port. "There's another bunch of floaters," he said. He looked back at Adams. "Should we cut out around them? We don't have water enough for everybody."

"What do you think we ought to do?" Adams asked.

"You know damn well what I think. Old Soft-heart Moore says let's give each guy a little sip of water. If it don't do anything but give him the will to hang on for a little while longer, it may be just long enough to keep him going until rescue gets here."

"You phony bastard," Adams said, grinning. "You had me fooled. I used to think, every time I saw you on the *Indy*, there's a typical regular Navy. A tough son of a bitch with a heart, if he has one, made out of stone. So what do you turn out to be? A decent guy with values."

"Man, you missed your call," Moore said, laughing. "You should of been a preacher. You know what I thought about you when I discovered I was stuck with you when everybody else got ate by sharks? I thought you were a weak little creep who'd cry himself to sleep every night. Man, I guessed wrong! To tell you the truth, Adams, you're a tougher guy than I ever was. You're a hard bastard, man. Underneath that smoothy way you talk and the way you look, you've got balls."

Adams was looking at the floaters. "We'd better not give them anything to eat, especially the biscuits. It would just make them thirstier. It would offset what little water we can give each guy. How much do you think we ought to give them?"

"Well, considering the amount we got left and the number of floaters up ahead there, and considering a fourth of them are probably dead, I'd say two inches maximum."

Adams said this sounded reasonable to him. "Two inches would have seemed like two gallons to me yesterday at this time."

Moore looked aft. Since he had quit paddling to discuss the dispensing of water to the floaters Tojo had surfaced. He was balancing gracefully on his long pectoral fins, his pig eyes staring at the men in the little survival boat.

"Stay right where you are, you son of a bitch," Moore said. "Because I'm going to put a forty-five right into each one of those sneaky little eyes."

He picked up the Colt's .45 caliber semiautomatic pistol he had taken from the sentry he had KO'd on Wittmer's raft.

Very carefully, he aimed the .45 at the big shark's left eye.

20

VERY CAREFULLY MOORE ZEROED THE .45 caliber semiautomatic's sights on the big surfaced shark's unblinking left eye.

Slowly he began to squeeze the trigger. When he was at the end of the squeeze, a fraction of a moment before the powerful gun fired, a wave slapped the little boat's bow.

The bullet missed.

"Son of a bitch," Moore said. Quickly, before the shark could submerge, he shifted the sights back to the shark's baleful little eye and squeezed the trigger again.

The firing pin clicked against nothing.

"Goddamn," Moore said bitterly, watching the big shark glide under the sea's gently rolling surface.

He jerked the magazine out of the gun. It was empty. He looked over at Adams. "I had him," he said, his teeth clenched. "If it hadn't been for that fucking wave, I'd of got him. I'd of got him with number two, too. I had him dead-centered both times."

He looked at the gun and its empty magazine. "How do you put this together? I'd bet a year's pay this gun was full-up when it left the *Indy*. Everybody kept their guns on full load. So what happened to the bullets I didn't fire? I fired one on the raft and one here. Which means there were four others."

"The only thing I can think of, I don't like to think of," Adams said.

Moore said, "If you mean those guys on the raft shot at guys who tried to get onto the raft after they decided they had all the guys they wanted on it, then you and me are on the same wavelength."

"It's a hell of a thing to think of," Adams said, "and maybe we're wrong. I hope we are. But that big chief would have shot you if he'd had a gun. And probably me."

Moore looked again at the gun in his hand. Then he threw it and its clip into the sea. "It's no good to us," he said, "and we might have stepped on it and pushed its front sight through the fabric. A hole in the bottom of this yacht is not a hole we need."

He went to the paddle seat on the forward port side of the little survival boat. He picked up the paddle, then he looked aft, toward Adams. "That damn shark is going to show up again as soon as I start paddling. He'll follow us to those floaters. If he starts eating one of them, which I'll bet he does, a dozen of his pals will suddenly show up to get in on it. Then, with those other guys right there, it's hard to say what they'll do."

Adams, sitting on the stern gunwale, was looking at the men in the water. "Look how low they're floating," he said. "That second guy, the one with the red hair—his mouth is just barely above the water."

He looked over at Moore. "I know what happened. I remember from boot camp. They told us that after a certain time in the sea a kapok jacket begins to waterlog. Eventually its packing becomes full of water. Then the guy wearing it is worse off than if he didn't have it in the first place."

Very likely, he continued, that redheaded man with the waterlogged kapok couldn't remove it. "If he tied those strings in a hard knot and they swelled from a long time in the water, I'll bet he can't untie them."

"Jesus," Moore said, looking at the redhead and the others. "I never thought about that. What a hell of a way to go. A slow drowning!" He turned back to Adams. "I wish I'd killed that shark. God, I hate to lead him into those guys."

Adams' face became pensive. "We're going to have to figure the odds. If we go into them we can use your knife to cut them loose so they won't slow-drown. They can hold on to the kapoks like we did that life-jacket bag when we first started this tour, and we can give them jackets from the dead guys, plus a drink of water. Against which there's Tojo. So what'll we do?"

"Tojo and his pals most likely won't eat very many of them," Moore said. "I figure we can save more guys than the sharks can eat. But, Jesus, it's a hell of a thing for the guys they do eat."

Neither man spoke for several moments. It was a tough decision. "I think we ought to look at it," Adams said, "like it was us out there, with our mouths just barely above the surface and kapok jackets that are going to drown us and we can't take them off. Here comes guys that can cut off the jackets so we won't drown. But sharks come with the guys. But they might not eat us. So it comes down to a sure death one way and a maybe death the other way."

"There's also the chance sharks might eat them even if we detour. Tojo isn't the only shark in this ocean," Moore said.

"Hell, let's go," Adams said, his face grim.

Moore dipped the paddle into the sea and the little boat glided toward the floaters with the waterlogged kapok jackets. Both men looked aft. Tojo was pacing them. "I wish I'd at least made him bleed," Moore said, looking forward again. "Then his buddies would have eaten him."

He looked over his shoulder at Adams. "That's something, isn't it? One of them begins to bleed and his buddies eat him."

Moore paddled to the floaters. Eight were dead, six were alive. The mouths and noses of five of the dead men were below the surface, their eyes barely above the water, open and seeming to be staring. Three corpses were even more submerged. Only the tops of their heads and their sea-washed hair was above the surface.

"God, what a way to go," Adams said. "Knowing you're drowning and not being above to take the jacket off that's drowning you . . . and the bastard pulling you lower and lower. A tiny little bit at a time."

"Wouldn't you think," Moore said, "the Navy would invent

some kinda life jacket that wouldn't soak up water like a fucking sponge?"

"They don't, right at first," Adams said. "They hold a guy up real good."

"Yeah, but, Jesus, they should have figured a guy might be in the water long enough for them to start soaking up the ocean."

Moore came to the redhead whose mouth was barely above the sea's surface. "Help me, please. Please help me," he begged.

He was Eddie O'Brien, seaman second class, six weeks out of the Farragut, Idaho Naval Training Station.

Moore reached over the gunwale and slashed one of the life jacket's straps. "Now get hold of it before I cut the other one," Moore said, "or you'll sink like a rock."

"Oh, God, thanks!" O'Brien said after Moore cut the other strap. "I was gonna drown. Like those other guys. I would of been dead in a couple hours."

"We'll get you a jacket from one of the dead guys," Adams said. "That one and the one you got ought to keep you going until help comes. Right now we've got a drink for you."

"A drink? Of water?"

"Good old drinking water," Adams said. "Put your hand on the gunwale, here, and I'll pour it for you."

Adams held the little collapsible metal cup to O'Brien's mouth so he wouldn't drop it onto the sea because it would sink.

"God, you don't know how good that tastes," the youth babbled. "I sure appreciate it. I feel like a new man already."

"Great, now just keep hanging on to that jacket," Adams said, "and we'll get you another one as soon as we cut everybody else loose and give them a drink."

The others, having seen O'Brien get a drink of water, were swimming toward the boat as fast as they could. "Everybody stay where you are," Moore yelled. "We'll get to you, but stay there."

He turned to Adams. "If they all get hold of the gunwales they might make you spill some of that water. Or maybe a couple of them would want another drink, or a bigger one, and raise hell. Some of them might be off their rocker from being in the water all this time with nothing to drink."

Moore turned toward a man who had kept swimming toward the little boat. "Stay there, damm it," he bellowed.

He looked around at the others. "Everybody that don't stay right where they are don't get a drink or their jackets cut loose."

The swimmer stopped. He would die if he kept coming. The man in the boat had said he would.

Moore paddled to the closest living floater. He was Adrian Harmon, storekeeper first class. He knew both Adams and Moore. "I never saw two more welcome guys," he croaked, his lips parched and cracked. "I couldn't get this fucking jacket off. My fingernails are too soft to untie the knots. The knots are swollen, anyway. So damn tight you'd need pliers to untie them. I tried biting the straps. Everybody else did, too. You can't, no matter how hard you bite."

Moore cut the straps of the garrulous man's waterlogged kapok jacket. "Put your free hand on the gunwale, here," Adams said, "and I'll give you a drink."

Harmon had just finished the drink when one of the floaters shrieked. "A shark bit me," he screamed. "Oh, God, help me!"

Moore and Adams and the men in the sea looked toward the source of the shriek. It had come from the man who had kept swimming toward the boat and who had stopped coming when Moore threatened to deny water to him and the cutting of his kapok jacket's straps.

He vanished below the surface. The water churned and flailed and a bloody froth came up. "That ain't nothing new," Harmon said, looking at the feeding frenzy. "Sharks been eatin' us ever since we hit the water. For four friggin' days they been eatin' us.

"You guys are lucky you got a boat. You don't know how doggone lucky you are. That was Denny Rice those sharks are eating over there. The guy handed out the mail. You guys knew him, didn't you?"

"We knew him," Adams said, "but we didn't recognize him from here."

"Well, that was him," Harmon said. "Can I have the water you were going to give him?"

Adams and Moore turned to the asking man. "No," Moore said.

The frenzy had ended. Only God knew where Tojo and the other sharks were now, or which man they'd attack next. Moore paddled toward another floater.

The sharks didn't attack again, and after Moore had cut the kapok jacket straps of the other four living men and Adams had given each of them a two-inch drink of water from the collapsible cup, Moore paddled to a dead floater and cut off his jacket.

"I wonder why that shark hit Rice instead of one of these dead guys. We've noticed before they'll hit a live guy when there's dead ones all around."

"I've thought about that, too. The way I figure it is, the live guys make some kind of movement that attracts them. The dead guys naturally don't."

The men in the little rubber survival boat cut the jackets from the dead floaters and Moore paddled to the nearest living man, Joe (Skeets) Gallagher, shipfitter first class, and gave him a jacket from one of the dead men. "Thanks, fellas," he said. "That one and the one I was wearing ought to keep me going.

"You guys got here just in time. The one I was wearing only held my nose a couple inches above the water. I had to close my nostrils with my fingers every time I dipped into a swell or I would have choked to death. One guy did, that I know of. He got to choking and a bunch more water got in his mouth. He did so damn much flopping around a bunch of sharks came. You can imagine how long he lasted then. Maybe you guys knew him. Wally Stitts, the big black diesel guy."

"I knew him," Moore said. "He wasn't my all-time favorite, though."

"How long would you have lasted if we hadn't showed up when we did?" Adams asked. "I guess what I mean is, how fast have those kapoks been pulling you guys down?"

"Well, pretty fast today. They didn't start until day before yesterday. In fact, until then they did a fine job holding us up. We were a lot better off than guys with the pneumatic belts. The kapoks held us up higher. But day before yesterday they started soaking up water. It was slow at first, but every couple hours you could tell they had pulled you down a little more.

"Today, though, they've been going real fast. You asked how long before my nose would have been under. I'd say before night. Maybe earlier. Are we ever going to be rescued?"

"Sure we are," Moore said. "We might all be old enough for the old sailors' home before they get here, but they'll get here."

"What's holding them up, for chrissake?"

Moore said he wished he knew.

"They know about us, don't they?" Gallagher asked.

"I hope so," Moore said.

"Well, Christ, why wouldn't they?"

Moore said Gallagher's guess was as good as his. "Well, so long, Skeets. See you guys on the beach."

Moore began to paddle toward the three rafts to which they had been going before they came upon the men with the waterlogged kapok jackets.

He looked aft. "He's back there," Adams said.

"He's quite a bit closer than he was," Moore said. "I wonder what that means?"

Adams looked at the big shark's dorsal fin. "I don't know," he said, "but I don't like it." He turned toward the rafts. "I'll feel a lot better when we can get on one of those rafts."

21

DOC HAYNES, SENIOR MEDICAL OFFICER of the torpedoed cruiser; Father Tom Conway, the sunken ship's chaplain; and twenty-nine enlisted men were on the three rafts toward which Moore and Adams were paddling, hoping to reach the rafts before sundown.

Lieutenant Commander Lewis L. Haynes, physician and surgeon, son of a Manistee, Michigan, physician, had been sleeping in his cabin when the Japanese submarine's first torpedo struck the *Indianapolis*.

Its terrible explosion hurled him from his bunk to the steel overhead of his little cabin. He fell back to the cabin's deck where he sprawled, dazed.

He was getting to his feet when the *Nakapo*'s second torpedo hit the *Indianapolis* almost directly under the doctor's cabin.

The doctor slipped his feet into his shoes; then, wearing only his pajama pants, he opened his cabin's door. Quickly, he closed it. The passageway leading to the main deck was filled with flames.

He looked back into his little cabin. Flames were jutting up the rents in his cabin's steel deck plating. Already they were burning the mattress and blankets on his bunk and the clothes he had hung over a chair.

He opened the door again and looked the opposite direction along the passageway. There were no flames, but it was filled with smoke. Dr. Haynes grabbed his life jacket and went into the passageway.

Its deck was tilting. Dr. Haynes, holding the life jacket in front of his naked chest, staggered down the smoke-filled passageway. Its deck was hot. A fire was raging under it. The doctor went as fast as he could; his feet felt as though he were walking on red-hot coals.

He stumbled. Instinctively he thrust out his hands to break the fall. They sizzled when they contacted the hot steel deck. "Oh, God," he said. A doctor needs hands and his were terribly burned.

He was groping along the passageway, holding his hands palms up, his feet agonized by the hot steel deck, when he came to a compartment's hatch. He knew it would have portholes and he had to get air or suffocate.

He opened the hatch, stepped over its coaming, and went to its sea-flanking bulkhead. He shoved his head out an open porthole and breathed fresh cool air until his mind began to clear.

Then he realized that a rope was banging against his head like the pendulum on a clock. He looked up, and in the light from the forward fires he saw that the line was fastened to something on the main deck.

The doctor grabbed the line the next time it came his way. Despite his burned hands, he pulled himself through the porthole; then, hand over hand, he climbed the line to the weather deck.

He lay on it, gasping, until he recovered from the effort of the climb, which had been compounded by the pain in his horribly burned hands. Then he staggered to a medic station that a chief pharmacist's mate was operating.

Haynes began to help the pharmacist's aide, jabbing morphine into the most agonized men. Twice he collapsed, but each time injured men revived him so he could relieve their horrible pains with morphine.

The torpedoed ship's list increased. Dr. Haynes' patients began to slide off the sloping deck into the sea.

Then, suddenly Dr. Haynes slid down the deck, under its starboard rail, and into the sea. Luckily for him, someone had put his kapok jacket around his shoulders and tied its thongs after the ship's list became severe.

The next hours were tormenting for the valiant young doctor. All around him men were screaming for a doctor. There was nothing he could do for them. He could not see them in the tropic night. He had no medical equipment. It is doubtful if he could have used it, anyway. The sea's salty water on the areas of his hands where burned skin and flesh had peeled off was agonizing.

Lieutenant T. M. Conway, chaplain of the big cruiser, was a Roman Catholic priest who had been an assistant pastor at a parish church in Buffalo, New York.

Father Conway had celebrated Mass on the fantail of the *Indianapolis* at 1000 hours that fateful Sunday, July 29. Afterward, at 1100 hours, he had conducted Protestant services, Doc Haynes helping him lead the singing of the hymns.

He had been writing a letter to a Nebraska mother assuring her that her son was recovering nicely from an emergency appendectomy when the first of the Japanese submarine's torpedoes struck the *Indianapolis.*

The explosion threw him against the bulkhead on the opposite side of his little cabin. He sat there on his chair, his head, which had struck the steel wall, hanging forward.

The second explosion brought him out of it. He dressed as fast as he could, knowing there would be dying men who would need absolution and anointing, and if they were conscious, the sacrament.

He could smell the acrid fumes of something burning below his cabin and he could hear men shouting and screaming.

He was running down a passageway toward a ladder that led to the main deck when the third torpedo hit the *Indianapolis.* It flung the priest to the deck, but because he was wearing a kapok life jacket, he wasn't injured beyond deep bruises on his knees.

He groped with his hands for the little box with the anointing oil and sacrament. The passageway's deck sloped sharply. It was totally dark. The passageway's little blue lights had gone out and choking fumes arose from somewhere below.

Father Conway found the little box and hurried toward the ladder to the main weather deck.

After he got onto the deck he went immediately to a young seaman who had been gutted by torn steel that had been blown off a bulkhead. He gave him absolution and held his hands while he died crying for his mother.

Father Conway was giving the sacrament to a boatswain's mate whose legs had been crushed when the *Indianapolis* canted so sharply to starboard that the priest and the dying boatswain's mate slid off into the sea.

Father Conway began to swim from one shrieking man to another, trying to comfort them, until he was so exhausted he could no longer swim.

Captain Charles B. McVay was in the sea, too, bobbling on the rolling waves, a kapok life jacket keeping him afloat.

He had been in his sea cabin when the first torpedo from the *Nakapo* struck the *Indianapolis.* His first thought was, many a torpedoed ship has stayed afloat. So he ordered the damage-control parties into action.

McVay began to put on his clothes. Then, he went out onto his ship's canting deck. The second hit had occurred and men were jumping off the *Indianapolis* into the sea. Thinking that it would be useless to order them to stand by, he yelled at them not to go over the side without life jackets.

Some ignored McVay. Panicked, they jumped into the sea where, without means of staying afloat, they swam until exhaustion overtook them. Then they sank to their deaths.

After the third torpedo the big cruiser listed sharply to starboard. McVay ordered an officer to check the inclinometer in the chart bridge. He reported a twenty-one-degree starboard list, and that the list was increasing rapidly.

Exactly twelve minutes after the *Indianapolis* took the first torpedo, McVay knew there was no hope of the ship remaining afloat. He ordered everybody topside, then he ordered abandon.

McVay didn't immediately abandon his doomed ship. He wanted to make sure everyone had gotten topside who wasn't trapped somewhere below. Additionally, he felt it was his duty to put life jackets on men too disoriented or too injured by the torpedoes and the subsequent fires and explosions to put them on themselves.

He was on the ship's red-painted hull tying a kapok jacket on an explosion-stunned young seaman who stood passively and uncomprehendingly with gaping mouth and distended eyes when a lurch catapulted him and the seaman off the hull.

McVay looked up at the canting ship and thought it would fall over onto him, but he didn't care. Better to be done with it now, he thought, than to face what will inevitably come if I survive.

The ship didn't fall onto Captain McVay. It sank almost straight down into the sea, and very quickly. He had looked around to warn the men whose voices he could hear to swim away as fast as they could. When he looked back, the ship was gone.

So he set out looking for something to cling to.

The men who had abandoned the *Indianapolis* were divided into groups depending upon the time and place they had left the sinking ship.

The big cruiser was underway from the time she took the first torpedo until the last moments before she sank. This scattered the men who jumped from her, or who slid, unwillingly, from her sloping deck.

Dr. Haynes, Father Conway, and Captain McVay, because they were among the last to abandon, found themselves with the largest group of survivors.

The agonizing hours until daylight were confusing and interminable. Injured men screamed for help. Sharks bit off feet and legs and hands, and feeding frenzies occurred in the midst of terrified men who hadn't known the ferocity and unending hunger of the Pacific's great white sharks.

Monday's dawn was welcomed. The water had been cold. The sun warmed the survivors. But most important, the survivors were no longer blinded by the tropic night. They could see. It made them feel better to be able to see who the others were, their proximities, the bright blue sky, the jetsam from the big cruiser, and every man tried to grab some floating thing that would help sustain him until rescue came.

But quickly the warm sun became painfully torrid. The sun's glare on the sea was blinding. The constant splashing of the sea's salty water onto faces, into eyes, up nostrils, and into mouths was annoying.

The sharks feasted continuously. A man never knew if he would be their next victim—if, suddenly, a foot or leg would be amputated by a shark's sharp teeth and quick hard bite.

Before midmorning Dr. Haynes, Father Conway, and twenty-one enlisted men came upon three rafts, two upside down, and a floater net.

Doc Haynes was hoisted up onto the first raft; he was A-one priority, being a doctor. Then he lifted Father Conway onto it and the two of them started pulling the rest of the men out of the sea onto the rafts, the first guys helping pull others until all had made it.

Then the rafts were tied together, but this didn't work. They kept banging into each other. So the men tied them with thirty-foot lines that allowed for the waves raising one or two while one or two were in a trough without grinding them on one another.

The nocturnal drifts had separated Captain McVay from Haynes and Conway. In the first gray light of dawn he and the men nearby came upon two rafts. They climbed onto them, discovering that they had landed on the water bottom side up. The raft's emergency water, food rations, flares, and medic kits were secured to their underside.

No one had realized that rafts to which emergency rations and other gear were lashed would land on the water wrong side up if dropped from a height exceeding two or three times the width of the rafts—much the same way a buttered slice of toast, because of the weight of the butter, almost invariably lands with its buttered side on the floor.

The men on the rafts were well off compared to the floaters. They could keep dry; the sea's salinity did not create sores or enlarge abrasions and wounds caused by the Japanese submarine's attack. They could walk from one end of the raft to the other, getting exercise denied to floaters or the men in the little yellow survival boats. They could salvage anything that floated past them. They could sleep well at night.

If they had water and food rations, their greatest concern was the interminable boredom.

Dr. Haynes had no time to become bored. The men on his

raft complex swam to injured floaters and brought them to his raft, where he cared for them as best he could, making it virtually a hospital raft. His terribly burned hands and lack of medicaments inhibited him, but he saved an incalculable number of lives.

Captain McVay was not idle, either. He kept the men on his raft occupied by fishing with equipment from two emergency fishing kits. He wouldn't let them eat their catches, even though the instructions in each kit, printed on paper impervious to water, read:

FISH IS FOOD AND DRINK

> If you catch fish you will not die of hunger or thirst. The flesh of fish caught in the open sea is good to eat, cooked or raw. It is healthful and nourishing. If you have caught more fish than you can eat, squeeze out or chew out the juice of the flesh and drink it. Fish juice tastes much like the juice of raw oysters or clams. It has been tested and found safe.

Despite what those papers said, Captain McVay warned the men on his raft not to eat the fish they caught. He had heard there were poisonous fish in the sea.

Fish wasn't needed for food, anyway. McVay's raft had ample food and water rations. But on Wednesday—the *Indianapolis* was torpedoed Sunday night—McVay ordered his men's rations cut in half, so they would last until rescue arrived.

Wednesday was the survivors' most difficult day. They despaired; several planes had flown over the survivors of the big cruiser but none had showed the slightest sign of recognition. No number of Very flares seemed to call their attention to the plight of the men in the sea.

Men died of exhaustion, despair, and thirst; for these unfortunates Wednesday was the limit of their endurance.

In the first light of dusk on that hot despairing day Father Conway died in Dr. Haynes' arms. The priest had worn himself beyond endurance swimming out to injured floaters and dragging them to the hospital raft.

About the time that Father Conway died, Moore quit paddling toward the three connected rafts. "We can't reach them before night," he said wearily. "Goddamn, I was hoping we'd get there."

"Maybe they won't drift during the night," Adams said.

Moore didn't reply. He was looking at the rafts. They were tormentingly close, but he couldn't paddle to them after nightfall. The tropic night, except for stars and a moon that would be dimmed by floating clouds, would be almost black. He wouldn't be able to see the distant rafts.

"They won't be there in the morning," Adams said dispiritedly.

"The drift will screw us again. It just naturally drifts rafts faster than a boat like ours."

Adams said they ought to enjoy a drink of water before they sacked out for the night. "It'll stay with us longer. In the daytime, when it's so damn hot, the sun evaporates it right out of a guy."

He poured two inches of water into the collapsible cup and extended it to Moore.

Moore held it as though he were proposing a toast. "Fuck the Japs," he said.

"Fuck the Navy," Adams said, holding an imagined highball.

"Fuck 'em both," Moore said. He savored the water, drinking it slowly. "Tojo hasn't gone below," he said.

Adams looked aft. The big shark was balanced on his pectoral fins. He was looking at the men in the raft.

Adams' hands trembled while he poured himself two inches of water. Always before, when the paddling ended and the little boat came to a stop, the big shark had disappeared into the sea.

22

SOON AFTER THE LAST LIGHT of dusk Moore and Adams fell asleep, sprawled on opposite ends of the little yellow survival boat. In the morning, if nocturnal currents hadn't drifted too far the raft on which Father Conway had died, and its connecting rafts, they would paddle to them.

They were impatient to get onto a raft. Tojo had become a scary menace. The big shark was keeping too close to the little boat. For whatever reason, it could mean no good to the boat's occupants.

The rafts would be significant for another reason. They would be able to walk on them. "To stretch our legs," as Moore had phrased it. They had been confined to the little fabric boat for an interminable time. "God, it'll feel good to be able to at least stand up," Moore said.

"This boat's so fucking small we can't even stretch out while we're sleeping without getting our legs tangled."

A little after midnight Adams suddenly awakened. The night was cool but beads of sweat had formed on his brow. Something had frightened him. It hadn't been a dream. He had been dreaming about flying to the Marianas on an Air-Sea Rescue seaplane.

He was in the little boat's stern. He looked aft. "Jesus," he croaked.

Tojo's head was inches from the stern's fragile gunwale. The big shark, balanced on its long pectoral fins, was looking into Adams' eyes. The moonlight reflected from his unblinking eyes and a tremor snaked down Adams' spine.

"Oh, God," Adams babbled. Only a thin fabric had separated him from the big shark. If the man-eating killer had bitten through that fabric he would have decapitated Adams, who had slept with his head against the stern.

Adams crawled to the little boat's bow. He shook Moore awake. "That fucking shark," he gasped, his heart pounding, "is right off the stern. Less'n two inches from it."

Moore sat up. He put a hand on the port gunwale. Then, quickly, he jerked it back. "What do you think he's up to?" he whispered, as if Tojo was listening and might respond with hostility.

"How would I know?" Adams said shakily. "All I know is, the big bastard's practically in here with us."

Moore's tongue flicked over his lips. "God, I wish I had my forty-five."

"You don't have it," Adams said irritably, "and wishing you did all the damn time doesn't do one damn bit of good."

Whatever they did, if they did anything, Adams said, would have to be with whatever they had in the boat.

"Which means either with my knife or the paddle," Moore said.

"Those are sure something to tackle a shark with," Adams said.

"Well, goddamn, swim over to Guam and get us a twenty-millimeter AA gun," Moore snapped.

"We'd both better calm down," Adams said. "We're not helping ourselves smart-assing each other."

"You're right," Moore said. "We've both got a case of GI nerves." He crawled to the little boat's stern. "Good God a'mighty," he croaked. Actually looking into the big white's murderous eyes was more terrifying than listening to Adams tell of it.

He kept looking into the shark's eyes. Then, suddenly, he turned away. They were hypnotizing him. "Jesus," he said, shaking his head as if to clear the hypnosis from it.

He looked over at Adams. "Do you think I could stab him just back of his head, underneath where the softest part of their skin is, and make him bleed enough to draw his hungry pals?"

Adams said he would be killing himself. "You couldn't swing that knife as fast as he could flip around and bite off your arm. Your hand, at least."

"You've got something there," Moore said shakily. Sharks were incredibly agile, and fast. In a tiny fraction of a second, or so it seemed, they could reverse themselves and come up under a victim, on a flank, or anywhere else. Adams was right. Before his knife's blade even touched the shark that big devil would have his arm bitten off.

The men sat on the stern talking on it. They looked back, then quickly away. It wasn't good to look into Tojo's devil eyes. "I wish I had a spear," Moore said. "I'd jab it through one of those eyes right into his head."

Adams didn't reply. Moore was always wishing he had something there was no way to get. It did no good thinking on it. What they ought to think about were realities—and there weren't very many realities on the little survival boat. Besides the knife, just the paddle.

The paddle would be about as effective against that big shark as a soda straw. Suddenly an idea occurred to Adams. "Maybe all we've got to do is paddle away from him. Real slow and easy. If it works, that'll be a hell of a lot easier than using force to get rid of him, even if we had something to use."

Moore said it was worth a try. "Anything's worth a try."

"Are you as scared as I am?" Adams asked the big gunner's mate.

"I don't know how scared you are," Moore said, "but I'll bet I'm twice as scared."

"I can't think of any worse way to die," Adams said.

"There ain't any," Moore said. "There absolutely ain't. I'll paddle."

Moore dipped the paddle into the sea. He shoved it aft. The boat glided forward. So did the shark.

He paddled again. Then once more. "He's staying right with us," Adams said.

"I'll try a couple fasties," Moore said.

He dug into the sea and thrust the paddle aft. The little boat moved forward several feet. He fast-paddled five more times. Then, breathing heavily, he looked aft. "That do any good?"

"Nope," Adams said. "He paced the exact same distance from us all the time."

Moore went to the stern and looked at the shark. "You mother-fucker," he screamed. "What the hell do you want?"

"Take it easy," Adams said, putting a hand on Moore's arm.

Neither man spoke for several minutes. Then Moore said, "How far back of a shark's eye would you say his brain is?"

"I don't have the slightest idea," Adams said.

"I was thinking if it isn't more than three inches, I could use my knife to make a three-inch stick-out piece on the butt end of the paddle, then spear him in the eye with it. I'd make it thick enough it wouldn't bust right off if I didn't get him straight in the eye . . . if it glanced off his head then went into his eye. I'd put a sharp point on it so it would slide in real easy."

"That would do one of two things," Adams said. "Three things! If his brain is right back of his eyes, like with people, it would probably kill him. Or else, if it didn't kill him, it would make him go away. Or it would make him so fucking mad he'd attack the boat. In which case you know where we'd be. So take a number. Which of the three would he do?"

"Or we could do nothing and hope he'll go away. Or if he doesn't, that he won't do anything to us. What do you think?" Moore said.

"God, I don't know," Adams said.

"He's bugging me, hanging in like that."

"Me, too, but, Christ, if we churn him up, then where are we? Where are we if we just sit on our ass?"

"I've got some change in my pocket," Moore said. "Feel like flipping on it?"

He took a half-dollar from his pocket, part of the change he had gotten at the *Indy*'s ship's service store Saturday evening after chow. He always bought an ice-cream cone—chocolate—after evening chow. A double scoop for fifteen cents. It had become a ritual with him.

Adams looked at the half-dollar between Moore's fingers. His lips were tight, his face drawn. "Flip the son of a bitch," he said. "Heads we make the spear. Tails we don't."

"All right," Moore said, his face grim.

He flipped the half-dollar. It fell onto the little boat's fabric bottom. It was heads.

"Okay, here we go," Moore said, taking the knife from his belt and picking up the paddle. "I won't cut it back so far we can't use it as a paddle. Like I mentioned, three inches."

It took almost an hour. "Okay," he said. "Here we go."

He went to the stern. The moon was brighter now. He could see Tojo's staring little eyes better than when Adams had awakened him.

He jockeyed himself on the stern seat, finding the most steady position. He gripped the spear in both hands. "Uh-uh, I can do it better with just my right arm," he muttered.

"Ready?" he said a moment later, his face taut.

"Ready," Adams said.

Moore sat there, gripping the spear, the muscles in his cheek twitching. He lowered the spear and turned toward Adams. "I can't do it," he said shakily. "He'll attack us if I do. I know he will! I can tell the way he keeps looking at me. God, I never saw such mean eyes."

His tongue glided over his lips. "He wanted me to try it . . . he was daring me!"

"Don't think about it," Adams said.

"Don't think about it! Jesus Christ, how can I help thinking about it? Take a look for yourself. Look into those devil's eyes."

"I already looked into them," Adams said. "Relax, Moore. If you think he would have attacked us, you sure as hell did the right thing."

Moore was terribly distraught. "God, I'm scared. I've never been really actually scared in my whole fucking life, Adams. But, Jesus, I am now. He'll do something to us. I know he will. I don't know what he's waiting for, but he's going to eat us."

Terror was on Moore's craggy face. He looked aft. "For chrissake," he babbled, turning back to Adams, "he's gone!"

Both men looked out onto the moonlit sea. There was no sign of Tojo. No protruding dorsal fin. No near-surface balancing on pectoral fins.

"I wonder if he'll come back," Moore said.

"I've got a hunch we'll know pretty soon," Adams said.

"Jesus, if we only could of got to them rafts."

"We tried," Adams said. "That's all anybody could have done."

The men sat in the little boat—Adams on the bow, Moore at the stern—for long silent minutes. Then Moore said, "It don't look like he's coming back. At least right away. I think I'll try to get some sleep. It'll be dawn in a couple hours."

Adams said he would try to sleep, too, but he wasn't guaranteeing he'd have any luck.

"Think about women," Moore said. "It'll take your mind off Tojo."

"I'd rather dream about some officer handing me a discharge and saying, 'Adams, the war's over. We don't need you anymore, so go home, you dumb son of a bitch.' "

A little after dawn Moore awakened. He looked at the sea adjacent to the little yellow boat. Then he looked farther away, in all directions. He awakened Adams. "Tojo's not out there," he said. "We must of spooked him."

"I sure hope so," Adams said, stretching his arms and yawning. "He was making mental cases of both of us."

The morning fog lifted. "I knew it," Moore said, looking at the rafts they had hoped to reach. They were barely visible. "That night drift must of been a bitch."

"We can't make it to them, can we?"

"Hell, no! They're too far, and if there's any kind of drift, we'd be screwed before we even got started."

Adams didn't say anything. He was looking aft, just back of the stern. Tojo was floating on his pectoral fins.

Moore, wondering what had drawn Adams' attention, looked aft. "God," he croaked. "He wasn't there a minute ago."

"Well, he's there now," Adams said, "and for chrissake, don't say if you just had your forty-five you'd take care of him."

"Don't make fun of me, you smart-ass bastard," Moore bellowed.

They glared at each other, each man's jaw squared. Then Adams said, "I'm sorry I shot off my fucking mouth. But seeing that shark the first thing in the morning— Moore, I wish to God you did have that forty-five."

"We're both right on the edge of flipping out," Moore said, "so let's forget it." He extended a hand. "No hard feelings, Adams."

Adams gripped his hand. "Thanks, pal. If I fly off the handle again, just give me a kick in the ass."

"Goddamn," Moore said, grinning. "I wish we were where I could."

Adams grinned, too. "So do I," he said. He looked at the rafts, and back at the shark. "I don't know how you feel about it, but I hope they rescue us today."

"Well, since we've got used to this cozy little yacht, and Tojo, back there," Moore said, "I'd kind of hate to leave them."

"That," Adams said, "is what is known as bullshit. We've got a little tiny bit of water left and two dried apricots. Why don't we have breakfast and then figure what we're going to do today?"

Moore said that wouldn't take a whole hell of a lot of figuring. "Since we've got no place to paddle to, we might as well just stay where we are and enjoy the scenery . . . and Tojo."

"Let's pretend he isn't there," Adams said.

"I'm not that good a pretender," Moore said.

"Well, then, don't look at him all the time," Adams said.

There wasn't much more than a swallow of water for each man. But it, and the apricots, made them feel better.

"I never asked before, and it's none of my business," Adams said, "but what are you going to do with that money you took from Ace McConnell's body? Assuming we survive this little adventure."

"You know why I wanted that money, Adams?" Moore said. "It's not because I'm a greedy son of a bitch. It's for Karen's wedding. I want my little girl to have a real wedding. It means a lot to a girl, having a fancy wedding. I never could have afforded it on Navy pay."

"You got a wife? You've never mentioned her, if you have."

"She died eleven years ago. When Karen was just a little kid. My sister in St. Louis raised her, along with her own kids. I've sent Bonnie some money every month. As much as I could because, God, I appreciate what her and her husband have done for my girl."

Tears came to the big gunner's mate's eyes. "I want more than anything to walk Karen down the aisle."

"You will, Charlie," Adams said, putting a hand on Moore's forearm. "And my wife and I are going to be there seeing that you do it right."

"We won't neither one be there if that damn shark attacks us," Moore said, looking back.

Tojo had submerged. Only his mutilated dorsal fin was above the sea. He was very close to the boat. His nose could not have been more than three feet from the boat's fragile fabric stern.

"I'm going to kill that son of a bitch," Moore said, his face taut, "and I've figured a way to do it."

He would lash his knife to the paddle's butt, he said, and slash Tojo's flank. Once he started to bleed, his buddies would finish him off.

"I'm going to tie that knife on real damn tight. We'll cut life-jacket thongs off some dead guy. I'll lash that knife to the oar as tight as I can with the thongs soaking wet. Then I'll dry them in the sun, which won't take long in this fucking heat. That'll draw the thongs real damn tight and I'll have a spear that I can do some good with."

Adams said it sounded great. "All we've got to do is get Tojo bleeding. But there's a little problem. We've got to find some floater that didn't make it."

Two hours elapsed before the men in the little rubber survival boat were able to see floaters. "There's seven of them," Moore said, looking at the men the drift had brought into view.

"What if none of them are dead?" Adams said. "We can't cut the jacket off a live guy."

"They're all dead," Moore said. "When I was on the crest of that last big wave I could distinctly see they weren't moving or anything."

He picked up the paddle. "Tell Tojo to start his engine," he said. "I'd hate to think he got left behind." He dug into the sea.

"Tojo started it," Adams said, looking aft.

They came to the floaters. Five were dead. Two were alive. "Let's take those poor bastards aboard before Tojo decides they're his next meal," Adams said.

"Okay," Moore said.

He turned to the floaters. "Don't swim toward us. Stay perfectly still. There's a shark back of us. We'll come over to you guys. And, remember, don't move."

The nearest floater, not counting the five dead floaters, began to swim toward the boat. "He's asking for it," Moore said. "The crazy son of a bitch."

Adams looked back. Tojo had vanished. He looked over at the swimming man. At any moment now, he would scream like they all screamed when a shark bit off a foot or a leg.

But he didn't scream. He kept coming and soon he put a hand on the little boat's port gunwale. "You guys should have come with me last night," he said. "I went over to Leyte. I'm going over there again in a little while. They got a hotel there. I'm going to drink some cold milk first. Like I did last night. Then a big steak dinner. I had fried chicken last night. You fellas want to ride with me? You can stay in my room."

Moore's eyes met Adams'. Their faces were sad with pity for this delirious man, who had been a yeoman on the *Indianapolis.*

"They got ice cream, too," the delirious man continued, his cracked lips in a smile. "You guys want to come with me? They got women there, too. Did I tell you about the chick I fucked last night? She was a redhead. Jesus, you shoulda seen her tits."

"We'll help you in," Moore said, "and we'll take you there. So give me your hand and—"

"You son of a bitch," the yeoman said, "you want to take her from me, that's the reason you want me to go with you. To steal my woman. That's gratitude, you prick. I took you there in my new red ragtop—you know how much that car cost?—and you tried to screw my girl. You know what? You better not try going with me this time. That's all I've got to say. You better not try it. I'm warning you, you woman-stealing son of a bitch."

He swam away, talking to himself.

"That was terrible," Adams said softly. "Just plain terrible. Do you think he'll ever be all right again—if he survives?"

"I don't know," Moore said. "Let's see how that other guy is. If we can, let's take him aboard."

He paddled to the other live floater. He was even more delirious than the yeoman. "There's a big island over there," he said, pointing. "They got a USO with free Cokes. Ice-cold Cokes with little bitty pieces of ice two inches thick on top. They got ice cream, too. And choc'lit shakes and big juicy hamburgers.

"They got shower baths upstairs and nice soft beds. You guys want to go with me?"

"We'll take you there," Moore said. "Give me one of your hands and when I start to pull—"

"Much obliged," the floater said, "but I can't go with you guys. I'm going with Nichols and McClusky. We're going to leave as soon as McClusky gets ready. Nichols got ate by a shark, so he's not going this time."

He began to swim away from the little boat. "I believe I'll have a Coke first," he said to no one. "Put a little more ice in it this time."

Adams looked into Moore's grim face. "That could have been us," he said, "if we hadn't found this boat."

"Let's get those thongs," Moore said.

He paddled toward the nearest floater, a brown-haired young man who had died during the night.

While he was cutting the thongs from the dead sailor's kapok jacket the man who had been going to Leyte screamed. Then the other swimmer screamed.

Moore tossed the thongs into the boat and paddled away.

Neither he nor Adams looked at the sharks' feeding frenzy.

23

MOORE HAD JUST FINISHED DRYING the thongs that bound the knife to the paddle's butt when a PV-1 Ventura, a twin-engine land plane piloted by U.S. Navy Lieutenant Wilber C. Gwinn flew over the survivors.

The Ventura was very high and Moore looked up at it and said he wished he had flares or a signal mirror. "A signal mirror would be better than flares this time of day."

"They wouldn't pay any more attention to us than the other planes," Adams said dispiritedly. "Some of the guys on rafts have got mirrors. We've seen their reflections. They didn't do a damn bit of good. The planes kept right on going. This one will, too."

"Well, goddamn, somebody is going to see us," Moore said. "Maybe the guys in that plane up there will be the ones."

"I wouldn't bet on it," Adams said. He didn't even bother to look up at the Ventura. What was the use?

There was basis in fact for Adams' negative thinking. The other planes that had flown over the survivors in the more than four days since the *Indianapolis* had been torpedoed had not been on visual patrol. Their crews only occasionally looked down at the sea. They relied on radar pips to indicate

Japanese submarines or surface boats. They hadn't seen the survivors or their flares or signal mirrors because such things don't show up on radar screens.

Lieutenant Gwinn, a California farmer's son, and his crew of four were based at Peleliu. They were on routine special patrol, a daily patrol with miscellaneous functions. They were to watch for unevaluated sightings, report weather conditions, report all surface ships and submarine activities, and harass the thousands of Japanese soldiers isolated on bypassed islands by preventing supplies from reaching them or evacuation ships removing them.

Gwinn and his men had taken off from Peleliu at 0820—it was Thursday, August 2—and soon they were flying at the usual eleven thousand feet and relying on radar pips to tell them if there was anything on the sea that was worth investigating or even reporting.

About 1100 hours clouds began to form. Lieutenant Gwinn had no desire to take his plane into a tropical storm, so he went down to a little less than five thousand feet.

Trouble arose with the experimental trailing antenna he had been ordered to use on this patrol. It was whipping wildly. Unless something was done, it would soon snap off. Gwinn turned control of the Ventura to his copilot, Lieutenant Warren Colwell, and went aft to see what he could do with the crazily lashing antenna.

While he was reeling it in, he glanced down at the sea. "Hey," he said excitedly. An oil slick was down there. An oil slick meant a Japanese submarine was in the vicinity.

He hurried back to the cockpit and told the copilot to drop to a thousand feet. "Open bomb bays," he said over the plane's speaker. "Prepare for attack."

This was exciting. Rarely had Gwinn and his men come upon anything demanding action any more dramatic than filling out a routine report.

"Want I should lace 'em?" George Northausen, the Ventura's machine-gunner, asked Lieutenant Gwinn.

"You bet," Gwinn said. "But wait'll I give the go. I want to get a closer look at them."

Northausen prepared his fifty-caliber machine gun to strafe the men on the sea and Lieutenant Gwinn took over at the Ventura's controls.

He put the plane into a dive, taking her to a little less than a thousand feet. He flew over the oil slick. He could see heads bobbing in the sea near the slick. "Where the hell's the Jap sub?" he said to his copilot.

"I don't see any sign of a sub," Lieutenant Colwell said.

There were no radar pips, either. "Take over again," Gwinn said to Colwell, "and bring her back over that oil."

Gwinn picked up his binoculars, and after Colwell circled for another run over the slick, he looked at the floaters. "For God's sake," he said. "They're Americans."

He swooped up his mike. "Secure bomb bays," he said. "Secure from combat stations. Those guys are Americans."

He turned to Colwell. "Take her up," he ordered.

He picked up his radio mike. "I'm radioing Headquarters to get the rescue guys here," he said to Colwell.

He spoke into the radio mike: ". . . sighted fifty Americans adrift at eleven-thirty north, one-thirty-three-thirty east . . ."

Moore and Adams stared with incredulity at the low-flying Ventura. "I don't believe it," Adams said, tears welling in his eyes.

"It's one of our planes," Moore babbled. "See the USN and the star and everything."

He wouldn't have been surprised, he said, the way their luck had been going, if it had been a Japanese plane whose gunners would strafe them with machine-gun fire.

There was rejoicing on the rafts and among most of the floaters. Some of the floaters, suffering the mental and physical effects of their fifth day in the shark-infested sea, didn't cheer. It was just another fantasy; they just thought they were looking at a U.S. Navy plane. They'd had other fantasies, most of them more interesting than the appearance of this blue airplane.

Moore and Adams watched the Ventura fly westward until they could no longer see it.

"Was that a real plane?" Adams said, smiling. "Tell me it was."

"It was a real genuine U.S. Navy Ventura," Moore said, "and what happened was, those fly-boys came down for a good look at us and then they radioed for rescue planes and ships."

"I hope you're right," Adams said, looking into the sky where the Ventura had disappeared.

"I know goddamn well I'm right," Moore said. "Man, you weren't dreaming and that was no imaginary plane. That was the real McCoy."

He began to laugh. He became almost hysterical. He wasn't going to die. He was going to be rescued.

He would walk his daughter down the nuptial aisle! And Adams would hold in his arms the little boy he had never seen!

"When do you think Air-Sea Rescue will be here?" Adams asked.

"It won't take very long for their planes," Moore said. "If a ship is anywhere close, it won't take very long for it, either. But if all our ships are quite a ways off, it'll take a while."

"Like tonight maybe?"

"It depends how far they are from us at the present time."

"I hope at least one of them is close," Adams said. "Not so much for us, but for the guys in the water. It's been plain hell for them. Just think of it. Going on five days in the water. Plus the sharks."

"Speaking of sharks," Moore said, looking out at Tojo, who had resumed a stance on his pectoral fins, his eyes looking at the little survival boat's occupants, "I think it's about time we gave Mr. Tojo a case of bleeds. I'd hate to think we left him here all sad and disappointed."

"It wouldn't bother me," Adams said, looking out at Tojo. "All I want is to get my feet on solid ground. Then I don't ever want to see an ocean or a shark again as long as I live."

"Well, I didn't make this spear for nothing," Moore said. "Plus which Tojo needs to be taught that bugging the piss out of guys in a survival boat is bad manners."

He picked up the oar to whose butt end he had firmly attached his knife. He looked toward the big shark. "Tojo," he said, "that plane not only screwed you out of a couple juicy meals but it made me decide it's time you joined your honorable ancestors."

"Be careful," Adams said, his tongue flicking over his lips.

"This would be one hell of a time to have something happen. When we're right on the edge of being rescued."

"Relax," Moore said, "and watch what this U.S. Navy hero is going to do to the shark that thought he had us by the balls."

He paddled closer to the shark, very slowly, very quietly, the knife which was lashed to the butt of the paddle reflecting the hot tropic sun with every stroke.

The shark didn't dive. This was something new . . . the little boat coming toward him instead of always going the other way. The big man-eater became curious; his eyes followed Moore's movements, and the shiny thing on the end of the paddle.

Slowly, lips taut, Moore positioned himself in the little boat's starboard midsection. From here, the way he had jockeyed the boat, he would be able to jab the spear deeply into the shark's guts. "Hang on, Adams," he said quietly, keeping his eyes on the big shark. "He's liable to kick up a storm."

Adams, sitting on the bottom of the little boat, gripped the gunwales on each side. He didn't like this. It was terribly indiscreet. They had it made. Why risk their lives for vengeance on a shark?

"Don't do it," Adams blurted. "Goddammit, man, you're risking our lives, and for what? For a stupid fucking shark? For God's sake, Charlie, think it through. We're the same as rescued. Don't blow it!"

"Knock it off," Moore said. "You're bugging me. I'm going to kill this baby . . . and nothing's going to stop me!"

"You son of a bitch," Adams said. "You're a Section Eight. You're as gone as those poor guys yesterday."

"Watch who you're calling a son of a bitch," Moore said, "and shut up. You're making me nervous. You want to remember Tojo won't hold still for seconds."

Adams looked out at Tojo. Dive, damn you! he reflected, biting his lips. Dive, you big stupid bastard!

Tojo didn't dive and Moore said, his eyes on the shark, "Tojo, you mother-fucker, you are about to have a great big bellyache."

While Moore held the spear, gripping it with both hands, waiting for a swell that would lift Tojo until his soft flank was exposed, Captain Frank Heberling, who had assured Lieutenant Kenneth Odell, his new communications officer, that no harm could come to the *Indianapolis*, sat at his desk at Headquarters, Philippine Sea Frontier, a cigar in his mouth.

Odell rushed into Heberling's office, a paper in his hand. "This just arrived from Lieutenant Gwinn, sir," he said.

Heberling, lolling in his chair, reached out for the paper. He began to read it, blowing a smoke ring between pursed lips. ". . . sighted fifty Americans adrift at eleven-thirty north, one-thirty-three-thirty east . . ."

The captain sat up in his chair. His eyes became wide. "My God," he said, "who the hell could they be?"

"I have no idea, sir," Odell said. "Lieutenant Gwinn, apparently, was unable to identify."

He had thought, for a moment, that he would suggest to Captain Heberling that they might be survivors from the long-overdue cruiser *Indianapolis*. But he changed his mind. Captain Heberling had been positive that nothing could happen to the *Indianapolis*, the time Odell had mentioned concern about the big cruiser.

Heberling began to write, hurriedly, on a pad. He tore off the paper on which he had been writing and shoved it out to Odell. "Get this off to Air-Sea Rescue, Marianas. On the double!"

"Aye, aye, sir," the young lieutenant said. "On the double."

He hurried toward the door, clutching the paper. He kept wondering if those men out there were survivors of the *Indianapolis*. Maybe he should have mentioned it to Heberling. Best he hadn't, though. The captain might chew out his ass again. Besides, the floaters could very well be from some other ship.

Before he got to the door Captain Heberling swooped up the microphone on his desk. "Now hear this," he barked. "Fifty American survivors in the sea at eleven-thirty north, one-thirty-three-thirty east. Roll it, and I mean roll it!"

Minutes later twenty-seven seaplanes began to fly seaward from PSF's little airfield, all of them carrying survival gear and floatable tins of food and water. Four had pharmacist's mates aboard with medic kits.

"I'm not asking," Adams said, clutching the little survival boat's gunwales and looking at Moore, who was about to drive his improvised spear into the shark that had been stalking them. "I'm begging! Please don't spear him. What if he attacks us? Charlie, this is no time to take a chance like that."

"Why don't you get off of it," Moore said, waiting, the spear poised, for the swell that would enable him to thrust the spear into Tojo's guts. "I'm going to kill him. And that's all there is to it."

"I hope that's all there is to it," Adams muttered dejectedly.

"Goddamn, shut up," Moore said.

A swell lifted the big shark. Moore thrust the spear. The knife sunk to its hilt into the shark's starboard flank. Moore continued the thrust. The entire knife and several inches of the oar slid into the shark.

Moore released his hold on the oar, flopped onto the bottom of the little boat, and gripped its gunwales, port and starboard, his head, and Adams', turned toward the wounded shark.

About this time, while several pilots and crews of Air-Sea Rescue, Marianas, seaplanes played poker in the cool earth-mounded former Japanese seaplane headquarters, a radioman with headsets who had been reading a comic book suddenly tossed it aside and sat up in his chair.

He began to write on his board. He tore off the sheet on which he had been writing, jerked off his headset, and ran to Lieutenant Commander Lawrence Callahan, who had been playing five-card draw with Lieutenants James Tripler, Thomas Solan, and Navy Correspondent David Stafford.

Commander Callahan read the message, the other card players looking over his shoulder. " . . . 50 American Navy personnel afloat 11:30N, 133:30E. Request immediate Air-Sea Rescue . . ."

The message had the count wrong. There were more than three hundred men in the sea. Lieutenant Gwinn had seen only about fifty. He had assumed that was all there were.

"Now hear this," Commander Callahan said into his PA mike after he announced the mission and the survivors' location, "I want everybody in the air in three minutes. And I don't mean four minutes!"

Tojo, the knife deep in his belly, churned the water, very nearly capsizing the little rubber survival boat while he tried to bite the knife out of his vitals.

He couldn't reach the spear with his teeth. He kept trying, going in a circle like a dog chasing its tail.

Blood and gore poured from his terrible wound. Other sharks, attracted by the smell of his blood, came speeding toward him. They began to bite great chunks of flesh from their impaled colleague.

Their frenzy tossed the little survival boat like a rodeo rider on a Brahman bull. Twice sharks came up under it, lifting it above the surface. Moore and Adams gripped the gunwales, terror on their faces.

Then, suddenly, there was nothing left of Tojo. The other sharks swam away and Adams said shakily, "You dumb bastard! Do you know how close we came to being dumped out . . . and what would have happened to us if we had? I'll tell you what would have happened. Those sharks would have eaten us. Right now we'd be in a dozen sharks' guts."

"It was a little rougher than I'd figured on," Moore admitted. "I naturally thought he'd swim out away from us. How'd I know he was going to go in a circle right next to us?"

"Well, it's over and we didn't get hurt," Adams said, "so I guess it's like that old saying, all's well that ends well."

"You got a case of flap-jaw there for a while," Moore said. "You called me some names. If it was anybody else, I'd bust their fucking face."

"Well, I never did enjoy being eaten by sharks," Adams said. "It makes me nervous every time."

Moore grinned and it was over. "I just thought of something," he said. "I'll bet the shark that gulped down the part of Tojo with the knife is going to be a very sorry shark."

"That could go on and on," Adams said. "He gets the bleeds. Some shark will eat the part of him with the knife and so on for a hundred sore-gut sharks."

Moore looked toward the east. Catalinas from Saipan

would get here first. They'd have less distance to travel than planes from Leyte.

"We made it," he said, a big smile on his unshaven sweaty face. "By God, we made it!"

"Somebody didn't," Adams said, pointing forty degrees off the little boat's bow.

Moore looked. Sharks were in a feeding frenzy. "What a hell of a break for that guy," Moore said, no longer smiling.

"He makes it through almost five days in the water, suffering every damn minute of it, and then just when he's about to be rescued, sharks eat him."

24

LIEUTENANT COMMANDER MOCHITSURA HASHIMOTO, IMPERIAL Japanese Navy, had arrived in Japan with his command, the submarine *Nakapo*.

He was the nation's hero. Japan, beset everywhere by the Americans, who seemed to have no end of resources and manpower, urgently needed a hero, and here was one who had sunk the flagship of the United States Navy's vaunted Third Fleet.

Hashimoto's victory was officially celebrated with a sword presentation at the swank officers' club at the Sasebo Naval Base.

High-ranking officers of the Imperial Navy were in attendance as were several generals of the External Challenge Forces of the Imperial Army who had been invited to show them that while their Army could not produce a significant victory the Navy had been able to bleed the Americans without the loss of even one Japanese.

Enormous quantities of sake were served and geisha girls attached to the Naval Ministry were there to function in their duties as morale boosters.

The party opened with the haunting strains of the "Song of

the Warrior," popular for centuries with the Japanese armed forces.

If I go to sea I shall return
a corpse awash

If duty calls me to the mountain
a verdant sward will mark my grave

For the sake of Japan I will not die
peacefully at home.

The song and the free-flowing sake lifted everyone's spirits. There were shouts of "Tenno Heika, Banzai" (Long Live the Emperor).

Rear Admiral Hiroshi Matsubara made a speech praising the *Nakapo*'s great victory, concluding with, "Let's all toast Commander Hashimoto and the men of the victorious submarine *Nakapo!*"

You incompetent old goat, Hashimoto reflected, looking at the little admiral, who was four-feet-ten and wearing three rows of service ribbons.

Hashimoto had no respect for Admiral Matsubara. He had been the cause of a monumental defeat for the Imperial Navy. Matsubara had been in command of the Third Column, the right-flank screen, in the cruiser *Agano* at the battle of Empress Augusta Bay on November 2, 1943.

The Americans were invading Bougainville. "We must fight desperately," Admiral Matsubara told the commanders of the ships in the Third Column shortly before the attack on the American invading forces. "If Bougainville falls, Japan will have taken a step backward on the ladder of victory."

The Japanese strategy was uncomplicated: Destroy thc invaders' troop transports and warships, then land a convoy of six thousand Japanese troops for a counterinvasion.

It was to be a full-scale nocturnal counteroffensive, but Admiral Matsubara had little experience in night battle and he put his ships on a collision course with the Japanese destroyer task force.

The *Agano*, leading the Third Column, slammed into two of the destroyers. The impacts crushed the *Agano*'s hull and forward deck and smashed two of the destroyers' port torpedo tubes and deck guns besides killing and injuring more than a hundred Japanese Navy men.

The Americans could hardly have inflicted more damage, and in the confusion, while Admiral Matsubara was trying to decide what to do with the crippled ships, and other ships coming up on them in the night very nearly collided with them and with each other, planes of the Fifth U.S. Bombardment Group attacked the Japanese.

The bombarded Japanese ships were in such disorder that when U.S. Navy Admiral Merrill's force of four cruisers and eight destroyers attacked them immediately after the bombardment, they were caught with no plans for such a contingency.

The Japanese ships groped like blind men, shooting with near hysteria in supposed directions of the American ships, wasting ammunition and squandering fuel in wild chases in which, twice, Japanese ships sideswiped each other.

After an hour the battered Japanese naval columns began to withdraw toward Rabaul, leaving their crippled ships, which American naval gunners quickly sank.

For the Japanese the battle of Empress Augusta Bay was a debacle. Later, Admiral Matsubara explained, "We were not a previously trained team," a tenuous defense that the Supreme Imperial Navy Command accepted.

The Sasebo party's sake flowed freely. Geisha girls kept the glasses filled. There were toasts to Japan's invincibility, her great armed forces, her valiant samurai, to Hashimoto, the emperor, and to one another.

This party is as big a farce as that stupid little admiral's speech about my great victory, Hashimoto reflected.

Japan isn't invincible. Her armed forces are incapable of defeating the enemy or even of keeping them from invading islands practically on Japan's doorstep.

The Imperial Navy has been stupidly inflexible. The Navy had thought the Americans were gullible enough to always play the Japanese game.

This had been a disastrous mistake. In addition to their continual buildup, the Americans were forever trying daring strategies and new tactics, such as skip-bombing, for which the Japanese had no defense.

It was true that Japanese technology was advancing rapidly—radar-controlled gunfire, proximity fuses, heat-homing artillery—but all of it too late to seriously harm Japan's powerful enemy, or even to catch up to the Americans' technology in these same areas.

"Fools like Matsubara," Hashimoto said drunkenly to Captain Haru Kogazaki, a former carrier force commander who sat beside him, "have lost this war for us."

"We have not yet lost the war," Kogazaki said, glaring at Hashimoto.

"We have lost it like you lost your carriers," Hashimoto said, "because the imbeciles on the Supreme War Council have been fighting the war with yesterday's tactics.

"They think that if a strategy works once it will always be successful.

"This has enabled the Americans to anticipate our moves.

"Our whole war has been conducted by men obsessed with illusions and miscalculations.

"And now defeat is inevitable."

Captain Kogazaki bristled. "We will fight to the last man," he snapped. "I, myself, will fight in the streets with just a bayonet in my hands, if necessary. We will make the Americans bleed."

"No doubt of it," Hashimoto said, "but when they are through hemorrhaging, they will have defeated Japan.

"When we lost Saipan, we lost this war, Kogazaki. It is all over but the funeral."

Like many another Japanese officer, Commander Hashimoto was convinced that Japan's cause had been lost with the fall of Saipan, the heavily defended Marianas island that had shielded the southern approaches to the Japanese main islands. Subsequent battles, even Hashimoto's sinking of the American cruiser *Indianapolis*, were anticlimactic. They merely delayed Japan's inevitable defeat.

So what did all these toasts mean? Why this party? Japan no longer even had a functioning Navy.

Hashimoto drank another sake, then another, as he thought about this. "God, we don't even have a Navy anymore," he said to Captain Kogazaki. "So what are those admirals up there at the main table trying to do? Deceive each other? Or play a pretend game like little children?"

The Imperial Japanese Navy had died with the sinking of

the unsinkable battleship *Yamato*, and no amount of sake and flowery toasts from the admirals could change that fact.

Brooding on the fate of that invincible warship diminished Hashimoto's esteem for the admirals even more. "The *Yamato* needn't have been sunk," he said to no one in particular.

"Even I, who have had small commands all my life, could have done better with the *Yamato* than those donkeys who were on her bridge.

"They could not have handled the situation more ineptly if they had planned and rehearsed it."

Hashimoto, continuing to think about the *Yamato*, drank more sake. "Stupid fool admirals," he muttered drunkenly.

On April 7, 1945, the giant 72,800-ton battleship *Yamato*—pride of the Imperial Japanese Navy—the light cruiser *Yahagi*, and eight destroyers sortied from the Inland Sea to attack the American forces that were defeating Okinawa in a desperate last-chance attempt to save the home islands from American invasion.

They had gone less than a hundred miles from the Inland Sea when American Task Force 58 hit the Japanese ships with remorseless fury, beginning with a ninety-minute aerial attack by 386 carrier-based American Hellcats and Avengers that dropped torpedoes and a seemingly endless number of 250-pound bombs.

The *Yamato* exploded in a column of debris and smoke twenty thousand feet into the sky. The *Yahagi* was sunk along with four of the destroyers. The other destroyers zigzagged back toward the Inland Sea in disorganized terror.

It had been a catastrophe. The last hope of the Imperial Navy had been destroyed less than halfway to its objective.

Commander Hashimoto's mood became dark. He tried to brighten it with more sake. This party was in his honor. He at least should be cheerful, or pretend to be.

He didn't become cheerful. He became drunk. He staggered over to Admiral Matsubara's table with the ceremonial sword. "I am returning this sword, sir," he said, "because my talent as a submarine commander had nothing to do with the sinking of the American cruiser.

"Our paths crossed by chance. Any inept officer could have sunk that cruiser."

Red-faced, Admiral Matsubara motioned to a geisha girl named Toshi to take Hashimoto to a bed.

She went toward Hashimoto and Admiral Matsubara, forcing a smile, said to the others, "A submarine officer must frequently abstain from love for such a long time that his judgment is impaired and he says things he does not mean."

Hashimoto pushed Toshi away. "Go screw that little sawed-off admiral," he bellowed.

An academy colleague, Iko Nagashi, deputy commander-in-chief, Combined Fleets, put an arm around Hashimoto and led him out of the room.

Only Hashimoto's achievement of sinking the *Indianapolis* at a time when Japan needed a victory so urgently saved him from a court-martial.

25

A SQUADRON OF TWELVE TWIN-ENGINE Catalina PBY amphibians from Air-Sea Rescue, Marianas, was the first to arrive at the site of the *Indianapolis'* survivors.

It was one hundred and seven hours after Captain McVay's order to abandon ship, and the sea and wind had spread the survivors for about four miles on a generally northeast-southwest axis.

There were many more men down there on the gently rolling Central Pacific than the rescuers had expected. "My God," Lieutenant Robert Frey, the squadron's commander, said, looking down at the floaters and rafts.

Frey radioed for more planes. "Also send surface ships. There are at least three hundred men down there!"

Priority should go to lone floaters, Frey decided. They needed rescue more urgently, he believed, than the men in clusters and on floating objects.

He ordered his pilots to begin rescue operations with lone floaters. "Make it quick," he said, "and when you get a load, take off immediately."

Each plane normally had a crew of seven, including two gunners at the PBYs' flexible fifties mounted in waist blisters.

In each plane a waist-gunner had been replaced by a pharmacist's mate whose function would be to give medical care to the survivors until his plane returned to the Marianas, where ambulances would be waiting to rush the survivors to a hospital.

On Frey's plane David Stafford, the Navy correspondent, had replaced the port blister's machine-gunner, the starboard gunner having been replaced by pharmacist's mate Louis Humlicek.

Stafford's experience as a machine-gunner had been limited to shooting sharks with a waist-blister fifty-calibre machine gun in a lagoon near the Japanese Naval Base at Truk while the PBY in which he was temporary crew was on routine patrol. This slight experience presumably qualified him for the rescue mission; there was no space for passengers. "Either you're a machine-gunner or you can't go," Frey had said, explaining that he wanted maximum space for the survivors.

Lieutenant Frey, who had been a Cleveland draftsman before the war, put his plane on the sea in the middle of a quadrangle of floaters.

The floaters swam to the seaplane as if they'd be left behind if they didn't hurry. They scrambled onto the plane, kicking holes in wings and fuselage in their anxiety to get aboard.

"Jesus Keerist," Corpsman Humlicek said, looking at the survivors who had come into the plane.

They had oozing saltwater ulcers, skin burns from the tropic sun, and oil burns in which skin had been peeled away exposing sun-purpled flesh that exuded a smelly fluid.

Their mouths gaped. The membranes of their throats and noses were inflamed. Their mouths, inside, were bright red. Their eyes, burned by the remorseless tropic sun and the sea's constant drenching, glowed like little red marbles. Two breathed with difficulty. Pneumonia, Humlicek said.

Humlicek gave each man a half-cup of water. Then Lieutenant Frey asked them the name of their ship.

"The *Indianapolis*," the survivor with crew-cut red hair said. "Five days ago. Where the fuck you guys been? Just sitting on your ass? Jesus Christ, man, do you know what five days in that fucking ocean is like? Never knowing when a shark is going to bite off your leg—"

He began to cry. Humlicek put an arm around him and led him aft. Meanwhile Copilot Mark Ewald had taxied the Catalina to another area of lone floaters.

Lieutenant Frey and his navigator, Ensign Joseph (Happy) Houlihan, extended their hands to a floater who had been hanging on to a cork life ring. He was Myron Keever, and he had been in the *Indianapolis'* coding room.

While Frey and Houlihan were lifting him out of the water, a shark suddenly appeared in a surface arc that brought him to Keever. He leaped up and bit off Keever's feet six inches above his ankles and continued the arc without slowing his pace.

"Oh, my God," Houlihan croaked, staring at Keever's blood-gushing stumps.

He and Frey quickly lifted Keever into the plane and with efficient haste Humlicek put tourniquets on the horribly bleeding stumps. Then Humlicek said, "He needs plasma and—"

He didn't say the rest of it. He had looked at Keever's face. It had the waxy look of a just-died man.

Humlicek put his stethoscope's tubes in his ears and probed for a heartbeat. There was none. The corpsman looked up at Lieutenant Frey. "He's dead," he said.

"If we'd just been a couple seconds sooner," Houlihan said, "we'd have had him up where that damn shark couldn't have got him."

"Sharks been eating us guys all the time," the redhead of the first rescued group said, coming forward and looking at Keever's body. "That's what the mother-fuckers do: they bite off your feet and then they come back and eat the rest of you."

"Have they eaten very many of you guys?" Frey said.

The redhead began to laugh. "Have they eaten very many of us guys! Jesus Christ, Lieutenant, they ate most of us!"

He began to laugh again.

"That's going to be the tough part," Humlicek said, turning to Frey. "What it's done to their minds."

"Can you do anything for him? To stop that crazy laughing? It's getting to me."

Humlicek said he'd put the redhead in dreamland. "That is, if his heart can stand it. I'll check on it right away."

He put his stethoscope to the delirious man's chest. Then he nodded to Frey. He took the redhead aft again and injected him with a sedative.

Meanwhile Frey looked down at Keever's body. "Throw him out," he said to Houlihan, his face grim. "We can better serve the survivors by taking a living man back with us."

Houlihan jockeyed the corpse to a hatch and tossed it out into the sea. Almost instantly sharks came. They began a feeding frenzy. "For chrissake," Frey said. He had never seen anything like it.

He ran to the starboard machine gun and fired sweeping back-and-forth bursts into the frenzied sharks. The powerful gun, fired at such a close range, fragmented the feeding sharks.

Others came, attracted by the massive spills of blood. Frey shot at them, killing them, too. More sharks came. Frey did not fire at them. Killing sharks wasn't his mission, he realized.

Moore and Adams, sitting in the little yellow survival boat, watched Lieutenant Frey machine-gun the sharks. "That sure beats the hell out of a homemade spear," Moore said.

"God, that was terrible, watching that shark bite off that guy's feet," Adams said. "Just when he was being rescued. That's irony if I ever saw it."

"It was a tough break, all right," Moore said. "The guy damn near had it made."

"That was him they threw out, wasn't it?"

"It was him. I noticed he didn't have any lower legs."

"I'm not getting out of this boat until I can put my feet on one of those planes," Adams said, shaken from witnessing Keever's terrible amputations. "If they ask us to swim over to their plane, I'm going to tell them I won't do it."

Frey's PBY taxied to several other lone floaters. Quickly Houlihan and Glenn Sievers, radioman first class, pulled them into the big seaplane.

The last man, a fire controlman second-class whom everybody on the *Indianapolis* called Swede, sat on the plane's deck, after Houlihan and Sievers lifted him out of the sea.

"Go on aft," Lieutenant Frey said. "We've got a medic who'll look at you."

"You'll have to help me," Swede said. "I don't have my legs anymore. Sharks ate them."

Frey's eyes met Houlihan's. Then Frey pointed to Swede's legs. "What are those?"

Swede looked at his legs. Astonishment swept over his broad blond face. "They must of grown out again," he said. He looked up at Lieutenant Frey. "That proves the power of prayer." He got up and walked aft.

Frey watched him, wondering how many of the survivors were suffering mental distresses because of their ordeal. Then he turned to his copilot. "Let's take 'em away," he said.

Frey's PBY wasn't the first of his squadron to begin the flight back to Saipan. He was the fourth. The lieutenant had wasted time machine-gunning the sharks that had frenzied over Keever's body.

The last two planes of Frey's squadron were taxiing for their takeoffs when the first of the amphibians arrived from the Philippine Sea Frontier, the delay being caused by the greater distance.

Like the Saipan planes, they began to pull lone floaters from the sea, ignoring men in clusters and on rafts and survival boats.

Moore and Adams sat in their little boat, watching the activities. "They're doing the right thing, taking those guys first," Adams said, "but I can hardly wait until they get to us."

"Unless they get some boats here," Moore said, "it will be quite a while before they get everybody. Each plane is only taking eight guys."

Adams turned to Moore, "Charlie, are you going to ship over when your enlistment runs out?"

"I've been thinking about it," Moore said. "Especially since that first plane came. I think I will. I think I'll go for thirty. I'll be doing downhill all the way. I've already got over twenty-two years in the bag. You going to sign up again?"

"I didn't sign up the first time," Adams said. "They signed me up. In other words they said Army or Navy, and I said Navy. Hell, no, I'm not going to ship over! Do I look like a Section Eight?"

"Uh-huh," Moore said, grinning.

"I ought to bust you in the chops."

"Let's get drunk first."

Adams, his heart light, said that sounded great. "What are you going to do, then?"

"Sleep, man. With my legs stretched out. Do you know how long it's been since I've been able to stretch my legs?"

They talked on what they would do when they got to Pearl or San Francisco or wherever the Navy would take them from the Forward Area. "First," Adams said, "I'm going to phone my wife. And then I'm going to go to a restaurant and order a serving of everything they've got. Then I'm going to a hotel and sleep. And if anybody wakes me up I'll kill him."

"You forgot a bath," Moore said. "You need one. You stink."

Adams said just one bath wouldn't do the job. "It'll take a whole big bar of Lifebuoy and an hour under a shower. I'm so sweaty and sticky I feel crusty. You'll need two bars of soap, the way you stink."

Both men laughed. The apprehensions of their terrible ordeal were over. There was nothing to worry about anymore. Soon they would be given water and food and be flown out of this damn shark-infested ocean.

The PBYs from the Philippines flew away with the men they had retrieved from the sea.

"It gives a guy a funny feeling, not seeing any rescue planes," Adams said. "Like there really hadn't been any. It wasn't just a dream, was it?"

"It was no dream. They were for real," Moore said. "I don't like the way these swells are building up. Jesus, I hope they don't get so big those PBYs can't land on them."

"They won't bother ships," Adams said. "Maybe a ship will get here before long."

"That depends on how far away the closest one was when they got the word. It could be tomorrow before the first one gets here."

"Maybe we won't need a ship," Adams said, his face lighting up. "There's another bunch of PBYs."

He nodded toward the east. Moore looked. Twelve PBYs were in the first wave. Another squadron was behind them.

They were the additional planes Lieutenant Frey had radioed for when he saw the number of men in the sea.

They landed on the rising swells and began with the efficiency of men trained in air-sea rescue to pull lone floaters out of the ocean.

Before the last of them had flown off with their cargoes, PBYs came from the west. Then more from the east.

Both contingents made shuttle runs. The swells, ten feet now, running from the northwest, impeded the rescues. Sometimes two hours were required to load a plane; before the swells, they could be loaded in minutes.

"I wonder how many guys they're missing," Adams said.

"I don't know how they can help missing at least some of them," Moore said.

When the little boat was on the crest of swells its occupants could see seaplanes everywhere. When they were in troughs all they could see were walls of bright blue tropic ocean.

For lone floaters it must have been tormenting, hoping they were seen by rescuers when they were on crests and hoping, then, that the big amphibians could wallow the rough seas and take them aboard.

Ships were on their way to aid in the rescues. The destroyer-escort *Doyle* had been in waters off the Palau islands, when its bridge got a voice radio contact with a PBY that appeared over the little ship.

The pilot reported the survivors' location. "The hell with waiting for an official okay," the ship's CO, Lieutenant Commander W. G. Claytor said. "Let's go help those guys."

He ordered a flat-out toward the survivors.

Another destroyer-escort, the *Dulfilho*, was on patrol east of Leyte Gulf. Its CO, Lieutenant Commander A. H. Nienau received an order from Philippine Sea Frontier to proceed immediately to the site of the *Indianapolis* survivors.

Nienau ordered his little ship to go at an engine-shaking twenty knots, a little slower than the newer *Doyle*.

Other U.S. Navy ships in the general area were ordered to assist in the rescue of the survivors and soon seven ships were speeding toward the site.

But the closest ship was a little more than two hundred miles from the survivors. It could not arrive before nightfall.

Night came. The PBYs used their powerful floodlights to locate floaters, holding the lights on them until they were lifted out of the sea.

Then the *Doyle* arrived and, a little later, two more ships. Adams and Moore, riding the swells—now running at twelve feet—became apprehensive. Would one of the ships, unable to see their little boat, slice the fragile little craft and throw them into the sea?

It could well be their final disaster. If they weren't swept into the ship's screws and mangled they would be in peril of attack by sharks. Twice during the rescues, subsequent to Keever's horrible amputations, they had heard the screams of men who were being attacked by sharks.

"It was going too good," Moore said. "We should have known something would happen. Such as these fucking swells."

"I wish it was daytime," Adams said. "I'd feel better if we could see what the hell's going on."

The night was interminable. Floodlights on ships and planes kept sweeping the tossing sea, looking for survivors.

Eleven times floodlights stopped on Moore and Adams, then went away. Floaters had priority.

At 0300 hours the floodlight from a Marianas Air-Sea Rescue PBY swept over the men in the little rubber-survival boat, came back, and stayed on them.

"They're going to get us this time," Adams babbled.

"Watch it getting aboard," Moore said. "This sea's a bitch."

The PBY taxied toward the men in the little boat.

"Hold up your right hand," someone shouted.

A hand reached down. "Go first," Moore said.

Adams reached for the rescuer's hand. The swells swept the boat away. Then back. Adams clutched the hand on the fourth go and instantly he was jerked up onto the Catalina's starboard wing. "Watch you don't punch holes," his rescuer said.

Soon Adams was in the big seaplane. "What do you need?" its pharmacist's mate said, his eyes gliding over Adams.

"Nothing," Adams said, "until my buddy gets here."

Moore came aboard moments later. "What we need," Moore told the pharmacist's mate after a rescuer brought half-cups of water, "is something for the sorest asses in the United States Navy.

"If you've ever sat for four days on a rubber gunwale that's constantly wet with salty seawater and hotter than hell you know how much we're hurtin'."

Moore and Adams were the last men aboard. The PBY's pilot began to taxi for a takeoff.

He had a hard time becoming airborne. His plane was heavily loaded. The swells were still twelve feet and an eleven-knot wind had come up.

After he got the PBY into the air Adams said, "Charlie, you ugly old bastard, tell me I'm not dreaming."

"It's for real, short man," Moore said, looking out a port at the lights of the ships and planes that were probing the black tropic night for other survivors.

A little after dawn Adams and Moore were in Navy 14, one of the more than a hundred connected-Quonset Army and Navy hospitals at Saipan.

They had, as Moore phrased it, "finally made the son of a bitch."

Epilogue

BEFORE THE JAPANESE SUBMARINE'S TORPEDOES struck the *Indianapolis* the big cruiser had a ship's company of 1,195 of which eighty were officers and 1,113 were enlisted men.

More than eight hundred survived the sinking of the mortally wounded ship. For five ghastly days they floundered helplessly in the torrid tropic sea while sharks ate them at the rate of a hundred a day.

When rescue finally came only 316 were alive.

It was the greatest sea tragedy in the history of the United States Navy.

At 7 P.M. Tuesday, August 14, 1945, announcement of Japan's surrender was broadcast to the people of the United States. One hour later the Navy Department released Communiqué 662: "The USS *Indianapolis,* a heavy cruiser, has been lost in the Philippine Sea as the result of enemy action. The next of kin of casualties have been notified."

In nearly nine hundred homes "regret to inform you" telegrams were delivered . . . in some cases the doorbell rang while the family was celebrating the end of the war.

Immediately after learning of the *Indianapolis* debacle Ad-

He took the *Indianapolis* to Guam, about a hundred miles south of Tinian. Here he was ordered to proceed to Leyte, Philippine Islands, where he would report to Vice Admiral Jesse B. Olendorf, Commander Task Force 95. At Leyte the crew of the *Indianapolis* would undergo seventeen days "refresher training," presumably for the invasion of Kyushu, the first of the main Japanese islands to be invaded.

McVay's routing orders: Depart Apra Harbor in Guam at 0900 Saturday, July 28. Proceed at 16 knots and arrive in Leyte Gulf 1100 Tuesday.

The voyage would be 1,171 miles true. Zigzag would, of course, add many miles.

The *Indianapolis* would have no escort. The line behind which ships could travel without escort was now the 130-degree north chop line, many miles north of the cruiser's course to Leyte.

When Captain McVay came into the navigation bridge, the *Indianapolis* was approximately midway on its voyage from Guam to Leyte. Adams and Keefer wondered why he had come into the bridge at 0300, three o'clock in the morning. "I've got good news, men," he said, smiling broadly. "We've got orders to secure from zigzag. As of right now."

Smiles swept over the enlisted men's faces. "Sir, is the war over?" Keefer asked.

McVay wiped the hot tropic night's sweat from his brow. "I hope so. I know you men do, too. But all the message said was 'Secure from zigzag.' "

Adams swung the helm to terminate the zigzag course of the big cruiser. "Isn't it a little risky, sir, securing from zigzag if the war might still be going on?"

He looked over at Captain McVay. "There could be a Jap sub out there. If there is, we'd be an easy target on straight course. The moon's coming out, too, sir."

Keefer said, "I'll bet the war's over. They wouldn't order us to secure otherwise. Would they, Captain?"

"They might," Captain McVay said. "In secure waters like these, they might."

He went to the navigation-chart bench, a metal shelf that had been welded onto a bulkhead at chest level. He looked at the chart. Then, without taking his eyes from it, he said, "Hold on two-six-two true."

the navigation bridge. He was barefoot, smiling, wearing shorts and nothing else.

Captain McVay was of medium height and trim build. He had a fair complexion, black eyebrows, and graying hair. He was good-humored and popular with his crew. At forty-seven, he was a graduate of the United States Naval Academy and had a successful, though not spectacular, record of diversified command.

McVay was pleased with his command of this big cruiser; it was an ambition fulfilled. With twenty-seven years' service, he hoped to exceed, or at least meet, the achievements of his father, Charles Butler McVay, Jr., a retired full admiral who had commanded the *Oklahoma, New Jersey,* and *Saratoga* during World War I, later serving as chief of the U.S. Navy Bureau of Ordnance, commandant of the Washington Navy Yard, and as commander in chief, U.S. Asiatic Fleet.

Captain McVay had been given command of the *Indianapolis* at San Francisco just four weeks ago. Under elaborate security the *Indianapolis* had left Hunter Point Navy Yard in San Francisco before morning colors on Monday, July 16, 1945, with a top-secret cargo. McVay's orders were to expedite this cargo with all speed to Tinian in the Mariana Islands. "Save this cargo at all costs," McVay was told. "Guard it even after the life of your vessel."

"What is it?" McVay had asked.

"You cannot be told," McVay was informed.

He thought it was a cannister of BW (bacteriological warfare). He was wrong. It was the atom bomb. It would be dropped on Hiroshima on August 7. It would kill thousands of Japanese.

"Expedite," CinCPac (Commander-in-Chief, Pacific) had ordered McVay. "Every hour you save will shorten the war."

The *Indianapolis* had delivered its secret cargo at Tinian ten days and five thousand miles from San Francisco, a small metal cylinder that McVay had kept in a senior officer's cabin secured by hinged strap steel that had been welded to the cabin's deck. Outside the officer's cabin McVay had lashed a life raft. If the *Indianapolis* were sunk the bomb could, hopefully, be saved.

"Report to Guam," CinCPac ordered McVay after he delivered his secret cargo at Tinian.